PEACHES AND CREAM

'Get off me, Mullins, now!'

'No,' Catherine answered. 'I shan't! I'm going to punish you, you spoilt, uppity little brat! I'm going to spank you and spank you and spank you . . .'

'Don't you dare!' Cicely hissed. 'Get off me, I say!' Again Cicely's body jerked as she tried to throw Catherine off, and again Catherine held on, twisting at Cicely's arm to draw out a squeal of pain and rage. Cicely went limp.

'Tell her to get off, Lottie! Tell her to get off!'

'Don't you dare, Miss Charlotte,' Catherine said. 'I'll not stand for it!'

'I can't!' Charlotte managed. 'I really can't!'

'That's right, Miss Charlotte,' Catherine said. 'You be a sensible girl and stay out of it. Now, where did that hairbrush go?'

PEACHES AND CREAM

Aishling Morgan

This book is a work of fiction.
In real life, make sure you practise safe sex.

First published in 2002 by
Nexus
Thames Wharf Studios
Rainville Road
London W6 9HA

Copyright © Aishling Morgan 2002

The right of Aishling Morgan to be identified as the
Author of this Work has been asserted by her in
accordance with the Copyright, Designs and Patents Act
1988.

Typeset by TW Typesetting, Plymouth, Devon

Printed and bound by
Clays Ltd, St Ives PLC

ISBN 0 352 33672 2

Summer 1920, Wiltonheath School for Girls, Devon

Charlotte Bomefield reached down to grip the hem of her dress. It was a long, shapeless garment, grey-blue in colour and decorated with a simple cross. Beneath it, her slender figure hardly showed, with no more than a hint of gentle curves at hip and bust. Wearing it, she felt she looked like a sick girl, and a sense of pride mixed with her vulnerability as she lifted it, displaying what was beneath to her companion.

Cicely St John smiled as Charlotte exposed herself. Lying back on the bed, she admired her friend, large brown eyes moving slowly, without hurry. Charlotte looked back, trying to stop herself trembling. The dress had come up to beneath her armpits, where she held it, showing the plain, loose cotton and lace of her drawers and chemise. Her nipples were hard, and she could feel the sensitive buds against the fabric, tickling faintly with the movement of her breathing. Her sex was also responding, her urgency growing, the cheeks of her bottom twitching in involuntary anticipation of what was to come. Again Cicely smiled, and patted her lap.

Moving forward, Charlotte found herself wondering how she could possibly allow anything so painful and degrading to be done to her. Cicely was going to spank

1

her, with a wooden brush used for polishing shoes. It was going to hurt, and it would leave her bottom a mass of bruises. She would be done bare as well, with the back of her drawers pulled open to display her little round bottom to the room, adding humiliation to her already abused feelings. None of that stopped her from draping herself across her friend's lap, or from leaving one leg trailing on the floor.

'This is going to be your last, you know,' Cicely said, 'maybe for ever so long. I think I had better make you especially sorry for yourself.'

Charlotte answered with a broken sniff, unresisting as Cicely's knee pushed up between her thighs, spreading them yet wider. The action forced her to lift her bottom, leaving it thrust high and tight against the seat of her drawers. Cicely's hand came to rest on one cheek, stroking with gentle intimacy. Charlotte let it happen, her eyes closed, her body limp, her mind full of the indignity of her position and fear of the coming pain.

'I shan't just open your drawers,' Cicely continued. 'I shall undo them, and part the curtains completely. I do like to see a full moon.'

Closing her eyes, Charlotte waited, painfully aware of every sensation coming from her body, the weight of her raised dress, the feel of her little breasts hanging down in her chemise, the gentle caress of Cicely's hand on her cotton-covered bottom. Again she wondered how she could let it happen to herself, why she never managed to resist her friend's cruelty.

Cicely took her time, exploring Charlotte's bottom and legs, squeezing the little fleshy cheeks and stroking the high cleft between them. After a while she hooked one of her own legs behind Charlotte's right knee, trapping her. Charlotte felt her sex spread by the action, and a wet, sticky sensation as the cotton pulled up against the lips of her vulva. Immediately, Cicely's fingers went between Charlotte's thighs, pressing to her

2

sex and feeling the little folds of flesh with the same lingering intimacy she had shown with her bottom.

'You do have quite the loveliest little cunt, Lottie darling,' Cicely said.

'Don't use that awful word!' Charlotte begged.

'Oh but I shall. It suits you so. Cunt, Lottie, cunt, cunt, cunt. A cunt so soft and neat, and she always seems to be wet for me. Maybe I should put my thumb up her and ruin you. Wouldn't that be ever so amusing?'

'No, Cicely, play by the rules.'

'You can be such a bore, Lottie. Think how it would feel with your maidenhead burst and the warm blood trickling down while I spank you. Doesn't it tempt?'

'Please, no, Cicely, please.'

'Oh, very well. If you must be prissy, then I shan't. You do know I'll have to take it out on your bottom, don't you?'

'You're a beast, Cicely, a super beast.'

'I know.'

As they had spoken, Cicely had continued to fondle Charlotte's vulva, squeezing and rubbing through the thin drawers. Now dizzy with pleasure, Charlotte could only lie inert as her friend began to prepare her for punishment. The single button that held her drawers fast in the small of her back was popped. They fell open, parting over her lifted bottom to let cool air to the shallow valley where the crease met her spine.

Cicely took hold of one side, then the other, opening the drawers like curtains to complete the exposure. Charlotte sighed, intensely aware of her bare rear view. The drawers were fully open, laid wide across Cicely's lap. Her sex was showing, the damp flesh suddenly cool as the air touched her. She knew her hole would be wet and open, the lips swollen, with the damp, pink wrinkles of flesh between them all on show, nothing hidden, utterly bare. So was her anus, the slim cheeks of her bottom too small and firm to provide concealment,

3

leaving the tiny, rude knot of dun-coloured flesh showing between them.

With Charlotte's bottom bare, her arm was taken, twisted up into the small of her back, tight, even as Cicely's leg tensed. Held firmly in place, Charlotte felt her fear and helplessness rise. Her lower lip was quivering, her breasts too, the nipples rubbing on the inside of her chemise to the movement. She shut her eyes, tight, as Cicely's body moved beneath her and she felt the cold, hard wood of the shoe brush pressed to her naked flesh.

She gave a stifled sob, fear running through her brain, along with her amazement at how she could subject herself to such pain and indignity. It was going to hurt, really hurt, and it was too late to stop it, too late to cry off as the awful brush touched her bottom, two gentle pats. It was the same signal Cicely always used, and Charlotte raised her bottom in response by instinct, hating herself even as she obeyed. She had started to snivel, and to kick her feet, her tension building inside her until she wanted to scream.

It was too much, the fear and humiliation, her senses of indignity and exposure, the rude feeling of being bare, of waiting for a beating, of knowing that every little flesh fold of her sex was on show to her tormentor and that all of it was about to be smacked. Then the brush came down and there was nothing but pain, the stinging slap ringing out around the room as her buttocks bounced to the impact, one noise followed an instant later by another as she screamed in reaction.

Again it happened, and again, as the spanking got under way, with the slaps of the brush in time to Charlotte's screams. Unable to hold herself back, she struggled and writhed in Cicely's grip, kicking her feet and shaking her head in her frantic efforts to dull the pain. None of it worked, her bottom held firmly in place, smack after smack landing on the wobbling cheeks as she screamed and howled her way through her beating.

Before long she had broken down completely, bawling her eyes out as she lay over Cicely's lap, the tears streaming down her face or splashing out over the bed covers as the hard smacks dislodged them. Her bottom was a ball of fire, smacked to the point where she had lost her mind with the pain, all sense of decency or dignity gone, bucking and writhing in the uncontrolled agony of her beating, her legs wide and her cheeks open, vulva and anus on plain show. Even when she released a fart she felt only a weak stab of humiliation, and another at Cicely's answering tut of disgust.

The spanking went on, mercilessly, smack after smack, delivered firmly across her naked seat. Her thighs were hit, too, even the lips of her sex, until her brain was hazy with the pain and her muscles could only twitch in helpless response. The bed beneath her was wet with tears; one shoe had come off with her frantic kicking; her chemise had ridden up, leaving her breasts bare and swinging in time to her spanking. Cicely had said nothing, just spanked happily away, until at last Charlotte began to push up her bottom.

Cheeks wide, vulva and anus offered to the blows, her screams had turned to moans, her blubbering to a steady, gentle crying, no less wretched or miserable, but open, abandoned. Cicely at once changed her tactic, releasing her victim's arm. Fingers delved between Charlotte's buttocks, spreading them, to leave her anus stretched taut. Two hard smacks were delivered to the little sweaty hole, making it pulse in pained reaction and wringing fresh gasps from Charlotte's throat.

With her anus smacked, Charlotte resigned the last scrap of her dignity, pushing her bottom yet higher and letting the little tight ring relax. Immediately the rounded tip of the shoe brush handle touched her ring, pushing in and stretching the moist flesh wide. Charlotte

5

sighed as she felt her bottom hole open to the pressure, the handle intruding into her back passage, deep in as her sphincter closed on the narrower part of the shaft. It was up her bum, the bristles tickling the sensitive, smacked skin between her cheeks, providing a sight she knew was both ridiculous and obscene.

She lay numb and broken across Cicely's lap, trembling gently, her breathing slow and deep, beaten and penetrated. Her mouth was open, hanging slack, spittle running from one corner. The fondling had started again, Cicely's hand now down between Charlotte's thighs, masturbating her as the brush wobbled to the motion. She'd been beaten, and now she was being made to show her reaction to it, her lewd, dirty response, writhing her sex against her tormentor's hand as her pleasure climbed slowly towards orgasm.

So many times it had happened, and so many times she had sworn it would never happen again. It did, always, almost every time they were together in private. Sometimes Cicely had to tease and taunt, or even apply a little force. More often it took only a command to lift the ugly school dress and get her bottom high for beating.

As her orgasm built in her head, she knew exactly why she did it. Nothing gave the same thrill, nothing whatever, no matter how hard she tried. Only Cicely could do it; only Cicely had the cruelty, the skill, the strength.

Charlotte was coming, her vulva squirming under Cicely's fingers, her breasts clutched tight in her hands, her burning bottom pushed high. She screamed once as it hit her, the sound trailing off into a babble of words and noises as peak after peak tore through her; Cicely's name, broken thanks, gasps and sobs, a long moan and once more her lover's name.

It was over, and she went limp, letting the ecstasy turn to the beautiful sense of contentment that came only when they had played together, when she had been punished. After pulling the brush from Charlotte's anus, Cicely waited, patiently, until Charlotte chose to move, sliding to the floor, turning, looking up into her lover's face with a tear-stained smile. Without a word, Cicely hitched up her school dress, tugging her drawers wide at the front to show off a nest of dark curls. Charlotte buried her face in them on the instant, probing between Cicely's sex lips with her tongue to find the little hard bud between. She began to lick and, as she did so, Cicely stroked her hair, sighing first, then moaning, until her thighs closed tight on Charlotte's head and she cried out in her own climax.

Spent, they climbed together on to the bed, cuddling up with Charlotte's head on Cicely's shoulder, chestnut curls mixed with straight, dark hair. Holding Charlotte close, Cicely reached out for her bedside table and pulled open the drawer. After rummaging beneath the contents, she extracted a cigarette case and matches. She lit one cigarette, then another, passing the second to Charlotte.

'That was divine,' she said. 'So far better than listening to some dreadful speech about deportment and our duty to the Empire.'

Charlotte snuggled closer. With her two brothers lost to the war in Europe, the idea of her owing anything more to the country only filled her with resentment.

'I can imagine old Mebbin now,' Cicely went on. 'She will be standing in front of seventy-two girls, imagining them clinging to her every word while in fact they're all dreadfully bored. She will talk of our role in Empire, and our responsibility, about finding good husbands and home making, about our duty to the poor and how we must set an example.'

'Do you suppose we shall be missed?'

'Oh, undoubtedly. I mean to say, we are prefects. I'm supposed to be on duty. So are you. In fact, that was what I came up to tell you, but it slipped my mind.'

'Cicely, we shall be punished!'

'Don't be silly, darling. We're leaving in a few hours. If you're scared of Mebbin, just walk out of the gate. It's ever so simple.'

'I suppose I could. It will feel strange, not having to answer to the Mistresses.'

'Not having to answer to anybody, lucky things that we are.'

'The Colonel.'

'Who is a senile old fool and desperately in love with you. Anyway, you'll be twenty-one soon enough, and Mistress of Ashwood.'

'And expected to marry.'

'I don't see why you have to but, if you must, you must, I suppose. Choose a wet one who plays golf or some hearty fellow who spends half his life in Africa or trying to walk to the North Pole. That way I can come and make love to you whenever I please. How are the sharks, anyway? Attentive?'

'Ever so. I had five letters just this week, one to a shark. Lester Jerton is terribly formal but really rather intense. I could bear the thought of Victor Cushat if it wasn't for the politics.'

'Frightful.'

'Reggie Thann is worse, and I'm certain Cyprian prefers men.'

'How perfect. Come to an arrangement, so that he may have his lovers; we can have ourselves, and all the time everyone will think us terribly respectable.'

'No, I couldn't, really. I mean, who knows whom he might bring to the house?'

'There is that.'

'Toby amuses me at least. His letter is really quite witty.'

'Oh, God, please, Lottie, don't choose Toby. He's quite horrid underneath all that charm. Anyway, he knows, I'm sure. He'd probably make us do it in front of him. He's like that.'

'Surely not.'

'Oh, believe me, he might. When we were little he used to make me eat worms.'

'That's hardly the same.'

'It takes the same sort of nasty little mind. Anyway, I couldn't bear to think of you married to my brother. For one thing he'd expect you to have about a dozen children. He'd want to play the local squire as well, and he'd insist on a large household. Spince and Mrs Mabberley wouldn't be anything like enough for him.'

'Well, he has much stronger prospects than the others. Just now at any rate.'

In response Cicely sighed deeply before drawing on her cigarette and flicking the ash on to the floor. Charlotte followed suit, wincing slightly as the movement pressed her sore bottom to the bed.

'And yourself?' she asked. 'What will you do?'

'I shall be an invert,' Cicely answered. 'Girls can get away with it, you know, in London. I shall buy a little flat in Soho or maybe by the river. I shall dress in men's clothes and have the most scandalous writers and artists to lunch. I shall be thought frightfully clever and witty. Some may even suspect, but they won't know.'

'Won't it be terribly inconvenient to be called Cicely? A more feminine name is hard to imagine.'

'I shan't call myself Cicely, silly girl. I shall choose Bertie, or perhaps George. Both are certain to scandalise the Mamas.'

'Be George. It's so much firmer than Bertie, more definite. I like the thought of being spanked by a George. If you were a Bertie it would just seem silly.'

'George St John. George St John, Esquire. Yes, why not? It has a certain style.'

Cicely stretched and blew a smoke ring, which they watched as it drifted lazily upwards, slowly dissipating in the breeze from the open window. Outside, Charlotte could hear the laughter of the younger girls who were not obliged to be at Miss Mebbin's inspirational talk to those who were leaving. They sounded carefree, also innocent, and for a moment her excitement at the prospect of leaving faded, to be replaced by a sense of loss.

'I shall make Toby buy us dinner this evening,' Cicely said suddenly. 'We can drive to Sidmouth or Lyme and have quails' eggs and lobster and Alsatian wine, and ever so much chocolate cake.'

Charlotte's melancholy faded as rapidly as it had come, the excited anticipation returning. She thought of driving in Toby St John's car, and the sea, of being dressed in nice clothes and of washing quails' eggs and lobster down with white wine. Nuzzling her face against the swell of Cicely's breast, she imagined the possibilities offered by becoming drunk together, of a hotel should Toby also get drunk, and a shared bed in the name of sensible economy. It was always so much easier drunk, so much easier to give in to her feelings.

The sounds from beyond the window changed abruptly, with older, more confident voices added to the girlish ones. Reluctantly, she lifted her head from Cicely's chest, knowing that somebody would inevitably be sent to find them and that her room was the first place they would look.

'We would be best to make ourselves scarce,' she said.

'Nonsense! Kiss me,' Cicely answered.

Cicely's hand settled on the back of Charlotte's head, pulling her in. Charlotte resisted for a moment before letting it happen, their mouths opening together in a long, sensual kiss. Her feelings rose again quickly and it was impossible not to take one of Cicely's breasts in a hand, stroking and feeling the nipple rise beneath the coarse wool of the school dress. Cicely responded with a still firmer kiss, Charlotte's caution fading rapidly as she gave way to her feelings. Her dress was still up, at the level of her thighs and, as Cicely's hand began to move slowly down her back, Charlotte knew exactly where it was going: to the bare, sore cheeks of her smacked bottom.

Sure enough, her dress was twitched up and it was showing again, the red cheeks naked to the air. Cicely began to stroke, caressing the flesh she had beaten so hard, no longer cruel, but very much in charge, soothing her punished lover. All Charlotte could do was melt into the caress, gently feeling Cicely's own body as hers was explored.

Charlotte did not hear the door open. Only when Cicely became suddenly tense did she realise anything was wrong, and the next moment they had broken apart and she was desperately trying to get her dress down and extinguish her smouldering cigarette. Miss Mebbin stood in the doorway, her face set in horrified surprise.

'You will attend me in my study, in ten minutes, both of you,' the headmistress snapped.

'Oh, please, we . . .' Charlotte stammered.

'No,' Cicely answered.

'No? How do you mean, no?' Miss Mebbin demanded.

'I mean no,' Cicely repeated. 'It's a substantive adverb signifying the negative, or some such thing. I'm sure you told us.'

'I am aware of the meaning of the word,' Miss Mebbin replied, her tone icy. 'The question is what you mean by it.'

'I mean,' Cicely went on, rising and quite casually drawing on her cigarette, 'that I shall not be coming to your study in ten minutes, nor twenty. Nor will Lottie. You may wait all afternoon if it pleases you, but you must do so without the benefit of our company.'

'You impertinent child!' Miss Mebbin snapped back, advancing on Cicely. 'You will do as I say and you will do it promptly!'

'I rather think not,' Cicely answered.

The two women stood facing each other at the foot of Charlotte's bed. For years she had thought of Miss

Mebbin as impossibly tall and impossibly stern, a towering figure who could never be answered back, let alone defied. Now, despite the cold anger in her face, it was impossible not to notice how small and frail she looked, with the tight bun in which she wore her hair barely reaching the level of Cicely's chin.

Neither said a word, and Charlotte hastily covered herself and disposed of her cigarette, at once grateful that Cicely's defiance would deflect the headmistress's rage from herself and guilty for entertaining such a mean thought.

It was obvious what would happen. Cicely would quickly break down under Miss Mebbin's icy stare and try to apologise, or make light of what had happened. It would make no difference. They would be taken by their hands and led down to the study. Once they were there, their dresses would be turned up and their drawers parted – well, not hers, because they were certain to fall down the moment she got off the bed.

Once there, with bare bottoms on plain view through the study windows, to pupils and any parents or siblings who might have arrived early, they would be caned. After that would come the lecture as they stood against the wall, with their bottoms still showing, then the letter to the Colonel, complaining of delinquency and, worse, of lesbianism.

Cicely neither moved nor spoke. Instead, she blew a smoke ring, no more than a puff of air between pursed lips. The wreath of smoke wavered in the air, settling gently over Miss Mebbin's head. Charlotte's mouth came open, watching the expression of cold anger on the headmistress's face grow to fury. She grabbed Cicely's hand, snatched the cigarette away and stamped on it.

'I shall allow you a last opportunity, St John,' Miss Mebbin spoke. 'You may present yourself in my study within ten minutes. Otherwise, the consequences will be severe, more severe than you may entirely understand.'

'Oh, you do talk nonsense, Mebbin,' Cicely answered. 'I mean to say, what could you possibly do?'

'I can make you very sorry for your impudence,' the headmistress replied. 'It had been my intention simply to deal with this as a matter of discipline. Now I find myself obliged to write to Colonel St John.'

'More nonsense,' Cicely said, addressing Charlotte. 'As if she could possibly have resisted the pleasure of describing her little adventure to the Colonel. Oh, do run along, Mebbin.'

Cicely turned towards the window, throwing Charlotte a glance that was intended to convey amusement but betrayed her tension. Miss Mebbin stood, speechless, but only for a moment. As Cicely reached for the cigarette case, she was caught by the wrist and jerked hard down across the bed.

'I will not have my authority undermined!' Miss Mebbin snapped as the girl sprawled across the bed, bottom up.

Charlotte scrambled hastily back to provide room for Cicely to be spanked, her shock tempered by a sudden and unexpected delight at the prospect of watching. It didn't happen. Instead of allowing herself to be pushed down, Cicely jerked violently, rolling over on the bed. Miss Mebbin held on, her face set in grim determination, struggling to get the unwilling girl into a good position for punishment. Cicely jerked and writhed, pulling this way and that, all her poise evaporated, with fear in her eyes as she struggled to keep her bottom pressed to the bed.

With her lips pursed in anger and her eyes blazing, Miss Mebbin fought to get proper control, twisting Cicely's arm in an effort to force her over. Cicely began to roll, turned inexorably bottom up, in a state of panic, beating the bed with her free arm and kicking out violently, her heel catching Miss Mebbin in the back. The response was a stinging slap, full in Cicely's face.

Cicely cried out in shock and pain, the tears starting from her eyes even as she wrenched herself free, slapping out at Miss Mebbin with all her force. The blow caught the headmistress across the mouth and she went back, letting go of Cicely with an exclamation. Screaming wildly, Cicely grabbed Miss Mebbin by the hair, tearing the bun free and throwing her off balance.

'Horrid, horrid, horrid old woman!' Cicely screeched, dragging the headmistress down across the bed. 'You're horrible! You're so horrible!'

Cicely was wild eyed, her face scarlet and streaked with tears, her dark, long hair in disarray. Throwing a leg across Miss Mebbin's body, she began to rain down slaps, wild and disordered, then purposeful as the headmistress's skirts were grabbed and hauled high over her bottom.

'No!' Miss Mebbin shouted.

'Cicely!' Charlotte gasped.

'I'm going to do it, I'm going to do it!' Cicely stammered.

It was an impossible outrage, unthinkable, and Charlotte could only gape as the headmistress's skirts and petticoats were pulled up, revealing knee-length stockings and a pair of voluminous, lacy drawers. Miss Mebbin was struggling, but Cicely held on, immobile in her strength and fury. The anger on Miss Mebbin's face faded, changing to a desperate consternation as the horrible realisation sank in. Cicely was really going to do it.

'Do not do this!' she hissed. 'Do not!'

There was command in her voice, but more fear. Cicely had stopped, and was gazing down at her victim's silk-covered bottom, breathing hard.

'I shall do it,' she said, speaking through clenched teeth. 'I *shall*!'

'You will stop this! You will stop this instant!' Miss Mebbin grated. 'Do you hear what I am saying, St John? I will prosecute. Stop!'

Cicely had taken hold of Miss Mebbin's drawers, and with the last word she pulled the curtains wide, exposing a trim bottom and a remarkably hairy vulva.

'Oh, my Lord, Cicely!' Charlotte exclaimed. 'You can't!'

'I've got to,' Cicely rasped. 'This is for all the things you've done to me, you horrid old woman, and to Lottie, too. This is for the hurt and the loneliness and the beastliness. This is for everything, for confiscating Lottie's rag doll and for making Alice Challacombe stand still until she wet in her drawers, and everyone and everything, and that time on the playing field in front of everybody with my bottom bare and there were men watching, men!'

Her voice had risen to a screech, and on the last word her hand came down on to Miss Mebbin's bottom, driven with all the force of her rage. Charlotte heard the slap and saw the tight bottom bounce to the impact, then again, and again, as Cicely rained down blow after furious blow, all the while with tears streaming down her scarlet cheeks and her mouth trembling with emotion.

Miss Mebbin said nothing, staring forward with her teeth set and her eyes wide in cold fury as her bottom was spanked to a furious, glowing red. Her silence only seemed to make Cicely more angry, slapping and slapping, with both hands, to make her victim's bottom cheeks jump and part, revealing the full, hairy vulva and a tight, brown knot of anal flesh. Charlotte could only watch in mingled horror and delight as the woman she had been terrified of for so long was given an ignomini-ous, bare-bottom spanking, not knowing whether to be scared or pleased, to cry or to laugh.

'Say sorry,' Cicely demanded suddenly. 'Say sorry and I'll stop.'

There was no answer. Cicely continued to spank, but less hard, only to grab for the shoe brush and start to belabour Miss Mebbin's bottom with it in renewed fury.

The reaction was instantaneous. The headmistress's eyes went wide and her mouth came open in a gasp of pain and bewilderment. Then she was babbling apologies, begging Cicely to stop between little broken gasps, her head shaking frantically all the time. Cicely seemed not to hear, spanking on and on, with the marks on her victim's bottom turning quickly from pink to red and an angry crimson at each crest. Miss Mebbin was pleading for mercy, screaming in pain, and suddenly, without warning, she had burst into tears.

Cicely stopped immediately; her anger vanished as she climbed off her victim's back. Miss Mebbin stayed where she was, sobbing into the bedclothes, not even able to cover her bottom, despite the clear view of her sex. Cicely glanced at Charlotte, suddenly guilty.

'I ... I'm sorry,' she said. 'Look, I just lost my temper, that's all. You shouldn't have tried to force me. Look, Lottie, I think we'd better go.'

Miss Mebbin got up slowly, her dress falling into place. Her cheeks were stained with tears, her lower lip trembling, and Charlotte found herself wondering how she could ever have found the tiny woman so daunting. Cicely stepped back, still clutching the shoe brush, her expression worried but determined.

Charlotte felt a new fear, not of the headmistress, but those she might call on, other women, even men. Then there would be no resistance, and Cicely, and she herself, would get what was coming to them.

'You will not get away with this, St John,' Miss Mebbin said, her voice cold but far from steady. 'I shall prosecute.'

'You wouldn't dare,' Cicely answered. 'Think of the scandal.'

Miss Mebbin said nothing, but walked swiftly from the room, brushing past Cicely. As the door closed the girls' eyes met. Cicely reached out a hand, which Charlotte took, and together they ran for the school gates, freedom and safety.

Summer 1920, Steeple Ashwood, Somerset

With her pretty, chubby face set in a smile of pure mischief, Catherine Mullins peered out through the tangle of foliage. Three men were visible, all big, muscular farmhands, stripped to the waist, their skin glossy with sweat as they worked. Beside them a bank of dark earth stretched back across a flat field, the new ditch beside it.

She had come out on the pretext of taking them their lunch, hurrying so that she could spend as long as possible watching them work before revealing herself. The day was hot, and she had been hoping they would have stripped down. Sure enough, there was plenty to see, and not just the firm muscles of their torsos, but hard buttocks packed into tight canvas trousers, and more.

All three were from the village, the eldest her uncle, the others his two sons. All showed the same thick, tawny hair, solid bodies and smooth skin darkened by the sun. All were well worth watching, and she could feel her eagerness rising with the wet, open feeling between her thighs. It was impossible not to think of the cocks so poorly concealed in their trousers, and especially that of the youngest, John. He had always taken pleasure in teasing her, and recently his jokes and remarks had taken on a more serious turn, until on the previous Sunday he had threatened to make her take his cock in her hand.

She had run, dashing away down the lane to the sound of his laughter, her face red with blushes, not stopping until she had reached her parents' cottage. Only then had she changed her mind, wishing she'd shown more courage and dared him to carry out his threat. Now, with the cock she had come so close to being made to touch showing clearly through his trousers, she was again wishing she'd been bolder.

At the sound of the distant church bells she drew back into the bushes, emerging a moment later on the path. The men turned, laying down their tools with grunts of satisfaction at the sight of the basket in her hands. She greeted them, smiling and blushing as their eyes moved quickly to her ample chest. Pretending not to notice, she put the basket down, opening it to take out the men's food.

'Bread and honey,' she said. 'Then there's a drop of cider, and milk for the boy.'

'Milk, what's this milk?' John demanded.

The others laughed at his discomfort, to Catherine's delight.

'Cider's for grown men,' she mocked. 'Milk's the better for them as isn't long off their mother's.'

'I'll show you who's a grown man, one of these days, Catherine Mullins,' he answered.

'It's best not to make promises you can't keep,' she replied.

He answered her with a look that sent the blood to her cheeks and a fresh urgency to her sex. She thought again of his cock, and of how it would have felt in her hand. With four brothers, the sight of men's genitals was familiar enough, and she knew what happened when they became excited. To actually touch was a very different matter.

They were no longer paying attention to her, just eating and discussing the drainage system on which they were working. She felt grateful, sure that it would be obvious how flustered she was, and that they'd know why. Looking away, she hid her face, feigning indifference.

'We'll be needing mattocks, once we're in among the poplars,' her uncle remarked, gesturing to a grove of trees a few yards beyond the end of the ditch.

'I'll fetch 'em over,' John answered quickly. 'I'll walk Catherine back while I'm at it. Wouldn't do to have some wicked old gypsy or whatnot get at her.'

'I'm very able to look after myself, thanking you, John Dunn,' Catherine answered.

John laughed and took a swallow of his milk, then grinned in response to a wink from his father. Catherine stood up, feeling very unsure of herself, aroused and a little scared, certain that John would make an advance on her if they walked back to the village together. There was no excuse not to go with him, and she found her fingers shaking as she packed the lunch things back into the basket. John had stood, taking his shirt from where it was hung across a branch. Catherine watched him put it on from the corner of her eye.

'Don't waste your time,' her uncle remarked to John as he walked over to her. 'There's plenty more work to be done.'

'I'll not waste it,' John answered. 'Come on, Catherine, don't keep your betters waiting.'

'Which betters would that be, then?' Catherine questioned as she fell into step beside him. 'All I can see is some mumpheaded boy who's no better than he should be.'

'Mumpheaded boy, is it?' John demanded. 'Why, I should take a strap to that big white arse for that, so I should.'

'You wouldn't dare.'

'Oh, wouldn't I?'

'No, and you know it.'

'I don't know nothing of the sort. In fact, I've a mind to teach you a few manners.'

She didn't answer, and he didn't press the point, leaving her more uneasy than ever. The threat of a belting had left her trembling, but more at the thought of having her bottom exposed to him than of the pain it would bring. Half of her wanted to keep on teasing, to goad him into it, the other half to run. What she was certain of was that once her skirts were up and the width of her bottom was bare in front of him he would quickly lose interest in beating her. He'd pull out his cock, and demand it be pulled at, the way boys liked it, probably with her smacked bottom still bare behind her.

'Here'll do,' he said suddenly as the path entered a thicket of elder and thorn bushes.

'Do? Do for what?' Catherine demanded in sudden panic.

'To belt your arse,' he answered. 'Come on now, get here, across this trunk.'

'I'll do no such thing!' she answered, stepping away from him.

'Then you'll tug my man, one or t'other, take your choice.'

'I'll tell Uncle Lias on you, John Dunn, and father. Then we'll see who gets the belting.'

'Get on with you, you fat baggage, you want it as much as I do myself. Don't think I don't see the way you look at me.'

He was walking towards her as she backed into the shade of the little thicket. His thumbs were in the top of his trousers, his fingers splayed towards a very obvious bulge. She could feel herself trembling, wanting to do it but scared, and unable to explain her feelings to him.

'Come on,' he urged. 'It's what you want, you know it is.'

'I would do it,' she answered defiantly, 'perhaps for a kind young man who bought me flowers, or some fancy

20

bonbons as it might me. Not for you, John Dunn. You'll have to make me.'

'Then so I shall,' he answered and grabbed for her.

Catherine twisted away, dashing between the trees. Behind her he laughed and gave chase. She realised at once that it was hopeless, her long dress catching on twigs and threatening to trip her at every stride. She stopped where the thicket met a grassy bank, and turned as he came towards her, grinning.

'You'll do it now, and no more teasing,' he ordered. 'Down on the grass with you.'

Catherine went, as afraid as she was excited, sitting herself down among the long, warm grass. He was fumbling with his fly, pulling at the buttons, the bulge of his cock bigger than ever beneath the material. She could feel a lump in her throat, and it was impossible to keep her fingers still. Then it was out, a thick, pale, fleshy cock, the wet red tip already poking from the foreskin. She reached out, tentatively, her fingers trembling, and took it, feeling the soft meat slip on the harder core within.

'That's my girl,' John sighed. 'Gently now, and pull on him. No, not like that: I'm not a cow. Up and down, nice and slow till he grows nice and hard.'

Catherine obeyed, the lump in her throat swelling as his cock grew in her hand, longer and harder, until the head was emerging fully from the foreskin with each tug. John blew his breath out, then pushed down his trousers and the garment beneath, exposing the pouch of his balls and a great deal of coarse, dark-brown hair. His cock was rock-hard in Catherine's hand and her own excitement was growing, making her want to spread her thighs to the big penis she was holding.

'Spill your dumplings,' he ordered. 'I've a mind to rut in between 'em.'

Catherine found her hands going to the laces that held her dress closed. It was too small for her, and she felt the tension go as her big breasts bulged out, free from restraint. John reached down, peeling her bodice open. Her breasts tumbled out, to lie fat and bare in the hot sun, her big nipples poking up, already engorged with blood.

'By God, but they're big ones,' John swore.

'Don't blaspheme, John,' Catherine answered. 'Not while . . . not while this.'

He just laughed, and kneeled down, pushing his crotch to her chest, his erection pressed in between her breasts. She caught the scent of his cock, sweat too, male and urgent, increasing her need to have him between her legs.

'Push 'em together then, stupid. Don't you know nothing?' he said and began to rub his cock and balls in her cleavage.

'I do know,' Catherine answered in automatic reproach.

She obeyed, squeezing her breasts around his turgid cock and the taut, rough sac of his scrotum. He took her by the shoulders, rubbing faster and faster, with the bloated tip of his penis poking in and out of the soft, creamy flesh of her breasts.

'Oh, you beautiful fat baggage,' he moaned. 'I'm going to have you now, right here and right now.'

'No, John!' she squeaked as his hands went to catch her up under her knees. 'No!'

It was too late: he had jerked upwards, sending her sprawling on to her back, her legs rolled up to her chest, her skirt falling to expose her bare sex, against which his erect cock lay.

'No, John, don't be foolish,' she stammered. 'I've no mind for a baby, John!'

'Nor I,' he said, spreading her thighs apart to bring his cock to her sex and fully expose her breasts.

The head of his cock was against her vulva, pressed to where her hymen half closed the wet, swollen opening

22

into her body. She could feel it, tense against her flesh, threatening to tear her. Her breathing was fast, uncontrolled, and she found herself unable to move, for all her fear.

'No, John,' she breathed, 'you'll give me a baby, you will!'

'I'm not stupid, girl,' he answered. 'Don't you think I don't know how to stop a brat?'

With that he pushed. Catherine gasped as her hymen burst with a sharp stab of pain and his cock was inside her, filling out her vagina to leave her wide-eyed and open-mouthed. He began to fuck her, holding her by the shoulders, his mouth pressed hard against hers in a bruising kiss. She cocked her legs wide, surrendering herself and trying to ignore the stinging, rasping pain of her torn flesh.

He was quickly urgent, and she began to wonder if he wasn't going to forget his promise and do it inside her after all, when he whipped out his cock. She was grabbed by the hair, wrenched down, her mouth stuffed with penis even as she opened it to protest, and then with sperm as he ejaculated down her throat. Slimy, salty come filled her gullet an instant before the head of his cock was jammed in after it. She was choking, gagging on his erection, the muscles of her throat going into spasms on his cock flesh, milking yet more come out of it. His hand stayed tight in her hair, forcing his penis well down her throat as she struggled to free herself, kicking and slapping ineffectually at his legs. He ignored her, groaning in satisfaction as he drained his cock down her throat and not letting go until the last drop had been squeezed out. Finally, he pulled back, leaving Catherine coughing and spluttering on the grass, with a curtain of come and spittle hanging from her lips and her mouth full of the revolting taste.

'Oh, I never had you for a cocksucker,' he sighed as he sat back.

'What choice had I?' Catherine managed once she had wiped the mess from around her mouth.

John simply laughed, pressing his rapidly softening cock back into his trousers. Catherine turned to him, trying to look angry but finding it impossible to keep the smile from her face.

Winter 1920, Ashwood House, Somerset

Charlotte sat up as she caught the sound of tyres on gravel. Across the room Colonel St John also looked up, replacing the glass from which he had been drinking Bual on the table as he did so.

'Visitors, d'you suppose?' he demanded.

'It will be Cicely,' Charlotte answered patiently. 'You know she's coming down for a few days.'

'Cicely? Cicely who? Oh, Sissy, my niece, of course. Why can't you call her by her blasted name? Sissy, splendid, nice girl.'

He pulled himself to his feet, walking heavily to the door. In the hallway the butler, Spince, had already opened the door, through which a canary-yellow Sunbeam was visible. Charlotte felt a flush of disappointment as she saw that the driver was not Cicely but a young man, only for the emotion to change to delighted surprise as she realised that it really was her friend, but in a neat, dark suit, cut to the latest fashion, for men.

She hurried to the door, struggling not to laugh at the look of passive disapproval on the butler's face. Cicely was already climbing from the car, pulling at her gloves as she did so. She wore a leather cap, and as she pulled it free Charlotte saw that her friend's hair had been cut short and was slicked back with gel. It was boyish, but would have passed as eccentric. Not so the suit, which was undoubtedly masculine, and the more so for the crisp white shirt and brocaded waistcoat beneath, the neat cravat of crimson silk, brilliantly polished black shoes and a pair of fawn spats.

Charlotte found it impossible to conceal her delight. Running down the steps, she spread her arms wide for her friend, hugging her close and kissing her without thought for the butler or even her guardian. Cicely returned the kiss, but pulled gently away before it could become too open, only to favour Charlotte's bottom with a gentle pat as they turned towards the house.

'You've really done it. How wonderful!' Charlotte exclaimed. 'Oh, whatever is Francis going to say?'

Colonel St John had reached the steps and was looking at them, with no animosity but a puzzled expression.

'Uncle Francis,' Cicely greeted him, and kissed him on the cheek, at which he pulled back.

'Toby? What the devil?' he demanded, peering at his niece.

'It's not Toby, dear Francis,' Charlotte said. 'It's Cicely.'

'Sissy?' the Colonel demanded. 'Why, so it is. I thought you were your brother. What the hell are you doing dressed as a man? Is it fancy dress tonight? Spince, have you laid out a costume for me?'

'No, it's not fancy dress, Uncle Francis,' Cicely answered. 'I'm afraid I'm an invert, and you must address me as George.'

'George? Why in hell would I want to do that? And besides, what's an invert?'

'An invert, dear Uncle, is a term coined by Karl Westphal, although I believe it's something of a mistranslation from the original German . . .'

'German?'

'It has nothing to do with Germans, Uncle, they merely invented the word. It means a woman who prefers the company of other women – sexually, that is.'

'Sexually? What, you mean you're a bugger? No, that's not right, is it? What, girls, like Lottie?'

'Especially Lottie. We've been at it for simply years.'

'Good God!'

'Cicely!'

'Oh, don't be so dramatic, Uncle Francis. It's no more shocking than the way you like us to read to you after dinner. He may as well know, Lottie. I mean, if we're in the same house he's sure to realise sooner or later. I prefer to be honest.'

'You mean everybody knows, in London?' the Colonel demanded.

'Well, no,' Cicely admitted, 'only my better friends. The others may think what they please. Most of them think it's just rather amusing, and it does mean that only the interesting people ever invite me anywhere. Thank you, Spince.'

She had handed her driving cap and gloves to the butler, who had remained silent and motionless throughout the conversation. He took them, gave a slight inclination of his head and stood back, holding the door wide as they trooped into the house, Cicely in the lead.

'Damn peculiar,' the Colonel remarked, his eyes widening at the sight of Cicely's bottom straining out the material of her trousers. 'Still, I'm damned if I ever saw a pair of trousers fit that snug on a boy.'

'There's no need for vulgarity,' Charlotte chided, allowing Cicely to take her arm.

The Colonel snorted in response, following them into the drawing room and returning to his glass of Bual. Feeling elated, and chokingly proud of her friend, she ordered Spince to fetch a bottle of Krug from the cellar. In the few months since leaving school they had written to each other, but had not met, and Cicely had kept the extent of her transformation to herself. It was not all that had changed. Always poised and cool, Cicely had become still more urbane, smoking cigarettes in an ebony holder and speaking casually of art and of the fringes of London society among which she found her friends. Charlotte was entranced, and hung on every word, the crush that had sustained her through school growing rapidly towards hero worship.

Over dinner Cicely declined the jugged hare, explaining that her principles no longer permitted her to eat meat. Despite the Colonel's open disgust, Charlotte agreed, refusing her own portion as she took in her friend's arguments in favour of vegetarianism, both moral and physical. Even cheese proved to be unreasonable, involving, as Cicely explained, the exploitation of animals for human ends. The Colonel merely laughed, helping himself to what the girls would otherwise have eaten.

Charlotte came to the end of dinner in an adoring trance, pleasantly drunk and more smitten with Cicely than ever before. Even the Colonel seemed impressed in a way, commenting that Cicely seemed to have matured remarkably fast. Rather than please her, the complimentary remark sparked an uneasy feeling, and as they followed the Colonel into the library she and Cicely shared a glance.

'Splendid, splendid,' the Colonel remarked, seating himself in a broad leather upholstered armchair. 'I take it your damn fool reservations don't extend to port, Sissy?'

'Anything derived from the plant kingdom is acceptable,' Cicely answered. 'It is to animals that we must accord respect if we are ever to become truly civilised.'

'Stuff and nonsense,' he answered amiably. 'Leave the decanter, Spince. The girls are going to read to me.'

'Very well, sir,' Spince answered and withdrew, turning the key in the lock behind him and sliding it back under the door.

'Really, Uncle,' Cicely said immediately. 'You can't possibly expect –'

28

'Can't I just,' he answered. 'I trust you've not grown too hoity-toity to help out your old guardian, even if you are a bloody what's it, an invert.'

'Francis, really!' Charlotte broke in.

'Don't be so damned mawkish, girl,' he answered. 'It's little enough to ask, isn't it, reading to an old man who can barely see?'

'You would be able to see perfectly well if you would get a pair of spectacles, Francis, dear,' Charlotte said.

'And look like some damn clerk? I will not!'

'It's hardly suitable, Uncle Francis,' Cicely remarked. 'I mean to say . . .'

'Suitable!' the Colonel barked. 'I'll remind you, young lady, that you gad about London as you please, without even a chaperone . . .'

'Oh, Uncle Francis, don't be so old-fashioned. Simply nobody has a chaperone nowadays.'

'. . . and dressed as a man to boot,' he went on, ignoring her remark. 'How suitable is that, eh? How many fellows d'you know who'd have been so damn lenient as a guardian, eh?'

'None, I suppose,' Cicely admitted.

'Well, then, show a little consideration in return, damn you.'

Cicely didn't respond, but made an elaborate show of placing a cigarette in the long ebony holder and lighting it. With the first draw she blew a smoke ring, which Charlotte watched as it floated lazily up towards the ceiling.

'Well?' the Colonel demanded.

'Oh, very well,' Cicely answered. 'I won't touch it, though, and that's that. You must do it yourself.'

'Myself? What do you take me for?'

'Well Lottie may, then. I suppose she has done.'

'Sometimes,' Charlotte admitted, colouring at the admission. 'What is it to be then?'

' *The Pearl*, I think, the bit where old General Coote has his granddaughter whipped. No, no, later, with the

French piece, in Issue Four, if I remember rightly. All girls together, eh, Sissy? More your style, eh?'

Cicely said nothing, but walked to the bookcase, reaching up to the highest shelf, from which she took a dog-eared magazine. Seating herself in the chair beside the Colonel's, she opened it and began to scan through the pages, one-handed, with her cigarette holder in the other.

' "Miss Coote's Confession",' she announced. 'Look, I'll skip the first part – it takes a while to become interesting.'

'Splendid,' the Colonel answered, easing himself into a more comfortable position in the chair.

Quite casually, he undid his trousers, pulling free a big, dark-skinned penis and a full, leathery scrotum. With a sigh of resignation, Charlotte carried a stool over and kneeled on it, leaning on the arm of his chair. Reaching out, she took her guardian's penis in her gloved hand. It moved at her touch, the head stirring sluggishly beneath the thick foreskin. Folding her hand around it, she began to tug, with impatient little jerks. The Colonel reached out, taking first his cigar and then his glass of port, intent on both smoking and drinking while his ward masturbated him.

'I'll start here,' Cicely said, 'where the girls are stripping Mademoiselle Fosse, if you're quite comfortable, Uncle Francis?'

'Quite,' he grunted, pushing his belly up to wedge his penis more firmly into Charlotte's hand.

'Then I shall begin. "We all gathered round her and, although she playfully resisted, she was soon denuded of every rag of clothing. We pulled off her boots and stockings; but what a beautiful sight she was, apparently about twenty-six, with nicely rounded limbs, but such a glorious profusion of hair, that from her head, now let loose, hung down her back in a dense mass, and quite covered her bottom, so that she might have sat on the end of it . . ." '

The Colonel's penis had already began to stiffen in Charlotte's hand, the tip showing each time she pulled down. The skin of his scrotum was tightening, too, with the big balls two plump bulges beneath the wrinkled flesh. She began to tug faster, hoping he'd come quickly and not make a fuss over his treat. Unfortunately, he seemed in no hurry at all, sipping at his port and puffing on his cigar as Cicely continued to read.

' "Then we commenced our game again, and she switched us finely, leaving long red marks on our bottoms when she succeeded in making a hit. Her own bottom must have smarted from our smacks, but she seemed quite excited and delighted with the amusement, till at last she said, 'Oh, I must be birched myself. Who will be the schoolmistress?' " '

'Splendid,' the Colonel cut in. 'What is it, four girls, five? All stripped and birched. What a sight, eh?'

'Don't interrupt, Uncle Francis, dear,' Cicely replied. 'You'll make me lose my place, and probably put Lottie off her stroke. Now, this Laura. I'll try to do the voices, the way you like. " 'Oh! Let Rosa! She will lecture you as if you were a culprit, and give us an idea of good earnest punishment. Will you, Rosa? It will amuse us all. Just see if you can't make Mademoiselle ask your pardon for taking liberties with you. Do, there's a dear girl.' " '

The cock in Charlotte's hand was rock-hard, the head now fully emerged from the foreskin, an angry red with a bead of dampness at the tip. She put her second hand to him, tugging frantically and stroking the rough skin of his balls. He would try to hold back, she knew, either until the story became very rude or until she lost patience. As she masturbated him, she was listening to Cicely, thinking of the birchings that had been administered to her own bottom and all the times she had taken her guardian in her hand while she read out some lewd passage from his collection of erotica.

' "Thus urged, I took up the rod and, flourishing it lightly in the air, said, laughing, 'I know how to use it properly, especially on naughty bottoms, which have the impudence to challenge me; now, Mademoiselle, present your bottom on the edge of the bed, with your legs well apart, just touching the floor, but I must have two of them to hold you down; come, Laura and Louise, each of you hold one arm, and keep her body well down on the bed. There, that will do just so. Hold her securely, don't let her get up till I've fairly done.' " '

The Colonel shifted forward and at the same time put down his cigar. His arm came out, around Charlotte's waist, then lower, taking hold of her bottom and starting to knead. She let him fondle her, squeezing his balls and tugging as fast as she could on his cock, which was so swollen with blood that the head had become shiny, and a rich purple in colour. Her wrist was starting to hurt, and she was sure he would come, yet he just continued to sip his wine and feel her buttocks as Cicely read on.

' ". . . till her bum was rosy all over, and marked with a profusion of deep red weals. Mademoiselle made desperate efforts to release herself, but Lady Clara and Cecile also helped to keep her down, all apparently highly excited by the sight of her excoriated blushing bottom, adding their remarks, such as, 'Bravo, bravo, Rosie. You didn't think she would catch it so. How delightful to see her writhe and plunge in pain, to hear her scream, and help to keep her down,' till at last the surprised victim begged and prayed for pardon, crying to be let off, with tears in her eyes." '

Charlotte set her lips in frustration. Her arm was hot with pain, her fingers numb where they gripped the big cock. The Colonel had been groaning at the description of the French woman's whipping, but as Cicely read on he relaxed again, taking another sip of wine.

'Get to another whipping, Cicely,' she demanded. 'You know he likes those best.'

Cicely stopped, turning the page. The Colonel gave a grunt of irritation, burying his fingers deeper into the cleft of Charlotte's bottom. Already her dress and petticoats were pushed well into her cleft, and the new motion spread her cheeks further, pressing cotton to her anus. The Colonel found the little hole and began to wiggle his finger in it, until a little bud of cotton had been pushed up her anus.

'Francis!' she protested, feeling a flush of resentment at the rude penetration of her bottom.

He merely grunted, pushing his finger deeper up her behind, petticoat cotton and all. Cicely was still turning the pages. In desperation, Charlotte kneeled forward, opened her mouth around her guardian's cock and sucked hard. Immediately the back of her dress was whipped up, the cotton plug pulling from her bumhole as her petticoats followed. His hand delved into the split of her drawers, finding her naked bottom and squeezing one cheek. She sucked harder still, eyes closed as his hand pushed in between her thighs, cupping the swell of her sex, his thumb pressing to her anus.

'Perfect,' Cicely said quite calmly, 'here we are: ". . . Frau Bildaur at once mounted me on Maria's broad back, and pinned up the dress above my waist, then the English governess with evident pleasure opened my drawers behind so as to expose my bare bottom, while the soft-hearted young German showed her sympathy by eyes brimming with tears." '

The Colonel's thumb invaded Charlotte's anus, squeezing in past the reluctant ring, and up. He began to massage her in her rectum, while squashing the flesh of her vulva between palm and thumb. She sucked frantically, masturbating his cock into her mouth with furious jerks, her head swimming with humiliation at the awful position she was in, a cock in her mouth, a thumb up her bared bottom and, worst of all, with her beloved Cicely watching and coolly reading out the dirty story.

' "My red blushing bottom must have been a most edifying sight to the pupils, and a regular caution to timid offenders, two or three more of whom might expect their turn in a day or two; although I screamed and cried out in apparent anguish it was nothing to what I had suffered at the hands of Sir Eyre or Mrs Mansell; the worst part of the punishment was in the degrading ceremony and charity-girl costume the victim had to assume." '

On the word 'degrading' the Colonel came, filling Charlotte's mouth with thick, salty sperm, which burst from around her lips to dribble over her hand as she finished him off with a last series of firm tugs. He grunted once, followed by a long sigh of pleasure as his body went slowly limp and his thumb pulled from her anus with a sticky pop.

Spring 1921, Fitzrovia, London

'Thank you ever so for lunch, Victor,' Charlotte simpered, patting her companion on the arm. 'It was ever so clever of you to find a vegetarian restaurant. You didn't mind too awfully, did you?'

'Not at all,' he answered. 'I expect it will make it easier to stay awake during the afternoon. Stanley Baldwin is expected to speak, and also to be at his most meaningless.'

'I would have thought sleep was the better choice, then.' Charlotte laughed, blowing a kiss as she turned away. 'Well, do have fun.'

'When shall I see you again?' he demanded.

'Oh, ever so soon,' she answered.

'Tomorrow, perhaps, for dinner?'

'No, not tomorrow, I promised Cyprian Yates he could take me to the Black Cat.'

'That awful man Yates? Surely not?'

'He did give me a scarf pin, with ever such a pretty stone. One must be civil.'

'Oh, really, Lottie! Friday, then? I can't make lunch, but –'

'I'm dining with Toby St John that day.'

'St John? But he's an absolute rat! What did he give you?'

'There is no call for unkind remarks.'

'I apologise, it was ungracious. Saturday, then?'

'Sorry, Victor, I'm due back at Ashwood that day. My train's at three or something like that. Look, I must go.'

'But when?' he demanded, almost whining. 'Look, Lottie, I have something most dreadfully important to say to you. It's . . . I mean to say . . .'

'I must dash, really,' she answered. 'Cicely St John was expecting me half an hour ago.'

She left, almost running as she turned into Charlotte Street, certain that she had avoided the embarrassment of yet another proposal. Two minutes' brisk walk took her to the door of the flat in Percy Street that Cicely was renting. It was on the top floor, a long attic room with large skylights, which let it flood with light both morning and afternoon. Cicely let her in, more languid than ever, and as smartly dressed, in Oxford bags with a brightly patterned cravat at her neck. They kissed, hands briefly lingering on each other's body with far more intimacy than Charlotte had shown Victor Cushat.

'Lunch with a shark?' Cicely demanded, disengaging herself.

'Yes, how did you know?' Charlotte answered as she sat down in one of the wide, basket-like chairs Cicely had bought.

'I can smell them,' Cicely replied. 'In due time I expect to be able to work out which it was, just from the scent. It wasn't Toby, anyway. Lester Jerton?'

'Victor Cushat.'

'Oh, I thought it was one of the stuffy ones. Are you going to choose, or will you become my lover and be damned to the world?'

'I don't know, Cicely . . . I mean, George. I'd like to, you know I would, but some things are expected of me.'

'You must do as you think best, of course, and I shall be happy so long as you visit me now and then.'

36

'Always.'

'I am glad. Now, I have a surprise for you, darling. I've decided to fuck you.'

'You have? I mean, how?'

'That you shall discover presently. I'm sorry about your maidenhead, of course, but if you won't make up your mind I really don't see how I can be expected to wait any longer. Besides, I don't care about the sharks. You may tell whichever you choose that it happened riding.'

As she spoke her hands had gone to her trouser buttons, which she began to open. Charlotte watched uncertainly, unsure what to expect. Cicely let her trousers drop and opened the flap at the front of the male drawers beneath, revealing a wide brass ring sewn into the fabric, with a puff of thick dark hair showing at the centre. She turned abruptly, standing at a large chest of drawers with her legs braced apart to keep her trousers up. With the tails of her jacket and shirt hanging loose over her bottom and her breasts hidden, she looked more masculine than ever.

'What are you up to?' Charlotte asked as Cicely pulled the drawers open.

Cicely didn't answer, keeping her back squarely to Charlotte, who could only see that her friend was making some sort of clothing adjustment. When she finally turned, it was to reveal a sight that left Charlotte gaping open-mouthed. There was a cock sticking out of Cicely's drawers, a huge rubber thing, bigger even than the Colonel's, the head a great bulbous dome, the shaft writhing with thick veins.

'Simply hideous, isn't it?' Cicely said.

Charlotte nodded dumbly, her eyes fixed to the grotesque rubber cock as Cicely advanced on her.

'Come on, darling, legs up,' Cicely ordered. 'It seems an absolute age since I saw that sweet little cunt.'

'Oh, Cicely, don't. You know how I hate that word.'

'All the better. It's such an intrusive word, isn't it? It's so immodest, and I'm sure it's what the boys say all the time, so I shall too.'

Cicely had reached her, and taken hold of her ankles, pulling them up so that her body slid down into the chair and her skirt and petticoats fell away from her legs. Her drawers where showing, her sex too, with the gap open, leaving her completely vulnerable to the huge phallus now rearing up between her open thighs. Cicely licked her lips, admiring Charlotte's sex.

'You are ever so pretty,' she said. 'Now I have no idea how the boys go about this. Do you suppose they have a little lick first, or dish out a spot of spanking? Or do they just stuff it in, and never mind if the poor girl's ready or not? Toby says whores use duck fat, but I'm sure he's lying. I mean to say, how could a whore afford to eat duck?'

'I am ready, I think,' Charlotte breathed, 'just from the thought of you. Let me see.'

She reached down, her fingers trembling as she pulled the split of her drawers wider and put her hand to her sex. The lips felt swollen and sensitive, and the middle was wet. Having slipped a finger into the hole, she drew it out, sticky with rich white mucus.

'Well, I am flattered,' Cicely said. 'Pop that in your mouth and we'll get fucking, shall we?'

Charlotte placed her sticky finger obediently in her mouth, tasting herself as Cicely took a firmer grip on her legs and rolled them high. The position left her bottom stuck out over the edge of the chair, with her vulva presented to Cicely's phallus. Shutting her eyes and sucking on her finger, she waited, a little afraid, but eager, filthy-dirty thoughts running through her head.

Something touched her vulva, something round and heavy, pushing in to stretch the little hole wide. She moaned in pleasure, waiting for her vagina to fill with the big, rubbery penis. Cicely pushed and it started to go in, stretching Charlotte's flesh until with a sudden stinging pain her hymen tore.

She gave a little scream as it happened, the noise turning to a drawn-out gasp as her vagina filled and Cicely's body settled between her open thighs. Their mouths met and they began to kiss, mouths open in their passion, Cicely jabbing the phallus in and out of Charlotte's sex. The terrifying thing felt huge inside her, and there was still some pain, yet the pleasure was greater, and better still for the feel of Cicely's male clothes against her body and under her hands.

For a long while, Cicely contented herself with fucking Charlotte's hole, until at last she pulled back, smiling, her short hair in a crown of spikes where Charlotte had mussed it up, her cravat askew.

'Oh, I've wanted this so long,' she sighed. 'How does it feel, Lottie, darling, with me between your thighs and a full cunt.'

'Lovely,' Charlotte admitted. 'Make me spend, Cicely.'

' "George", please. Do you imagine a Cicely would have a thing like this? Not for a minute. Maybe I should put it up your bum to teach you a lesson.'

'No, please. I'd split, I'm sure I would. My maidenhead went, you know.'

'Oh, wonderful; oh, let me see. Oh, so pretty. You've got blood, Lottie, on my cock. Oh, wonderful!'

Cicely had leaned back a little way, and was peering down at where the thick shaft of her rubber penis filled Charlotte's vagina. Charlotte smiled, despite the slight pain she still felt, happy because Cicely was. Once more the big phallus began to move inside her, Cicely now upright and watching it go in and out. Now thoroughly aroused, she put her hands to her chest, quickly unbuttoning her blouse and lifting the chemise beneath to bare her breasts. Cicely watched, still holding Charlotte by the legs, as breasts and then belly came on

39

display, soft pink flesh in a jumble of disarranged clothing.

'Now frig your cunt, darling,' Cicely said. 'I shall watch, and I shall talk to you also.'

Charlotte immediately put her hands to her body, one to a breast, the other between her thighs, touching first the straining mouth of her vagina with the thick plug of rubber within, then the little firm bump of her clitoris. She began to rub gently, thinking of what she was doing and wishing faintly that she'd been given a beating first. It would have been better, she knew, taking away the guilt she felt at surrendering her body to another woman and giving her both a warm physical glow and the wonderful punished feeling she had always enjoyed at school.

'You didn't spank me,' she protested. 'You always used to spank me.'

'Oh, you poor little thing. I suppose I was rather eager, but you can hardly blame me. You're so pretty, either way up. Bum up, then, darling.'

As she spoke, she began to pull on a leg, forcing Charlotte to turn on the cock. She went, scrabbling at the chair for balance with her insides twisting on the huge rubber penis, ending up open-mouthed and gasping, but bottom uppermost, still stuck firmly on Cicely's phallus. A few quick adjustments of her clothes exposed her bottom and she was ready.

'Now I shall fuck you as I take my belt to your bottom,' Cicely announced. 'Come on, girl, get your knees properly on the chair, and do pull your back in, make it round and open so that I can see your cunt and that rude little bottom hole. Yes, that's better, now rub at your cunt while I thrash you.'

Charlotte had followed every instruction, sticking her bottom out and pulling in her back. Again Cicely began to fuck her, and as the belt smacked down across her bottom her fingers once more found the damp crevice of her sex. She gave a little cry of pain, but started to masturbate, concentrating on the feeling of her body and thinking of the rude, intimate words Cicely was using.

The belting hurt, stinging blows making her buttocks dance and forcing her to wriggle on the big cock in her hole. Despite the pain it was wonderful, with the glorious indignity of having her skirts thrown up and her drawers pulled open to expose every rude detail of her bottom while her breasts pressed nude to the wicker of the chair and the huge phallus worked in her hole.

'Let's have it all out,' Cicely said, and quickly snipped open the button of Charlotte's drawers, leaving them to fall wide across the full breadth of her bottom. 'That's my girl, Lottie, stick it out; show me everything. Such a pretty cunt. Even your bottom hole is pretty, so darling, so tempting. The boys'll put their cocks in there if you let them, you know? It's what they do at school, filthy creatures that they are, so you may be sure that if you marry your husband will want the same from you. Think of it, Lottie, a man's penis up your bottom hole. How perfectly horrid!'

The belt slapped down again, harder than before, drawing a yelp from Charlotte and breaking the rhythm of her masturbation. Finding it again, she thought of what Cicely was saying, the filthy suggestion that she was making, that men might want to put their cocks in her tiny, tender anal opening. Even the handles of brushes had made the little ring feel strained and left her sore, and the thought of a fat cock like the Colonel's in her back passage was both terrifying and unutterably dirty.

'I've a mind to bugger you myself,' Cicely said, 'right up your little filthy hole, Lottie, right up, in your dirt.'

'Cicely!' Charlotte wailed in protest, but it was too late, she was coming, and her mind fixed on her lover's filthy suggestion.

'I'm called George, you little brat!' Cicely spat and brought the belt down across Charlotte's bottom with all her force.

41

The blow caught Charlotte just as her orgasm was about to explode in her head. She screamed, ecstasy and pain blending as she imagined the grotesque phallus now in her vagina being forced up her bottom, and how it would squash in her own filth. Mouth open, fingers clutching at her sex, she came, over and over again as Cicely beat her and rammed the phallus home, leaving Charlotte a whimpering, shaking mess, with tears of pure shame rolling down her face from what she had thought of as she came.

'You beast! You utter beast!' she sobbed. 'What a dreadful thing to say!'

'Oh, don't be so wet,' Cicely laughed. 'You spent, didn't you? And I'll put a pound to a penny it was over what I was saying. Don't forget I know what you're like, Lottie Bomefield, with your dirty little thoughts going round and round while you touch yourself off. Well, I'm right, aren't I?'

'Yes,' Charlotte sniffed as Cicely began to pull the phallus out.

'My turn now,' Cicely announced cheerfully. 'On the floor, Lottie, like the first time, when you fought. Remember?'

'Naturally,' Charlotte answered, climbing unsteadily down from the chair.

Still shaking hard, she composed herself and lay on the floor. Cicely came to stand over her, smiling down, her eyes full of excitement. The phallus was wet and streaked with white juice, ample evidence of where it had been.

'I'm ready,' she said. 'Make me.'

Immediately, Cicely's hands went to the rear of the crotch of the male drawers, tugging them wide to expose two slices of creamy flesh and a puff of hair. Charlotte swallowed, opening her mouth. Cicely squatted down, revealing twin sex lips and the dark knot of her anus a moment before her bottom was pressed to her lover's face.

An instant before Cicely sat down on her face, Charlotte realised what was about to happen. Her friend was too far forward, but it was too late, and her protest was turned to a muffled squeak as the rank taste of Cicely's anus filled her mouth. Twice she slapped her hand on the floor, but her lover took no notice, merely settling her bottom more comfortably into place.

'Lick me, Lottie, darling,' Cicely ordered. 'Lick me well. Lick me clean.'

Charlotte's whole face was smothered in bottom, her mouth open around Cicely's anus. For a moment she resisted, struggling to keep a last tiny vestige of her dignity, until Cicely wiggled her behind and that too was lost. Charlotte began to lick, tasting her lover's anus as the little tight bottom was squirmed into her face.

'Good girl,' Cicely sighed. 'Oh, you are such a dirty little thing, Lottie, such a dirty, dirty little thing.'

With as much bitterness as passion, Charlotte set about applying her tongue to Cicely's anus. Above her, she felt her mount slide a hand beneath the phallus and a moment later fingernails touched her chin as Cicely began to masturbate.

'A little more enthusiasm for your task, please, my darling,' Cicely urged. 'Come, come, I want that little tongue inside, well inside. Yes, that's my girl, right in, deep in. Oh, lovely; oh, to think of how that must taste for you, how perfectly, wonderfully horrid! Now come on, up with your legs, I want to see that little cunt of yours, too.'

Charlotte did as she was told, lifting her knees and opening her legs to let the skirt fall away. Cicely reached out, tweaking cloth to one side, and again Charlotte's sex was showing. Unable to stop herself, she put a hand to it and once more began to rub. All she could see was the gentle curve of Cicely's bottom, and her tongue was pushed well up the wet, muscular anal ring. It had

43

begun to pulse as Cicely grew more excited, squeezing on Charlotte's tongue as she licked at the hot cavity within. It was all too rude, too degrading for her not to bring herself off once more and, despite her smouldering resentment at what she was being made to do, she was soon licking eagerly and rubbing firmly on her clitoris.

'That's my girl. That's my Lottie,' Cicely breathed. 'That's right, my darling, frig your sweet little cunt while you lick out my bottom. Think what comes out of that hole, Lottie, and now your tongue's up it. Oh, it's where you belong, Lottie darling, it really is!'

Her words ended in a long moan and her bottom hole tightened on Charlotte's tongue, once, then repeatedly. At that, Charlotte's own climax started, building in her head, up and up as she pushed her tongue deeper and deeper into Cicely's wet, pouting bumhole. Cicely screamed, the moist hole of her vagina pressing to Charlotte's chin, fingernails jabbing into flesh, anus contracting, coming over and over, together, bottom to face, with everything focused on the glorious servility of one person licking another's anus.

For two days Charlotte stayed at Cicely's flat, falling ever more deeply in love and growing ever more worshipful. She was fucked repeatedly, in a variety of positions, but most frequently kneeling, with her bottom turned up to Cicely's gaze. Despite frequent threats, she wasn't buggered, but she spent plenty of time licking eagerly at Cicely's quim, and also her bottom, rather less eagerly.

On the Thursday she spent the day in just her drawers and chemise, not troubling to dress until shortly before Cyprian Yates arrived to take her to dinner. The evening was spent in dancing and small talk, with her thoughts constantly turning back towards Cicely. On her return, Yates's footsteps had barely faded on the stairs than she was pushed over a chair, belted for being out so late, and then fucked. Afterwards, Cicely confessed to her jealousy, making Charlotte more devoted than ever.

The Friday was spent nude, in Cicely's bed, a long, lazy day of frequent sex punctuated by long sessions just holding each other and talking. Only when the doorbell rang did they stop, Cicely putting her brother off as Charlotte dressed in frantic haste.

In the company of Toby St John, she was taken to the Café Imperiale, where he had booked a private room. Seated, he began to study the wine list, moving his index finger slowly down the long column of names.

'Not bad, not bad at all,' he pronounced after a while. 'We'll have champagne, of course, and I suppose we can drink Mosel now without being unpatriotic. After all, we did beat the buggers. Then they have some '99s, even a few '75s at a price. No, there's a 1900 Latour, which is truly splendid. We'll have that, then perhaps an old Rieussec and port to finish.'

'Do you seriously propose that we are to drink five bottles of wine between us?' Charlotte queried.

'Yes,' he answered. 'I propose to get you beastly drunk and then take advantage of you.'

'You shall do no such thing!'

'Well, not here, no, you silly girl. I mean, imagine the scandal. Not that we'd be the first, mark you, not if Frank Harris is to be believed. No, I'll have my wicked way in the back of the cab, or perhaps up against the wall in some sordid alley.'

'I have never heard such a thing!'

'No? I'm surprised, with half the chaps in London desperate to get into your drawers. Then maybe not, they're so damned formal, most of them. I don't suppose that idiot Jerton would know what to do with your cunt if you sat on his face.'

'Really, there's no call to be so coarse.'

'You make be feel coarse, Lottie, with those glorious little bubbies and that divine backside. By God, but I

45

wouldn't know what to do with you first. Yes, I do, it's that face, so pretty and so damned impudent. I'd make you suck on my cock, then see how self-satisfied you look.'

'Mr St John, you are disgusting! I shall leave if you don't stop it!'

'Oh, very well, if you insist. Now, let us choose from the menu to suit my selection of wines. Oysters, of course. One fills the shells with the wine and takes them down all at once. There's quite an art to it, at least if it is to be done with any style. I am the master, of course.'

'I shan't touch the oysters, thank you.'

'Oh, you poor thing. Caught a bad one, did you? Dreadful, that – it can put you off for life.'

'Not at all. It is against my principles to eat the flesh of dead animals, something you probably wouldn't understand.'

'The flesh of dead animals? What a perfectly beastly way of putting it! But don't worry, oysters are still alive when you eat them. Didn't you know?'

'Worse still. How awful, to eat a living creature!'

'Oh, what nonsense! They're shellfish, for goodness' sake.'

'Nevertheless, I shall have the asparagus soup.'

'Well oysters for me, anyway, and it would be a crime not to have a few plovers' eggs. With my claret I shall have the pigeon, which is excellent here. I recommend the same.'

'Absolutely not. I shall have a plate of salad, and perhaps a little rice.'

'Good Lord! No wonder you manage to keep that starving-waif look. It's what you are. Who's been filling your pretty head with all these damn-fool ideas? My sister, I suppose.'

'Vegetarianism represents an important moral choice.'

'Silly fad, nothing more. Now, if I was your husband I wouldn't stand for it. I'd expect meat on the table every night, save perhaps for the odd fish to make a change.'

'Well, you shan't be my husband, so the matter need never arise.'

'No? Do better, can you? I'll be Lord Cary when poor old Pater shuffles off, you know, and it can't be long.'

'What a thing to say about your own father!'

'Well, be realistic. He's been in Holford bin for nearly ten years. He doesn't even know who I am. Mark you, nor does Uncle Francis half the time. I hope to God it doesn't run in the family.'

'Well, if it does that certainly makes a good reason for not marrying you.'

'Nonsense! I take after my mother, I'm sure of it. I'd hate to think I'd ever look like Francis, never mind Pater, and I'm certainly a great deal more handsome than either of them were at my age. No, of course you must marry me. Life won't be dull, that I can promise, and I'm really quite a fine fellow, when all is said and done. Kind enough at any rate.'

'That is not what Cicely says. She told me that you used to make her eat worms.'

'Worms? Certainly not, what a disgusting thought! No, you're perfectly right, I remember now. So I did. Ha, ha, yes, I recall the look on her face, a perfect picture!'

'Well, I think you are quite horrid.'

'Oh, nonsense. All part of the rough and tumble of life.'

'Well, that just goes to show how unsuited we are for one another, then. I think it's a perfectly beastly thing to do.'

'Well, marry Victor Cushat then, or Reggie Thann; I don't care. You'll spend your life knocking on the doors of slums and being civil to people you'd normally cut dead in the street. Or you might have Lester Jerton and die of boredom, or Cyprian Yates, so you can watch him bugger boys against a background of lilac plush. I'm not joking, you know: his whole flat is upholstered in the most frightful taste. That old queen Quigley helped him design it.'

'I know. I have called on Mr Yates.'

'You have? Alone? Scandalous! Well, don't turn your back on him, that's all I can say. Your bum's a sight too boyish to be safe.'

'Toby!'

'It's true, damn it. Don't forget that I was at school with the fellow.'

'Then doubtless you enjoyed each other's company.'

'Aha! *Touché.* You see, you do have some wit, for all that you're pretty much the typical feather-brained flapper. You'd be wasted on anyone but me, that's for sure.'

'You must think what you please.'

'I shall have you one day, Charlotte, stripped down to the raw, on your back with those fine legs wide apart. Damn, but you'd look good like that, or maybe on your knees with that pert arse in the air. One of the best ways to put a woman that, kneeling, or crawling.'

'It is not a pleasure you are ever likely to enjoy, Mr St John.'

'Oh, reserved for my sister, is it?'

'That's outrageous! I wish to leave immediately, if you would be enough of a gentleman to call me a cab.'

'Oh, do sit down. I know what you two get up to, my dear. Drawers down and tongues up each other's cunt at every excuse.'

'Mr St John!'

'Please, Lottie, do spare me the affronted lady act. I mean, there's Sissy strutting around London, dressed as a fellow and calling herself George, if you please. You're her closest friend, and as soft as butter. One doesn't have to be so very clever to work out what goes on between the two of you.'

'Nonsense.'

'It's pointless to deny it, Lottie, and it's another damn good reason why you should marry me. I know, you see, and I'm prepared to tolerate it. Why, it might even be fun to watch now and again.'

'That is precisely what Cicely said.'

'Aha, so you admit it? You two are lovers!'

'I . . . We . . . That was a cruel trick, Toby St John!'

He laughed, slapping his hand on the table in delight at having confirmed his suspicions. Blushing in confusion, Charlotte struggled to hide behind her menu, which only drew fresh laughter from him. When she finally managed to raise her eyes he was grinning from ear to ear.

'So the dirty little secret's out, eh?' he said. 'I knew it!'

Further embarrassment was spared by the waiter arriving to take their order. Confused and insecure, Charlotte was also angry with herself, because his conversation had left an uncomfortable damp patch in her drawers.

Summer 1921, Steeple Ashwood, Somerset

Stepping from the carrier's cart, Catherine Mullins found herself smiling with pride and satisfaction. They had been to Bridgwater, and now, for the first time in her life, she wore a pair of drawers beneath her dress. It felt strange, with the wool tickling her thighs and bottom, as if a petticoat had caught between her legs and wouldn't pull loose. It also felt good, something to be proud of, and also evidence of her maturity.

Most of all, she wanted John Dunn to know that she was wearing them, and that her dress could no longer be turned up to reveal a bare, chubby bottom and the curls of her sex. Not that she had any intention of telling him, let alone showing him, but if they were to get a moment alone there was every chance he'd make her lift her dress, or simply do it for her.

It was already late in the afternoon, but she knew he had been working on the Bomefield estate for several days, cutting hedges and felling dead trees. It seemed more than likely that he would still be there, and quite possibly alone.

Explaining to her mother and sisters that she wanted to stretch her legs, she set off on the path that bordered the estate, full of anticipation for the exposure of her new garment and what was likely to follow. John would demand she show him the split, she was certain of that. Once she had made a decent amount of fuss and called him a few names she would coyly pull it open, showing him her quim or her bottom, as the mood took her. Once she was bare, it wouldn't be long before his cock was out, and popped inside her.

Feeling naughty and thoroughly pleased with herself, she kept her ears strained for the sound of voices or axes. Neither came, and when she reached a junction in the path she hesitated. One route led back to the village, the other across the estate and, although there was no real reason why she shouldn't be on it, her presence would need explaining. On the other hand, if he was working at the far side of the land, which seemed likely, he was certain to come that way. Feeling naughtier still, she chose the estate path.

From where she was it led, arrow-straight, along a bank, with a ditch to one side. The water was perfectly still, until she reached a point where a field drain joined it, splashing into the larger stream. She paused, watching the water gush and bubble from the clay pipe with a tinkling noise that reminded her of the sound of pee falling into an already full chamber pot. As she moved on she became aware of the tension in her own bladder and wondered if she should turn back for her cottage, or find a private spot where she could do it in the open. The second choice was clearly the better, and she walked on, intent on a distant clump of poplars, which she hoped might offer enough shelter to allow her to pee without embarrassment.

By the time she reached the trees she was wriggling her toes in her boots, with her urgency too strong to be denied for much longer. The copse was thinner than she had hoped, with no undergrowth and signs of having recently been cleared, which suggested than John and other men might be nearby. She bit her lip in frustration, hesitating and throwing a worried glance to where

51

the path disappeared between two high hedges of clipped yew.

Nobody was visible, and it was going to be the work of a moment to squat down among the poplars, pull up her dress, split her drawers and let it out on to the ground. Unfortunately, it meant her bare bum would be on view to anyone who came along the path. Still she hesitated, her knees pressed together, despite her knowing she had little choice. Blushing with embarrassment, she grabbed at the front of her skirt but stopped as the portly figure of Colonel St John emerged from between the hedges. She curtsied, smiling and bidding him a good afternoon even as she wished fervently that he would go away.

'And a good afternoon to you too, my dear,' he answered her, his eyes moving immediately to the swell of her breasts beneath her dress. 'I know you, don't I? You're little Catherine Mullins, unless I'm greatly mistaken, aren't you?'

'Yes, sir,' she answered.

'Well, you've grown up, I must say,' he went on, his eyes still lingering on her chest. 'Good heavens, yes. Out for a constitutional, are we?'

'Yes, sir, I mean . . .' Catherine stammered, struggling for a reason why she was on the estate path.

'Walk with me a while,' he went on. 'Not often I have a pretty girl for company these days, you know, now that my wards spend so much of their time in London. Mark you, Lottie's down. You remember her, I'm sure.'

'Yes, sir, I know Miss Charlotte, sir.'

He walked on, and she fell into step beside him, unable to deny his request. She was knock-kneed with pain, the straining sensation in her bladder growing by the moment, her embarrassment far too great to allow her to squat by the path with him there.

'Now there's one who could take a leaf out of your book,' the Colonel went on, apparently indifferent to her distress. 'One only has to glance at your figure to see that you eat a proper diet. Plenty of you, the way a young woman should be. Damn me, but you're blessed in the top hamper.'

He had turned, eyeing her breasts with undisguised relish. As he moved his arm she thought for one moment that he was going to touch her, and with the shock of that her control went. The pee erupted from her bladder, full into her new drawers, filling them almost instantly and pouring out from the divide in a noisy stream.

'I say, had an accident, have we?' he said as she felt her face go scarlet with embarrassment.

'No . . . I mean, yes, sir,' she stammered, clutching at her dress as the piddle splashed out beneath her.

The yellow fluid was forming a rapidly growing pool on the hard ground, and as she looked down in abject misery she saw a wide trickle of it start to snake out from beneath her dress towards his feet. She had wet herself, in her new drawers and, worse, in front of one of the most respected men in the district. It was still coming, too, in fitful bursts as she struggled to control her bladder, only to realise that it was hopeless. She let go completely, her stream immediately doubling in force to squirt out through her soiled drawers and on to the front of her dress. The Colonel watched the wet patch spread with ill-concealed amusement.

'Dearie me, couldn't hold it, eh?' he said, stepping quickly back to avoid the advancing stream. 'You poor little thing. Well, I suppose you had better run along home.'

Catherine ran away along the path with the piddle still dripping from the hem of her new drawers, her face burning with blushes and her hands clenched in the sodden material of her dress to keep it off the ground. Behind her she heard the Colonel give an unmistakably lewd chuckle.

* * *

Charlotte slipped down into the warm embrace of the bathwater, stopping only when it reached the level of her chin. Slowly the discomfort of the journey from London down to Ashwood left her, to be replaced by a drowsy feeling of contentment. The two weeks she had spent in the city had been a whirl of parties, dancing and at-home invitations, with all five of the sharks vying for her attention. She had given in to none, using every technique at her disposal to avoid their proposals. Even Toby St John had failed, despite his best efforts to get her to himself, mainly because he made no secret of his intentions if she did allow it.

If he had failed, then his sister had not. They had slept together each night, with Charlotte naked more often than not, and never fully dressed unless one or other of the men was expected. Her bottom had been kept almost permanently warm, and her mouth full of the taste of her lover's sex, while Cicely's particular pleasure was to make Charlotte kiss her anus before a date, particularly when it was with her brother.

Despite missing Cicely, she was not sorry to have returned to Somerset. For one thing she felt she needed to order her thoughts in peace, allowing her to decide on one man or another, or none at all. The choice was not easy, with her sense of duty weighing against her personal needs. Among the sharks, Toby St John remained the favourite, his confident, open admiration doing as much to excite her as to shock her. Behind him came Cyprian Yates, who was at least good company, and seemed the one least likely to make demands on her in married life. The others were placed well behind, with the dull and serious Lester Jerton marginally preferable to the two politicians.

Now, relaxing in the hot bath with her eyes closed and her body almost completely afloat, she thought of her choices and what they would imply in the way of sexual contact. Toby was embarrassingly open about what he wanted. Essentially, it was complete access to her body, in every orifice, including her anus, when and where he wanted it. In return, he would turn a blind eye to her relationship with his sister. Indeed, his intention of watching them together was one of his favourite erotic boasts.

Cyprian had been far less open in the expression of his admiration, but again and again she had caught him looking at her bottom and also those of handsome young men. If she chose him, it was clear that, if they had sex at all, it would involve the regular insertion of his penis into the tight hole between her bottom cheeks, something that both frightened and titillated her. He also seemed likely to tolerate Cicely. The other three would mean a life of respectable boredom and, if any of them expected sexual pleasures other than for straight-forward procreation, they had not revealed it.

She had begun to soap herself beneath the level of the water, sliding the smooth, hard bar over the flesh of her belly and breasts. Gradually the action grew into a lazy, self-indulgent masturbation, with the soap bar moving lower until she had begun to grind it against her sex. She slumped down into the bath, leaving just her face above water, and as she did so she let go of her bladder, feeling the warm pee gush out into her hand. It felt good, naughty as well as a pleasant relief.

Her legs came up, the soap bar pushing lower still, to ease between her bottom cheeks and press to her anus. It felt good, slippery and smooth, and her finger followed, tickling the tiny hole until it came open. The soap stung her as she penetrated herself, but it didn't stop her, the finger moving deeper up her bottom.

Her thoughts were mixed, with as much shame as pleasure, not simply for what she was doing, but for what had been done to that same sensitive hole by others, and how much she had enjoyed it. There was not only the Colonel's habit of molesting her anally while

55

she masturbated him, but Cicely, who seemed to take a special pleasure in it. There was also the thought of what she might do, if only the right person caught her at the right time, when she was not only alone but in the sort of mood that craved lewd attention.

She was smiling, easing her finger in and out of the tight tube of her rectum, with her thumb turned up to her sex, stroking the fleshy folds between her outer lips and exploring the mouth of her vagina. She could feel the ragged edge of her torn hymen, bringing back memories of her lost virginity, although she was uncertain whether what Cicely had done to her technically meant that she was no longer a virgin. Realistically, she knew that she wasn't, which brought a new flush of shame.

It had been so lewd, so dirty, and she had felt so helpless, so wonderfully used. She came, finishing herself off with a long moan of pleasure, her mind locked on the awful moment when Cicely's cock had torn her hymen.

As the orgasm tailed off, she felt guilt and shame for her thoughts, but physically only a great sense of relaxation. She lay still, only her head and bottom touching the enamel of the bath, just thinking, until a faint noise broke into her reverie.

She sat up, opening her eyes and frowning in annoyance. There was no evidence of anything that might have caused the noise, yet the moment was gone, while the bathwater seemed suddenly cold. Putting the interruption down to a bird outside the window, she got out of the bath, selected the largest of the towels from the airing cupboard and wrapped herself in it. After a moment of hesitation, she decided to dry herself in her bedroom, only to find Colonel St John in the passage, watering the collection of orchids in the window bay. His face was red, and she recognised the quality of the leer on his face as soon as he turned to her.

'Been diddling yourself in the bath, eh, Lottie?' he asked.

'I have not!' she retorted. 'What a thing to say!'

He merely laughed, and snatched suddenly for her towel. His fingers closed on air as she jumped back.

'Not now!' she exclaimed. 'Really, *must* you behave so crudely?'

'Now and then, yes. Come, now, let's have that towel off for a spot of spanking.'

'Francis! You are drunk!'

'So I am, and all the better for it. Come on, girl, out with that ripe little bum. I've a mind to give it a good tickling.'

'Really, Francis, the servants will hear!'

'They're all below stairs.'

He grabbed for her again as he spoke, and this time caught the edge of her towel. She clung on, trying to keep it around her and not be pulled in to where he could get down on the window seat and take her down across his lap.

'Aha, caught you now!' he declared. 'Let's have it out, then, and a spot of spankee to get up our appetites.'

'No! Do let go! You are beastly drunk, Francis, and Spince might well come upstairs, or Mrs Mabberley!'

'Hmm, maybe you're right. Wouldn't do to see the young mistress getting it across the tail. Give them the wrong idea, eh? Come on, then, into the bathroom with you.'

'That is not what I meant!'

He had a firm grip on the towel, and pulled her struggling into the bathroom, with her only choice to release the towel and run naked and down the corridor. She didn't take it, and was quickly back inside the bathroom with the door locked behind them. He went to the edge of the bath and sat down, patting his knee with his broad red face showing a wide and lecherous grin. She set her mouth in a firm line, only for her resolve to vanish in feelings of helplessness and bitterness.

'Oh, very well, if you really must!' she said. 'But really, you are an incorrigible beast!'

'No more than you, my girl, as well you know,' he answered. 'Now, come down across my lap and we'll soon have that little bum afire.'

'Not hard, then, I'm wet, and you know how it stings.'

He nodded, apparently in agreement, and she draped herself reluctantly across his knees, pushing her bottom up into a good position for spanking. She was blushing hot, and her mind was full of consternation and resentment, which became abruptly stronger as the back of the towel was twitched up to expose her bare bottom. His hand closed on her flesh, squeezing one cheek as he gave a self-satisfied chuckle before rising and landing across both with a hard slap.

'Ow!' Charlotte yelped. 'Must you? That stings so very dreadfully.'

'So it should,' he answered. 'Where's the pleasure in spanking a girl if it doesn't hurt her, eh?'

A second smack fell, harder still. Charlotte yelped again, letting go of the towel in an effort to protect her bottom. Immediately he caught hold of it and tugged it away, lifting her briefly to get it out from underneath her body even as she realised her mistake and made a grab for the edge. She caught it, but it was wrenched out of her grasp and she was nude.

'Not naked, no!' she protested miserably.

'Why not?' He laughed. 'Always best to be spanked in the nude, that's what I say. Good for your sense of humility. Now come on, bottom high, yes, very pretty, and here we go.'

He began to spank her again, slap after slap across her quivering bottom, with her wriggling and kicking her legs in her pain. He talked to her, too, telling her

58

how much he enjoyed spanking her and how pretty she looked in the nude with her bottom bare and rosy pink. His words produced a stinging humiliation nearly as bad as the effect of the spanking, and made worse because she could feel a growing lump pressed to the soft flesh of her middle. He was becoming excited, and it was quite obvious who was going to be expected to help with his condition.

With her resentment of his treatment of her body absolutely burning in her head, she waited for the inevitable. Her bottom was growing warmer, her sex too, until she was fairly sure that if he didn't stop soon she was likely to disgrace herself by masturbating while she attended to his cock. A nude spanking, still wet from her bath, was simply too much in tune with her needs to be easily denied. Her bottom was hot, and she was getting the urge to stick it up to the smacks and to spread her thighs in open surrender.

When he did stop it was only to adjust himself, pulling his now stiff cock free of his trousers so that when she once more settled into her spanking position it made a hard, hot rod against the soft flesh of her middle. The spanking resumed, now with her body rubbing on his erect penis as she wriggled and squirmed in her pain.

She knew she was lost for certain when he paused to fondle her bottom and she couldn't find it in herself to protest. His fingers had gone down between her buttocks, lingering on her anus before going lower, to cup her sex and give it a vigorous rub that left her gasping.

'My, but you'll be ripe for your husband when he gets to you,' he remarked. 'You've quite the hottest little cunt I've ever had the pleasure to feel, except maybe for that fat whore in Peshawar.'

Charlotte could only moan in response, unable to resist as she was masturbated from behind. He began to slap her again, using his free hand and still rubbing at her sex, a technique suspiciously familiar from the way Cicely handled her. It was nice though, too nice even to want to stop, although he had begun to rub his cock on her belly as he frigged her.

With pleasure and self-disgust warring in her head, she simply took the easier course, letting it happen as the slaps became harder and his rubbing more vigorous. She knew she was going to come, and there was a great bubble of shame welling up in her throat. The tears were starting in her eyes but she was sticking up her bottom, meeting the smacks. His thumb found her anus, the ball of it pressing to the little hole, adding the dirty shame of having it touched to her feelings.

Her bumhole began to open under the pressure of his thumb. The thought of the same lewd action being performed by a cock filled her head and it was all too much. Even as she burst into tears she had started to come. A moment later she was sticking her bottom up and begging him to spank her harder, writhing her sex against his hand and wiggling her bottom in wanton ecstasy, with every vestige of decency abandoned as she imagined what it would be like to be spanked and then buggered. As it happened her anus gave, his thumb pushing inside to draw a last, high-pitched squeal from her at the very peak of her orgasm and circling in the open mouth of her anus as it ran through her.

She had barely finished her orgasm when he was pushing her to the ground. She went willingly, fully aware of what she was going to be made to do. His cock was rigid, protruding from his fly with the hairy mass of his scrotum sticking out beneath. Without hesitation she took hold of it, moving into a comfortable kneeling position between his open legs as she started to suck, her bottom stuck well out to allow him to admire her reddened cheeks.

'Shame you have to be kept a virgin,' he grunted as she began to get her rhythm. 'I'd be more than pleased to fuck that little tail.'

Charlotte carried on sucking, not wishing to admit the loss of her virginity and so risk having the big cock now in her mouth pushed up her vagina. There was also the possibility that he might decide to bugger her, and with that thought she sucked harder, determined to make him come quickly. He sighed in contentment, responding to her eagerness, then taking her firmly by the hair and pushing his cock deeper into her mouth.

'I'm going to show you a trick I learned from that whore I mentioned,' he said. 'Sit back a little and down. Yes, that's my girl.'

He had guided her as he spoke, using the grip in her hair to adjust her head until his cock filled her throat, jammed right to the back, far deeper than she had intended to take it, far deeper than was comfortable. She could feel her throat squeezing on the fat head, with the thick, rubbery mass of the peeled-back foreskin coming behind, pushing deeper. Suddenly, she began to gag, her body reacting by instinct in an effort to swallow the meaty penis that was blocking her throat.

'I said you could do it,' he grated in absolute satisfaction at the desperate, breathless swallowing motions as her throat went into spasm.

She tried to pull back, struggling to breathe, choking on the great bloated penis in her mouth, only to have his grip tighten and yet another inch get forced into her straining gullet. He was ignoring the frantic scrabbling of her hands on his legs and belly and the drumming of her feet on the bathroom floor. Jerking himself back and forth in her mouth, he went deeper with each push, with her gagging over and over until suddenly he grunted and she felt an explosion of thick, slimy sperm into the back of her throat. For one instant there was relief, until he jammed his cock yet further down the sperm-slick passage. Her stomach lurched; she farted loudly; a gush of pee squirted from her bladder to the floor beneath her, and with a last, agonising stab of unbearable shame her vision went blurred, then red.

She was falling the instant he let go of her hair, his cock sliding from her mouth, the sperm exploding after it as she went into a fit of coughing. Clutching at her throat, her eyes tight shut, she slumped sideways. She was unable to control her body, piddle still spraying from her quim, with great, heaving spasms running through her as she dribbled a mixture of sperm and saliva out on to the floor and over his boots.

'I say, do mind what you are doing!' he exclaimed, and with that it was simply too much, her senses going as she collapsed slowly on to the floor.

The next thing she was aware of was the Colonel's hand planted across her cheek in a gentle slap, then his voice, full of concern.

'Are you all right, Lottie? I say, Lottie.'

Charlotte opened her eyes, watching his face swim slowly into focus.

'Ah, good, that's my girl,' he said. 'I knew you wouldn't be out for long. Here, have some water.'

He pressed a glass to her lips, which she vaguely recognised as the one he kept his false teeth in even as she sipped at the water. Her head had begun to clear, with her feelings of shame and resentment returning. Not only her bottom, but her vulva and mouth were sore, while her neck and chest were soiled with sperm and she was kneeling in a puddle of urine. After a while she tried to throw him a dirty look, but failed.

Gradually she came round, propped up on one elbow with the come still dribbling down her chin. He watched her, his face full of concern, and finally passed her a handkerchief. She took it and wiped her face and chest, wishing she could be really angry with him but finding it impossible. Her own orgasm had been simply too good to deny the pleasure she had taken in what they had done. It was also hard to deny him his own enjoyment in return, which did seem to be fair play.

At last she felt ready to move, retrieving her towel and wrapping it protectively around her body. The Colonel watched, still with his cock and balls hanging from his fly.

'Fainted there for a bit,' he remarked after a while. 'How d'you feel?'

'I didn't faint,' she managed, making her voice deliberately resentfully. 'Well, I wouldn't have done if you hadn't made me choke!'

'Choke? What nonsense! No girl ever choked on a little honest jism.'

'But I did choke on it!'

'Oh, you do talk nonsense. You don't eat properly, that's your trouble. Now come on, up you get. You're to have a glass of port.'

'A moment. I'll be all right presently, but I still feel rather faint.'

'Well, you look damn pale, that's for sure, positively ghostly. It's this damn muck you eat, I tell you. Wouldn't feed a rabbit. You're not getting enough protein. I believe there's a spot of game pie in the pantry, and the servants were having stew and dumplings earlier, unless I'm greatly mistaken. Once you're dressed I'll have Spince send up a portion of each. That'll put the roses back in your cheeks.'

'I couldn't possibly. It would be wrong of me.'

'For goodness' sake, girl! It's our damn nature to eat meat. What d'you think it says in the Bible, about dominion over the beasts of the field and the birds of the air or whatever it is?'

'What it says in the Bible is neither here nor there. It represents an ancient, patriarchal creed of no relevance to modern society. I am an atheist, and so is Cicely.'

'Atheists! By God, Lottie! I'd thrash this silliness out of you if you weren't in such a sorry state already. Maybe I'll do it anyway, and Sissy too.'

'That would be cruel.'

'Cruel to be kind, that's what it would be. Well at least have a glass of milk, damn it. You can't say that does an animal any harm, can you, now?'

'Nevertheless, it is not ours to take.'

'Milk, not ours? What the hell are you talking about? Who do you think gives the damn cows their lives? Besides, cows need to be milked. A fine state they get into when they're not.'

'Only because their children have been cruelly slaughtered.'

Children? Calves, you mean? Don't be absurd. Anyway, you're more valuable than some damn calf, and you need to eat properly. Milk's the stuff. Old Archie Maray used to swear by it, even bathed in the damn stuff, so I hear. Fit as a fiddle until the day he died. Mad as a hatter, but fit. Drowned in his bath, poor chap. Seventy-five, I think he was, or seventy-four.'

'I shall be fine presently. Indeed there would be nothing wrong at all if you didn't always insist on being so rough with me. It really is rather horrid of you. After all, I do oblige you.'

'Certainly you do, as any dutiful ward should. As to my being rough, you know damn well you wouldn't get half the delectation from it if I wasn't.'

Charlotte didn't answer, unable to deny what he was saying.

Autumn 1921, Steeple Ashwood, Somerset

Catherine Mullins pushed open the press house door, stepped within and shut it quickly behind her. Immediately the bitter wind that had been blowing across the levels all day was shut out, to be replaced by warm, still air, rich with the smell of apples. The building was a great, high barn, at the centre of which stood a massive stone trough, piled high with apples and straw. These were being crushed by a great round stone supported on a central shaft and drawn slowly around by the donkey whose musky scent mixed with that of the apples. Men were working in the building, a half-dozen of them, all young, including John Dunn, tending the press and the great barrels used for fermentation and storage. To one side stood a wooden tub, full to the brim with used apple pulp.

'And about time, too,' Peter called out.

'You should be thankful I'm here at all,' she answered. 'Besides, I don't call this work. Not besides looking after our bees, which is what I've been at all morning.'

'Certainly it's work,' John answered her. 'Hard work.'

'Lifting a mug to your face? Hard enough for you, I dare say, John Dunn,' she answered him, drawing laughter from the others.

He put down the mug from which he had been drinking and gave the boy next to him a light-hearted punch. This was another John, who responded in kind, leading to a brief tussle before they broke apart, laughing.

'You need to grow up a little, the lot of you,' she said. 'You're doing men's work, best to behave like men.'

'Oh, we're grown up enough,' the biggest of them, Sam, answered her, 'and, from what I hear, Cousin John's proved it to you!'

There was general laughter as the blood rushed to Catherine's face. She put down the basket she was carrying and immediately a hand took hold of her bottom, squeezing one plump cheek through her dress. She slapped it away, turning to find John grinning at her, which left her struggling to keep a smile from her face.

'Get on with your work, the lot of you,' she chided.

'Work goes at Harold's pace, no more no less,' Sam answered her, jerking his thumb at the donkey.

'Haven't you anything to do besides tend the press?' she demanded.

'All done,' Will, the youngest, told her.

'Except for the drinking!' John added.

'Looks like you've done enough of that,' Catherine retorted. 'Anyways, here's bread and cheese for the lot of you.'

Their attention turned to the food, breaking off chunks from the bread and cutting wedges of the hard yellow cheese. Catherine poured herself a mug of cider and sipped from it as she waited for them to finish. They continued to tease her, John especially, showing off and hinting at what he had done with her. She returned comment for comment, but with six of them it was impossible to hold her own and the blood was soon hot in her face. They noticed, and the teasing immediately grew worse.

'So what's she like, Cousin John, for real?' Peter asked as he swallowed the last of his bread and cheese.

The question was earnest, breaking the light-hearted air of the teasing. John shrugged in response, his mouth still full of food as he answered.

'I'd have thought you'd know,' he said.

'Me?' Peter demanded.

'You, why not? Not particular, is she?'

'Why, John Dunn!' Catherine broke in. 'What a thing to say!'

Her face was now a furious crimson, and it was impossible not to glance at Luke and Sam, both of whom had talked her into taking their cocks in her hand more than once. Luke was looking the other way. Sam returned a dirty grin.

'Come on, John, for real,' Peter urged.

'Find out for yourself,' John answered coolly. 'Ask her nice enough and I dare say she'll take you in the storeroom and tug you off.'

'I'll do no such thing!' Catherine stormed as a gale of laughter greeted the suggestion.

'Why not, wrist too sore from it?' Sam demanded.

'No,' John put in, 'more like from frigging her own cunt!'

'Does that, does she, the dirty baggage?' Peter asked.

'Sure she does, most nights,' Sam answered. 'You must have heard her, for sure.'

More laughter followed, and Catherine found herself unable to speak for embarrassment and sheer outrage. More often than not she played with herself when she went down on John's cock, but she'd never imagined he let anybody else know. She also made a habit of it in bed, and the realisation that the others had heard was, if anything, worse.

'How can you say such things?' she demanded, finally gaining her voice. 'I ought to tell Father, and Uncle Lias, too. I ought to, and have the lot of you thrashed!'

'Don't take it hard, Catherine, love,' John answered. 'Why, most girls'd be flattered for the notice of six fine young men.'

'Call yourselves men?' she snapped. 'Why, you're no more than a lot of dirty little boys!'

'There she goes again,' Sam said. 'Reckons we're not men. Well, I say we should take her in the storeroom and prove it to her.'

'Fine idea,' John answered, 'a tug all round, and she can see who's man or not. Who's for it?'

'I'll do no such thing,' Catherine answered, getting to her feet only to find the massive Sam stepping between her and the safety of the door.

'Come on, Catherine, there's no harm in it,' John urged. 'At the least give me a tug. I could use it, after all this talk.'

'You've no one but yourself to blame for that,' she answered hotly.

'No,' he answered, 'I've you to blame for that, my girl, with your fat tits and the way you waggle that big arse. It's more than any man can stand.'

'I'm built the way I am. I can't help that!' she exclaimed.

'Hear that, boys? She can't help it.' He laughed. 'Why, that's the best yet, the little tease. Come on, Catherine. Here, I'll give you a start.'

With two quick motions he freed his cock, which was already half stiff. She took a step backwards, only to bump into Sam.

'I'll not do it,' she snapped, 'least of all with you lot leering at me.'

'In the storeroom, then,' he said. 'Can't see why the others shouldn't watch, though, and join in, too. I don't care, for sure.'

'I'll not!' she answered.

'Come on with you,' Sam urged. 'There's no call to act the fine lady, not with us.'

'Come on, Catherine,' another said. 'We don't want to put it up your cunt or nothing, just to do it in your hand.'

'I'll not!' she repeated, folding her arms across her chest. 'And, if you don't let me out this moment, I'll be telling Father and Uncle Lias both.'

'Let her go,' Will said. 'She's not game.'

'Oh, but she is,' John answered. 'You've a lot to learn, young Will. Now there's a thought, Catherine love. Take Will and I on, at the least. He's not had a girl at all, I don't think.'

'I have that!' Will answered but only drew laughter from the others.

'No,' Catherine said firmly. 'It's not decent, it's not, with all you lot here.'

'Now that's just hard-hearted, Catherine,' Sam said. 'Give poor Will his first. It's no loss to you, after all.'

'I'll not do it,' she said defiantly. 'Now let me out!'

'Fair enough,' Sam said, 'but you're regular cruel, you are.'

'Cruel enough to need a lesson,' John said, 'so here's your choice, Catherine. Help us with our cocks or it's in the pressings with you.'

As he spoke Catherine jumped to the side, intent on a dash for the door and safety, only for Sam's huge arms to close around her, trapping her own. She kicked back, but he only laughed and hoisted her clear of the ground.

'What's it to be?' John asked. 'Our cocks or the spoilage tub? Your choice.'

'Let me down, you great bully!' she stormed, but for all her efforts she failed to sound really angry, and with that she was lost.

'In the tub with her!' Peter called, and the others joined in immediately.

'No!' she squealed. 'No! I mean it, boys, no! You'll ruin my dress!'

'Fair enough, we wouldn't want that,' John answered her. 'Get it off her, then, boys!'

Catherine shrieked as hands grappled for the fastenings of her dress. She fought, but it was useless. There was a hysterical giggle in her voice and her protests only made them laugh. Her dress was quickly pulled up over her head, leaving her blind. Eager hands immediately closed on her bottom and breasts, then the dress was off and she was in two scraps of cloth, chemise and drawers, along with her knee stockings and shoes. Cries went up to strip her.

'No!' she screamed. 'That's not decent! No, not that!'

She ended her protest in a shriek as rough hands wrenched open her chemise. Her huge breasts spilled out, and as they came bare she felt a sudden thrill, making her fight more furiously than ever. They held on, and despite her screams and desperate struggles she was dragged to the tub of apple pulp. The level was close to the top, a great mass of crushed skins, pips and pulp, mixed with the straw from the press. She tried to kick, but two of them caught her legs, spreading them wide as she was lifted from the ground. Her drawers fell open, exposing her quim. With the knowledge that the furry mound and fleshy pink folds of her sex were on show she redoubled her struggles, kicking and writhing in their grip, but only succeeding in making herself look ridiculous as well as rude.

'No, you mustn't!' she squealed as she was moved over the big tub, still kicking. 'That's for the pigs, that is! It'll spoil!'

'Nonsense, dare say you'll improve the flavour,' Sam said and the others laughed. 'Come on, boys, on three! One! Two . . .'

'Stop!' Catherine screamed. 'Stop! I'll do it!'

It was too late: both of those holding her thrashing legs had let go, and as her full weight came on to Sam he dropped her. She went into the pulp, bum first, screaming in shock and despair as she hit with a splash, to the sound of their raucous laughter.

Sitting in the mess, she could only clutch on to the sides of the tub, her face set in disgust as the apple pulp squashed up into the opening of her drawers, over her quim and up between her buttocks. All six men were convulsed with laughter, slapping their thighs or clutching their sides, Peter and John so overcome that they fell to their knees in helpless mirth.

Trying desperately to look cross, Catherine began to pull herself out of the mess with a sticky, sucking sound, only for Sam to take her by the shoulders and push her firmly back down. Wet apple pulp squashed into the entrance of her vagina. She opened her mouth in wordless shock, her eyes closing, only to open abruptly as a hand locked in her hair and something hot and firm was shoved into her mouth.

It was John, holding her by the hair as he forced his erect penis into her mouth to the sound of the others' catcalls and claps. She slapped at his thighs, kicking her feet in the muck as she struggled to get off his cock, but only provoked yet more laughter.

'What's the matter? You said you'd do it,' he demanded as he began to feed his cock in and out of her mouth.

Catherine wanted to speak, to say that it wasn't fair, that she'd agreed only if she didn't go in the pulp, that she'd never said she'd do it in front of the others and, most of all, that she'd never promised to suck cock. All she managed was muffled noises as John fucked her head, easing his erection back and forth between her pursed lips.

She was near nude in front of them, her breasts on show, her quim on show, with her bottom sitting in wet, squashy apple pulp. It was just too much, and with a last, angry slap at the surface of the pulp she gave in, starting to suck on John. They saw and cheered, hands going to trousers fastenings, first Sam's, then the others', with Willy last as he conquered his shyness.

John was grinning in triumph and pleasure as she sucked on his erection. She looked up, still trying to seem cross but failing miserably, not that they seemed to care one way or the other. Her arm was taken and her hand put to Sam's cock. She began to tug at it and reached up for another, taking Willy. His expression as he began to stiffen in her hand was not just of pleasure but of gratitude, making her feel motherly and less unhappy about what she was doing.

Without her hands to support her, she began to settle into the apple pulp, the cool mush rising slowly over her quim as she tried to keep all three men satisfied. She could feel it in the mouth of her vagina, and between her bottom cheeks, where something hard was tickling her anus. Her shame and chagrin at what had been done to her was fading as her excitement rose, and she found herself wanting to squirm her sex into the pulp, also to spread her thighs. With the last of her modesty she tried to stop herself, only for Willy's cock to jerk in her hand and hot sperm to splash out over her breasts. It was too much, and, with three lines of white sperm streaking her breasts and a single thick streamer hanging from one nipple, she opened her legs.

Peter's hand found her quim almost immediately, cupping her sex and slipping two fingers into her hole. A fair bit of apple pulp went up with them, wading into her vagina. John pulled her head back, keeping just the tip of cock in her mouth despite her efforts to take more in. She looked up, finding him grinning down at her as he began to masturbate into her mouth. Giving in to the inevitable, she took hold of his balls, feeling them and still jerking clumsily at Sam's cock.

Luke kneeled down by his brother, taking a handful of pulp and smearing it over Catherine's breasts, first one, then the other. As her nipples stiffened fully under the pressure of his fingers and the slimy feel of apple pulp and sperm, she began to mouth on the head of John's cock, suddenly desperate for his sperm despite the taste. He obliged, finishing himself off with a flurry of hard tugs to fill her mouth with hot, salty spunk. It burst from her lips as he pushed his cock down her throat, into which he did his second spurt. She swallowed, sucking hard until he pulled back, to leave her with her mouth full of sperm bubbles and a curtain of it hanging from her chin.

The other John was erect, and watching with obvious delight, but hesitant to actually touch. Catherine smiled at him, reaching out to take his cock. For a moment he hung back, until her soft, eager fingers closed on his erection. She began to masturbate him, pulling him close until she could get him into her mouth.

She had given in, completely abandoned to the hands on her body and the eager cocks. It didn't matter that Peter and Luke were fondling her body, nor that Sam was hard in her hand, even that John's cock was in her mouth. It was too good to resist, and she was soon pulling the two men in, taking turns with their cocks in her mouth, one at a time, sucking on one and jerking at the other. Sam came, all over her hand, then John, full in her face. Luke and Peter immediately took their places, taking the same treatment, hand and mouth, until at last they came, almost together, covering her face, breasts and hands with thick, sticky come.

Catherine was in heaven, and thinking of nothing but the demands of her body as her slippery hands went to her sex, two sperm-soiled fingers sliding straight into the wet, open hole of her vagina. She was going to masturbate, in front of them all, and she just didn't care. She spread her thighs wide to the room, slapping a handful of pulp on to her quim and mushing it in. More went over her breasts, smeared on to the fat globes and rubbed over her nipples, before her hands went back to her sex, one to spread her lips, one to masturbate with.

'The dirty strumpet!' Sam exclaimed.

'Six men and she needs to diddle herself!' Luke added.

'Let's give her a seventh!' John put in.

She barely heard them, aware of their presence only as an audience to make what she was doing even ruder. Her eyes were closed, her fingers working on her quim, her head full of the cool, squashy feeling of the pulp in her vagina and over her breasts. When a thick, soft cock was placed in her hand she instinctively began to tug at it, realising it belonged to Harold only when it had stiffened to impossibly large proportions. By then she was so close to orgasm that she didn't care, but kept tugging at it, delighted by the sheer maleness of the monstrous thing as it grew in her hand until her fingers could no longer circle it.

Her thighs were wide open, her hand slapping on her sex, smacking at her clitoris and catching the little bud over and over with her fingers. The boys had stood back, gaping at her as she started to come. She was groaning, calling out her ecstasy, and at the last moment jerking her head around to stuff the end of Harold's cock into her open mouth. At that instant it erupted, spraying an enormous quantity of thick white come full in her face. Immediately she was sucking at it, gulping down the sperm, then rubbing the huge leathery head over her face, smearing the mixed come across her features as she snatched frantically at her quim in unbearable ecstasy.

When her orgasm finally began to subside it was replaced by a great rush of shame. Harold's cock was still in her hand, the last of his come dribbling out over her breasts. She dropped it hurriedly, her lower lip starting to shake as her eyes flicked from one amazed face to another. They were all looking at her, gaping, not even John Dunn finding the words for a joke or witty remark.

74

Winter 1922, Fitzrovia, London

Charlotte hesitated, considering the virtues of one shawl and then the other before deciding that it was better to do without and hope that her cloak would be sufficient against the cold February wind. As she had dressed, Cicely had watched, smoking and saying nothing.

They had spent the afternoon together, the first for some weeks, a passionate four hours in which they had taken up their relationship exactly where it had left off. Barely had they been inside the flat than Charlotte's clothes had been off for a brief but firm spanking followed by a lengthy period with her face buried between Cicely's thighs. The second session of lovemaking had been slower, the third slower still, with Charlotte penetrated from the rear as Cicely used a candle to drip wax on to her upturned buttocks.

Only as the light began to fade towards dusk had Charlotte started to tidy herself up in preparation for the evening. Cyprian Yates had promised to take her to dinner and she had accepted, finding his offer considerably more worthwhile than those of his rivals. Across the summer and early autumn, all five men had continued to press their suits, and it was becoming increasingly hard to delay a decision.

'Where is he taking you, the Black Cat?' Cicely demanded lazily.

'I have no idea,' Charlotte answered. 'I suppose so, in the end. I think we're having dinner at his club. Ladies are permitted to dine as guests on Friday evenings.'

'How very modern.'

'Yes, isn't it? I had better hurry; he'll be here shortly.'

'Oh, he can come up, I don't mind. After all, he's one of the few men in town who can even speak to me without going beetroot-coloured. Your man Cushat even crosses the street to avoid me.'

'I suspect he thinks it will spoil his career to be seen talking to an open invert.'

'No doubt.'

There was irritation in Cicely's voice, and as she spoke she stubbed her cigarette out with a sudden motion. Charlotte made a mental note, deleting Victor Cushat's name altogether from her mental list. He had been a weak candidate in any case, but she knew that any marriage in which her husband was unable to tolerate Cicely would be certain to fail. The bell sounded moments later, while Charlotte was still arranging her make-up, and Cicely went to the door, quickly returning with Cyprian Yates.

'Well, I am honoured,' he remarked, curling himself on to the sofa and reaching for one of Cicely's cigarettes. 'Not only am I invited into the pit of Sapphic depravity, but before the face-painting process is entirely complete. Honoured indeed.'

'The what?' Cicely demanded. 'The pit of Sapphic depravity?'

'Not my words, dear girl, not at all, but Reginald Thann's. I would never have allowed myself to utter anything so unnecessarily melodramatic, not to say inaccurate. This, after all, is an attic, so how can it possibly be described as a pit?'

'Beastly man,' Cicely commented. 'I suppose he doesn't like me being friends with Lottie.'

'Doesn't like?' Cyprian echoed. 'He simply detests it, my dear. It's jealousy, of course, pure and simple, while

'I dare say he allows his imagination to run wild, even if by its very lack it fails to run as far as it should.'

'He can think what he pleases,' Cicely answered.

'I have no doubt he will,' Cyprian went on, 'no doubt at all. Anyway, we must not let Thann concern us. He is simply beyond the pail. I at least am ready to accept your love for one another, to which I trust you are ready to admit. I mean to say, you do, don't you, Charlotte, my dear?'

'I am not at all sure that is any of your concern, Mr Yates,' Charlotte answered him.

'Oh, no, please don't take offence,' he continued. 'The thing is, it would be simply dreadful if you weren't lovers. So frightfully dull, don't you know, a confirmation that life holds that little bit less piquancy. Do tell me you are lovers.'

'And yourself?' Cicely answered. 'You are widely supposed to prefer men.'

'Men? Certainly I prefer men. How anybody could do otherwise has always astonished me. Make, if you will, the comparison. Man is lithe and strong, a creature of power and grace, long of leg and firm of muscle, the most magnificent of God's creations. Woman, by contrast, is short and dumpy, broad at haunch and chest, a creature lacking all pretension to elegance. Were that not enough, there is the matter of personality, of character. Contrast the steadfast, reliable man against a sex not only entirely unpredictable from moment to moment but uncommonly prone to minor maladies, which I have always felt to be evidence of a lack of judgement.'

'You are hardly flattering, Mr Yates,' Charlotte answered.

'My dear, pray do not be offended,' he went on. 'When I say women, my dears, I speak, of course, in the most general terms. Both of you have certain of the masculine qualities, which, my dear Charlotte, is why the thought of marrying you becomes bearable.'

'Is that a proposal, Mr Yates?'

'A proposal? Well, yes, I suppose it must be.'

'Well, if so, it must be the most insulting one I have ever heard! Do you seriously expect me to marry someone who openly admits to despising the entire female sex?'

'Well, yes, frankly. I did say that you are better than most, and there is a far more important consideration, which I really must discuss with yourself and young George here.'

'Which is?' Charlotte asked, casting a quick glance towards Cicely, who was busy lighting a cigarette.

'As you know,' he sighed, 'I have some level of social status to maintain. Certainly my family expects me to marry, and indeed to produce offspring in the fullness of time. Meanwhile, my personal preferences are tolerated only so long as I make no open display of physical affection towards my lovers, and then barely. Now, if you and I were to be married, Charlotte dear, we could exist in outward respectability; honesty also, at least towards one another if not the world, which is in fact a great deal more than most could truthfully claim. Marry me, Charlotte, and accept that social approval which is surely slipping from your grasp with every day you are rumoured to be George's lover.'

Charlotte said nothing, hesitant now that she was faced with an open admission of what she had suspected for some time. Cyprian continued to smoke, Cicely also, and Charlotte found herself wondering how much had passed between the two of them since her last trip to London. Certainly Cyprian's manner had changed, as he had never previously made an open admission of his homosexuality. The scheme was tempting, and in many ways seemed to solve all her problems, yet she found it impossible to accept immediately.

'I am naturally very flattered by your proposal, Mr Yates,' she said evenly after a while, 'but it is not a matter to be taken lightly. Allow me a little time and I shall give you a fair and fully considered answer.'

'That's my girl,' Cicely said.

'Proper to the last,' Cyprian added.

With a strong underlying feeling that the two of them had thoroughly manipulated her, Charlotte allowed herself to be taken to Cyprian's club, the Stegander. Cicely came with them, something else that Charlotte suspected was by prior arrangement.

The club was among the streets to the south of St James's Park and, despite the building's air of respectable antiquity and a doubtful glance at Cicely from the doorman, they were admitted and shown to a table.

Their success at getting in set a mood of both mischief and triumph, for it was clear that the doorman actually believed Cicely to be a man. Charlotte could see why, since not only was her friend in immaculate dinner dress but had bound her chest, completely concealing her small breasts, and had pushed a carefully folded handkerchief down her trousers to create a reassuring bulge. Only her delicate jaw and smooth face betrayed her femininity, but so convincing was the effect that Charlotte found herself wondering if the doorman's doubt had not been based on age rather than sex. Certainly Cicely made a very pretty boy.

They ate lightly, with nothing on the menu designed to suit their tastes and Cyprian abstaining from meat as well. Copious amounts of champagne more than made up for the lack of food, and Charlotte quickly found herself growing tipsy and once more wondering what had been decided for her. She knew that the suggestion of marrying Cyprian would become more acceptable with drink, and determined not to make a decision that evening.

From the Stegander they moved on to the Black Cat, and from there to a cellar bar used by London's misfits and intelligentsia. By the time they returned to Cicely's flat, both girls were having trouble walking, and were leaning heavily on Cyprian, who himself was less than steady. Already hands were beginning to wander, and Charlotte was too drunk to be embarrassed by the breach of propriety. Inside, the intimate touches quickly became open groping.

With no thought for anything but the physical responses of their bodies, they rolled together on to Cicely's bed, laughing and fumbling at each other's clothes. Charlotte found herself the main object of attention, her dress quickly pulled down at the front and her chemise opened. Cicely began to suckle her, mouthing at her nipples and at the same time pulling up her dress. Her sex was quickly bare, her drawers pulled wide with Cicely's hand pressed to her quim. The pose left Cicely kneeling, her bottom stuck up, bulging out the seat of her dress trousers into a taut ball.

Cyprian was watching, but not with his eyes on Charlotte at all, but on Cicely's bottom. He began to stroke it and she made no move to stop him, then to squeeze her buttocks and slap at them, and still she let him. Charlotte was indifferent, drunk and lost in the pleasure of being suckled and masturbated by her lover, only vaguely aware of what was going on.

Shortly, through the haze of drink and arousal, she became aware that Cyprian was trying to get Cicely's trousers down. His hands were under her stomach, lifting her as he fumbled for the buttons. Cicely stopped sucking, lifting her head, but she made no effort to resist. Her eyes were unfocused, with no more than a hint of mild consternation in her expression as her buttons were popped open and her dress trousers eased down, drawers and all, over her slim, white haunches.

He did not pull them all the way down, but left them at the level of her upper thighs, with just her bottom sticking out, looking more boyish than ever with its frame of disarranged male clothing. Kneeling up, he

80

steadied himself on the wall, his eyes fixed to Cicely's neatly rounded buttocks and his hand fumbling with the buttons of his own dress trousers. With the fly undone, he released his cock, a long, pink pole, slimmer than the Colonel's with a small, pointed head, as if it might have been designed for insertion into bottom holes rather than quims.

Even in her drunken state, Charlotte realised that he was going to bugger Cicely. His eyes were locked on her bottom, one hand bobbing quickly up and down on his erection, the other in his mouth, collecting saliva. Charlotte held on tight to Cicely, pulling until their mouths met. Cicely was eager, passionate, then suddenly tense; she broke away, her mouth and eyes coming open in shock, rising, only to be pushed firmly back down on to Charlotte.

Cuddled tight, Charlotte held on, knowing that Cyprian was trying to force his cock up Cicely's bottom. As it happened, Charlotte felt every push, every shudder, through her lover's body. Cicely was gasping and sobbing, her breathing heavy and irregular, but she never tried to stop it. When at last the pained reaction died away, Charlotte knew that his cock was fully in. She held on tight, and Cicely's body began to rock slowly to the even motion of buggery.

There was a cock up her lover's bottom, and her own thighs were spread wide around both of them, putting her firmly at the bottom of the pile. It felt wonderful, utterly debauched, utterly uninhibited, and servile, too, as if she was no more than a soft bed for their pleasure. She felt dirty, wanton, eager to please and do the lewdest of things, to be made to do the lewdest of things to them in return. An idea came into her head, something that would really put her in the place she wanted to be, and with a last kiss to Cicely's open mouth, she began to wriggle out from beneath them.

Getting unsteadily to her feet, she tried to focus on the scene in front of her. Cicely was half on the bed, half off, her trim bottom lifted, only the actual buttocks visible. With the male clothes and her short hair, she looked much more like a youth than a girl, and it was plain why Cyprian had chosen her bottom for attention.

After dropping to her knees, Charlotte crawled closer, pressed her face between stomach and buttocks as Cyprian kneeled back to accommodate her. Cicely's trim bottom cheeks were well open, the straining pink ring of her anus clearly visible, taut around the cock within, the flesh pulling in and out as she was buggered. Charlotte was hardly able to focus, the image of cock and anus splitting and blurring, only to become clear as she forced her eyes to co-operate. Pressing her face fully down between Cicely's buttocks, she began to lick at the junction of penis and bumhole.

Cyprian moved further back, using his thumbs to spread Cicely's bottom cheeks and let Charlotte get at them more easily. Cicely sighed deeply as Charlotte's tongue found the taut anal skin, lapping eagerly. Still Cyprian pulled back. His shaft emerged, the foreskin, the neck, wet and slimy. Charlotte lifted her head a little, knowing what she was going to do even as his cock pulled out, flicking up to stand proud over Cicely's gaping, well-buggered anus. Charlotte's mouth was coming open, unable to resist the prospect of sucking a cock that had just been up her lover's bottom. She took it in, sucking down the rank, earthy taste, taking all she could until his cock was clean and pink, a solid rod of saliva-wet flesh as Charlotte turned her attention to Cicely's anus. Cyprian began to amuse himself, alternately probing at mouth and bumhole, enjoying the drunken lust of the two girls. He was pulling at his cock as well, his fingers making a ring around the base of his shaft, and became gradually more urgent. Again and again he slid his erection up Cicely's bottom, only to pull out after a few pushes, leaving the hole gaping wide and dribbling fluid. The moment it was free it would go

82

in Charlotte's mouth, to let her suck before being stuck back into the hole beneath. When he finally came, it was in the mouth of Cicely's anus, filling the open hole with milky sperm before putting his cock in Charlotte's mouth to be sucked clean one last time. She did it quickly, her own pleasure at breaking point with her fingers fluttering between her thighs, and the instant he pulled back her mouth was on Cicely's bumhole, sucking up the spunk, probing with her tongue and at last coming herself as she cleaned her lover's sodomised anus.

They pulled apart slowly, and Cicely turned to share Charlotte's filthy mouthful in an open kiss, rolling the mess together over their tongues before swallowing their mouthfuls. Charlotte was then pressed down between Cicely's thighs and made to lick, kneeling as she did it in the same pose in which she might have sucked a man's cock. Cicely came quickly, but it didn't signal the end of their play.

After stripping with fumbling eagerness in the cool darkness, they tumbled into bed together, laughing and groping blindly in drunken lechery. Piled nude beneath the covers, the three of them let themselves go completely, fingers and tongues exploring without restraint, put into mouths and over nipples, poked into quims and up bottoms. Charlotte was as wanton as the others, simply too far gone to care, as was Cicely, as eager for Cyrpian's cock as for Charlotte's quim. Cyprian was buggered with Cicely's rubber phallus, and both girls were fucked, Cicely's virginity lost without her really noticing and Charlotte finally passing into drink-sodden oblivion with Cyprian's cock still inside her vagina from the rear.

Spring 1922, Ashwood House, Somerset

Propped against the bathroom door with her arm, Charlotte struggled to contain her nausea. She had nearly been sick, and felt too weak to stand unaided, while her head was spinning and her vision blurred. It was not the first time it had happened, but the attacks had been growing steadily worse.

'Are you unwell, my dear?' the Colonel's voice sounded from behind her.

'Quite all right, thank you,' Charlotte answered.

'Nonsense,' he answered. 'You're as weak as a kitten, and damn pale. Look, I keep telling you, you must eat properly, and none of this damn vegetarian nonsense. You need steak, and suet pudding!'

Charlotte had heard it all before and merely shook her head. The dizziness was clearing, slowly. Walking carefully into the bathroom, she sat down on the edge of the tub. The Colonel followed.

'By God, I wish Sissy wouldn't fill your head with such arrant nonsense,' he snorted. 'She'll be here presently, which is what I came up to tell you. She phoned just now to say she's coming, along with that appalling fellow Yates.'

'Cyprian Yates?'

'That's the one. I expect he'll propose to you again, and I'll tell you now, my girl, if he does he'll not get my permission. The fellow's a sodomite, I'm damn sure of it.'

'Oh, really, Francis, I'm sure he's no such thing, merely of the artistic temperament.'

'Huh, little enough difference if you ask me. Anyhow, they're motoring down and hope to be here for dinner. Oh, and there's a fine scandal in the village. D'you recall Catherine Mullins? Plump girl, year or two younger than you, plenty of hair and everything besides. Well, seems some village lad or other's put her up the stick. Seems she'd had half the boys in the village and nobody can rightly say who the father is, herself and all, ha ha.'

Charlotte nodded, an uncomfortably large lump coming up in her throat as he spoke. Placing her hand on her stomach, she felt the hard swelling that had been growing steadily larger and harder with time. When she had first noticed it she had tried to deny it, even to herself, but that was no longer possible. She, too, was pregnant.

After the night at Cicely's flat, she had turned Cyprian down, unable to face marrying someone who not only preferred men, but seemed to prefer Cicely as well. He had not given up, and had written repeatedly since, pressing his suit in ever more elaborate language, which did nothing to change her opinion. Now, with his child growing in her belly, there seemed to be little choice. It was also clear that she was going to have to tell the Colonel before Cyprian spoke with him, and with the news of Catherine Mullins's accident it was clearly the best time.

'I have something to say, something terribly important,' she managed as he made to leave the bathroom.

'Eh? What?' he demanded.

'I am not unwell,' she said quietly, 'not unwell at all. I'm . . . That is . . . Oh, dear . . . Look, I'm in the same condition as Catherine Mullins.'

'What! Pregnant? No!'

85

'I'm afraid so.'

'How? I mean, who by? Yes, damn it, who by?'

'Cyprian Yates.'

'Yates! Damn him! What'd he do, get you drunk and force himself on you? Good God, but I'll flay the bastard alive, see if I don't!'

'I was drunk,' Charlotte admitted, 'but I wasn't forced. I just didn't know what I was doing.'

'No damned difference!' he stormed. 'Oldest trick in the book, damn him. Get a woman drunk enough and she'll couple like a stoat, more often than not. Damn it, girl, haven't I taught you anything? How many times have I told you? Never let a man get you alone, and if one does, and he insists, then take it in your mouth!'

'I wasn't alone, Uncle Francis: I was with George.'

'George? Who the hell's George?'

'You know who George is, Uncle Francis. Cicely.'

'Sissy? What, you mean to say the bastard had you in front of Sissy?'

'He had her, too. We were all a little drunk, I'm afraid.'

'A little drunk? You go in for some sort of Roman orgy. You let yourself get pregnant and you tell me you were a little drunk! By God, you must have been sloshed to the eyebrows!'

'It's happened, so please do stop shouting.'

'By God, I've a right to shout, but yes, no gain in it, eh? He'll have to marry you now, of course. I'll still take a horsewhip to the slimy, misbegotten rat! Good God, I suppose the fellow'll expect to live here as well! We'll need new staff, a wet nurse and who knows what besides? Look, Lottie, you're sure, are you?'

His tone had changed abruptly from fury to concern, but as she gave a miserable nod in response to his question his face became redder still. Turning suddenly on his heel, he stamped away down the corridor, leaving her to reflect on her condition.

The rest of the day was spent in nervous silence. The Colonel kept to the library, even ordering his lunch there, while Charlotte spent most of her time in the garden. By teatime she was straining her ears for the sound of Cicely's car, and she grew increasingly impatient afterwards, only to find herself hoping it was somebody else's when she finally heard it.

Walking rapidly around the side of the house, she saw the bright yellow of Cicely's Sunbeam, parked carelessly in the carriage sweep. Cicely herself was climbing out of the driver's seat, and waved cheerfully as Charlotte approached. In the other seat was Cyprian. Both were dressed in tweeds, almost identical in cut and colour. Both also wore cravats, scarlet in Cyprian's case, powder-blue in Cicely's.

Charlotte returned her lover's wave, trying to appear nonchalant as she wondered desperately what she should say. Cicely greeted her with a kiss, Cyprian with a grin, and as Charlotte saw that Spince was already opening the front door she realised that she had to speak quickly.

'Look, Cyprian,' she hissed, blushing at what she was about to say. 'We're going to have to marry now. I'm in trouble!'

'My dear thing, you're not!' he responded. 'How frightfully awkward!'

'Oh dear,' Cicely added.

'Well, we must marry,' Charlotte went on quickly. 'I've told the Colonel, and he's furious, but –'

'I'm afraid it's not possible,' Cicely interrupted her.

'Not possible? But we simply must . . .'

Charlotte stopped, alarmed by the sincerity in Cicely's voice.

'Lottie, darling,' Cicely went on, 'it's not possible to marry Cyprian because I already have. You see, darling, you're not the only one in trouble.'

* * *

Catherine Mullins tried to fight down her nervousness as she walked along the lane towards the rear of Ashwood House. She felt both surprised and flattered to have been asked to apply for a position as a maid, especially after disgracing herself in front of Colonel St John. Yet the summons had come.

Her mother and sisters had spent the best part of the morning fussing over her and ensuring that she looked her best, and that her swollen belly showed as little as possible. It hadn't really worked as far as concealment went, but in a smart yet demure blue dress, a bonnet and even gloves, she was sure that at least her dress could not be faulted.

The lane ended at a jumble of buildings in the shade of several yew trees. At the centre was a yard, with what she took to be the servants' door leading from it. She knocked, her nervousness growing as she waited and yet more when at last it was opened by a portly man in a formal black coat. Recognising him as the butler, Spince, she bobbed a curtsy and allowed herself to be ushered inside.

'Colonel St John and Miss Bomefield will see you immediately, in the library,' he announced, his voice curiously high-pitched for such a large man.

'The Colonel? Miss Bomefield?' she queried, having expected to be interviewed by the housekeeper or just possibly Spince himself.

Spince did not reply, and she followed him along a dim passageway to a door that opened into the hall and from there into the library. Inside, Colonel St John was seated in an armchair, with Charlotte standing behind him.

'Catherine Mullins, sir, miss,' Spince announced.

'Very good, Spince,' the Colonel answered. 'That will be all.'

The door closed behind Catherine and she found herself shuffling nervously on her feet. Both of them were looking at her and, while she was used to men focusing on her body rather than her face, she was surprised to find Charlotte doing the same. With the blood rising rapidly to her cheeks, she waited for them to say something.

'Now, Catherine,' the Colonel said at last. 'I don't want you to be embarrassed, so I'll come straight to the point. We know all about your little difficulty and, as you know, we've chosen to offer you the chance to take service with us.'

'Yes, sir, thank you, sir ... miss ...' Catherine managed, glancing down to the swell of her belly, which made her pregnancy impossible to hide. 'I'm ever so grateful, sir.'

'And so you should be,' he continued. 'Now, you'll live here, of course, and I believe that Mrs Mabberley has already made up a room for you. As to pay, what do you say to a pound a week, along with all the tuck you can eat?'

'A pound a week, sir?'

'Yes, a pound a week, that's what I said.'

'Yes, sir, why, thank you, sir. You're very good to me, sir ... miss.'

'Exactly, Catherine, very good to you indeed. Now, in return for our charitable attitude, we expect good service, which I'm sure you will provide. We also expect loyalty, exceptional loyalty, and discretion also, for reasons that will become apparent in due time. Now, if you can't give that loyalty and discretion, there's no place for you here. That means no gossiping in the village, none at all. What you see and hear at Ashwood goes no further, or you're out on your ear. Do I make myself clear?'

'Yes, sir, absolutely sir,' Catherine answered hastily.

'Good. Now as long as we understand each other, we shall all get along just fine. Any questions, my girl?'

'Yes, sir,' Catherine stammered. 'What are my duties, sir?'

'For the time being, to do as Mrs Mabberley says. Run along and see her.'

Catherine left, trying to walk backwards out of the door and curtsy at the same time. Spince was outside and she followed him as he set off to the servants' quarters, where she was shown into their parlour. It was a small room, square and illuminated by a single window opening high in the wall. A floor of polished planking matched plain wooden furniture, save for a single upholstered armchair, into which Spince lowered himself.

The other occupant of the room was a squat, heavily built woman, her body enveloped in black bombazine. Catherine recognised her as the housekeeper, Mrs Mabberley, and curtsied. Mrs Mabberley replied with a curt nod. Not quite sure what to do, Catherine remained standing.

'So we're to have little Catherine Mullins as our maid, are we?' the housekeeper said after a long pause. 'Now, why the Colonel and Miss Bomefield are being so very generous, I can't imagine. Still, it's not my place to ask, so I'm stuck with you and I suppose I'll just have to make the best of it. Not that you need think you'll be lying idle until the baby's born. There'll be plenty for you to do, and I'll have no dawdling, you understand.'

'Yes, Mrs Mabberley.'

'Your mother's a useless baggage and I dare say you're no better, so odds are before too long I'll soon be putting my spoon across your backside, condition or no condition. If you don't fancy it, then you'd best do as you're told. Now then, first off, you'll need to know how to address others. The Colonel is sir to you, or Colonel St John and sir on top of it if there's other gentlemen present. The lady is Miss Bomefield, not Miss Charlotte, whatever they may say in the village; it's a sight too familiar a way to be talking of their betters. When speaking to myself it's to be Mrs Mabberley, and

Mr Spince the same. The outdoor staff you're not to speak to unless there's call for it. You'll learn their names by and by.'

'Yes, Mrs Mabberley,' Catherine answered.

'Now,' she went on. 'Catherine's no name for a maid, too grand by far, and Catherine's too flighty. You're to be called Jane around the house, same as the late Mrs Bomefield always used to call her scullery maid. That'll be from Mr Spince and myself, as well as any other staff who happen to address you. The Colonel's not one to stand on formality, and he'll call you as he pleases, Miss Bomefield the same.'

Catherine nodded as Mrs Mabberley continued.

'Now, just as important, you need to know your place. It may be that the quality took you on out of Christian charity, but that's no cause to go giving yourself airs. In this household you're the bottom of the heap, and make no mistake. Follow three words and you'll save yourself a parcel of trouble: obedience, diligence and quickness. Do you understand?'

'Yes, Mrs Mabberley. Obedience, diligence and quickness.'

'Well, you say you do, but I'm not so sure. What do you think, Mr Spince?'

'I think we should test the three,' Spince answered, 'and, if she doesn't get it right, put the spoon to her behind. Have her put a coat of polish to the floor, and do it without her clothes to show willing.'

Catherine's mouth came open in shock and she turned to Mrs Mabberley, expecting support against the outrageous suggestion. The housekeeper merely nodded, acknowledging Spince's suggestion before turning back to Catherine.

'Come on, girl, what are you waiting for?' she said. 'You heard what Mr Spince said, didn't you? Now off with your clothes.'

'But, Mrs Mabberley!' Catherine protested.

'Answer me back once more and I'm fetching the spoon,' the housekeeper said. 'Now you'd best peel off, if you know what's good for you.'

Catherine's hands were shaking as they went to the button that held her dress at the throat. She glanced from one to the other, hoping at first that it was simply a joke or a test of her obedience, then merely for some sympathy. There was none, only cruel amusement.

Gingerly, she began to undo her dress, blushing scarlet before she had revealed anything. One by one the buttons came open, exposing her straining chemise and then the bare swell of her pregnant belly. With the buttons loose, she shrugged the dress from her shoulders, letting it fall to her hips before pushing it down to pool around her ankles on the floor. She stopped, hoping that having her in her underwear was enough.

'Come on, girl, get on with you,' Mrs Mabberley ordered. 'It's not your place to get virtuous about your body, that's for certain. Besides, those are a sight too fancy for a girl of your station. Off with them, right now.'

'All of it? Must I?' Catherine asked.

'I'm a kind woman,' Mrs Mabberley replied, 'and I realise this is your first day, and also that you're not too bright, but if you gainsay me one more time I'll send you for the spoon.'

Catherine quickly put her hands to her chemise and once more began to strip.

Spince watched it all, his little protuberant eyes moving up and down her body, never missing a detail as she stripped. When her chemise came open and her heavy breasts swung free he licked his lips, and there was a cruel smile on his round, owlish face as she struggled to get her stockings off without revealing more than she had to. At last she was nude, stark-naked from head to toe, standing shivering in front of them with her hands covering as much as she could.

'Too modest by half,' Mrs Mabberley remarked. 'Hands on your head, girl, and turn around, nice and slow.'

Catherine obeyed, trembling as they inspected her body. With her back to them she was made to stop, and Spince reached out to pinch her bottom, taking a piece of the soft flesh between finger and thumb. Catherine winced, but stayed still, wondering just how far they were going to go with her.

'Fine fat piece, I must say,' Mrs Mabberley remarked. 'Get along with you now, you little tart, there's no need to show it off more than is called for.'

'Yes, Mrs Mabberley, sorry, Mrs Mabberley,' Catherine stammered.

'Now you're to scrub and polish the floor,' the housekeeper went on, 'till it shines, mark you. You'll find what you need in the kitchen.'

'Yes, Mrs Mabberley,' Catherine answered and ran.

In the kitchen she searched frantically for the things she needed, sure that one of the ground staff would come in at any moment, or look in through one of the windows and see her. The thought was hideously embarrassing, and she rummaged frantically through the cupboards until at last she had collected everything. Only then did she realise that there was no way of fitting the pail beneath the tap in the sink. In desperation she began filling a saucepan and pouring the contents into the pail, only to be brought up short by the housekeeper's voice from behind her.

'Whatever are you about, you foolish girl?' Mrs Mabberley demanded.

'Filling the pail, Mrs Mabberley,' she answered.

'Well I've never yet seen it done that way. Run outside and use the pump, stupid.'

'Outside?'

'Yes, outside. Do you think it matters if the keeper or a lad sees you in your birthday suit? My, but you do have some flights of fancy.'

Catherine hesitated, but as the housekeeper reached up for one of the big wooden spoons that hung from pegs on the wall she ran. To her immense relief the yard was empty, and she scurried to the pump and back, filling the pail as fast as she could and all the while thinking of what she was showing, breasts and bottom, legs and quim, but most of all the round bulge of her belly. Back inside Mrs Mabberley was waiting, with her cruel smile set on her face, still holding the spoon. Catherine hurried to pick up her things, bending.

'Stay right there, my girl,' Mrs Mabberley said.

Catherine froze, acutely aware of her uplifted bottom as the housekeeper advanced on her. The spoon was lifted, and brought down hard on Catherine's naked rear, making a smack that echoed from the walls and was followed by her shriek of pain.

'Hurts, doesn't he?' Mrs Mabberley said. 'Now get on with you. There's more where that came from.'

Catherine hurried, taking her things into the butler's parlour. Mrs Mabberley followed, still holding the spoon, and sat back in her chair. Quickly wetting a rag, she went down on all fours, her heavy belly and ample breasts swinging beneath her as she began to wash the floor, all the time thinking of the way her bottom was stuck out and what she would be showing from behind.

Both of them watched complacently, obviously enjoying themselves but giving no outward display of emotion. After a while, Spince reached out for a decanter of port, pouring first his own glass, and then one for Mrs Mabberley. They sipped port as Catherine worked, washing, scrubbing and then polishing, all the while with Mrs Mabberley giving her instructions and the occasional encouraging pat with the spoon.

At last, with the floor gleaming and slippery, she was told to stop. She was trembling, and she could feel the heat in her sex from being made to expose herself so blatantly and to work in the nude, a secret she was determined to keep to herself. Not that it was going to be easy, with her nipples hard and her wet, swollen sex on show, while, from the size of the bulge in the butler's trousers, it was obvious that she wasn't the only one who was aroused.

'Might I dress now, please, Mrs Mabberley?' she asked, sitting back on her haunches.

'Dress?' the housekeeper replied. 'I'll tell you when the time comes to dress. For now, I've another task for you, which again is best performed in the nude. In fact, I'm about ready now. Come on, girl, get that pretty face in where it belongs.'

As she spoke, Mrs Mabberley hoisted up her skirts and petticoats, revealing thick legs in wrinkled stockings held up by elaborate garters, an expanse of fat white flesh and a confection of linen and cheap lace, frothing out to conceal what was beneath. Catherine swallowed nervously as she realised what she was going to be made to do, then again as the housekeeper's hands went to the drawers. The fold was pulled open, exposing a fleshy pink quim, fat and moist in a tangle of coarse black hair. A strong natural female aroma caught Catherine's nose, mixed with the crude floral smell of cheap scent. She made a face.

'Best get used to it,' Mrs Mabberley said. 'You'll be spending plenty of time there. Now come on, or do I have to beat you first?'

Catherine shook her head, swallowed and shuffled forward to between Mrs Mabberley's knees. She hesitated, knowing full well what was expected of her, but unable to put her face to the housekeeper's fat quim without being made to do it.

'Hoity-toity piece, are we?' Mrs Mabberley demanded and grabbed Catherine by the hair.

An instant later her face had been forced full against the hot, reeking quim, muffling her squeal of surprise. With her feet kicking and her arms waving wildly, the grip in her hair tightened, pressing her nose to Mrs

Mabberley's clitoris. She tried to lick, poking her tongue into the big, musky hole of the housekeeper's vagina, only to find it impossible. Her whole face was being used to masturbate on, her head jerked from side to side with her nose bumping across Mrs Mabberley's sex. She could barely breathe, and the motion was making her bottom wobble and her breasts and belly swing, much to the butler's amusement, as she heard his laugh, as high-pitched as his speaking voice.

She struggled to hold herself still, but could do nothing to stop Mrs Mabberley using her face. Instead, she decided to make the best of it, reaching back to find her own quim despite knowing that the leering eyes of the butler would be fixed on it. Spreading her sex lips with her fingers, she began to masturbate.

'Keep your hands to yourself, you little strumpet!' Mrs Mabberley ordered. 'I'll have none of that.'

The spoon cracked down on Catherine's bottom and she quickly took her fingers away. A sense of unfairness was added to her woes as the housekeeper continued to make use of her nose. Then, as she heard the creak of the butler's chair and saw him move from the corner of her eye, came the realisation that she was going to be fucked.

Giving in to the inevitable, she stuck her bottom out, trying to hold it still as her body was shaken in the housekeeper's grip. Spince settled himself behind her, took her buttocks in his hands and spread them, pushing close so that his belly bumped against her bottom. His hands went lower, tickling her skin as he adjusted his trousers, until the firm head of his cock nudged between her buttocks.

'Ah,' he sighed. 'Nothing like a girl who's going to pup, eh, Mrs Mabberley? There's nothing you can do to her as hasn't already been done.'

'Very true, Mr Spince,' the housekeeper answered. 'Now, Jane, why don't you give me a little lick while Mr Spince enjoys your fine fat bottom?'

Mrs Mabberley let go of Catherine's hair even as Spince's cock found its target and slid easily up the wet passage. As her vagina filled, Catherine began to lick. Soon her bottom was bouncing to the butler's pushes, each of which forced her face into the housekeeper's quim, making it hard to use her tongue properly. Taking a firm grip on the housekeeper's massive thighs, she steadied her head, allowing herself to go to work properly on the big, fleshy quim to which her face was pressed.

'Not the first time you've licked cunt, is it, my girl?' Mrs Mabberley demanded. 'Who was it, you little slut? Your own sisters, I'll be bound. Dirty little strumpets, the lot of you.'

Catherine didn't answer, unable to admit the truth. Spince had begun to groan in pleasure, and his fat belly was slapping on her bottom, the flesh of gut and buttocks wobbling together as he fucked her. It was getting faster, and her licking became more urgent as the motion of the cock inside her brought her pleasure up and up. Mrs Mabberley was moaning too, her hand back in Catherine's hair, gripped tight.

Both were going to come and, as Spince's groans turned to a piglike grunting, Mrs Mabberley once more took control of Catherine's head, using her nose to masturbate on. Shaken like a rat in a dog's jaws, her bottom bouncing, her breasts and belly jiggling, her face plastered into the housekeeper's quim, Catherine could only let them use her, enjoying her body without the slightest consideration.

Spince came first, deep up her, and finished off by whipping out his cock and rubbing it in the sweaty crease of her bottom, smearing sperm and quim juice over her anus and up between her big cheeks. A moment later Mrs Mabberley also came, grunting out loud and calling Catherine a dirty tart, which seemed horribly unfair when it was she who was using Catherine's face to masturbate on.

97

Even when both had finished, Catherine's face was held to the housekeeper's quim, her hair released only when the butler had sat back in his chair. Catherine pulled back, wiping a moustache of Mrs Mabberley's juice from her upper lip. Her knees were still well apart, her open quim stuck out, dribbling a mixture of her juice and the butler's sperm on to the floor.

'Now you're to clean up your mess, Jane,' Mrs Mabberley ordered, nodding to the butler.

Catherine turned, to find Spince holding out a stubby cock, the dark, wrinkly skin smeared with white juice and a blob of come still on the tip. Obediently, she crawled over, opening her mouth to take it in and sucking his penis clean, then his balls, as he leered down at her. Juice was still dripping from her hole, leaving a trail on the floor, which she found when she had finished licking at the butler's genitals.

'Messy strumpet, aren't you?' Mrs Mabberley chided. 'Come on, then, clean it up. What are you waiting for?'

Catherine glanced at the housekeeper, then at the pool of dirty white fluid on the floor. Mrs Mabberley pointed at it, once more picking up the big wooden spoon. Catherine got quickly down, her bottom going up towards the butler. With her face screwed up in disgust, she poked her tongue out into the pool of slimy white muck, tasting the salt and the blend of male and female tastes.

Mrs Mabberley chuckled, watching in high amusement as Catherine lapped up the pool of come. There was plenty of it, as much hers as the butler's. She was gagging on the taste as she swallowed it down, but her sex felt hot and ready behind her. She was wondering if she dared masturbate, but something in Mrs Mabberley's face suggested that it would earn a rebuke at the least, maybe a smacking with the spoon.

She held back, telling herself she'd run to somewhere private as soon as she could and do it there, denying them the pleasure of seeing how excited their abuse had made her. As she continued to lick up the spunk she tried not to think dirty thoughts, only to feel something firm press to her quim, the round, smooth toe of Spince's boot. With a despairing sob she began to rub herself on it, unable to resist despite the agonising shame that immediately filled her head.

Spince chuckled at her reaction, pressing his foot more firmly between her thighs. Closing her eyes in abject misery, Catherine began to wriggle her bottom on to the hard boot. Spince laughed out loud at the sight, but her clitoris had begun to catch on the lip of the boot sole and she was already coming. The climax hit her and her mouth came open, pressing to the floor to suck up the mess, then to rub her face in it, grovelling and filthy, nude, dishevelled and used, on the floor with her face smeared in three people's come and her cunt spread wide on one of her tormentors' boots . . .

The orgasm went on and on, her pleasure mixed with burning shame at what she was doing and at what had been done to her, but far too good for her to stop, until at last the agonising sensitivity of her clitoris had simply become too much and she was forced to pull away. Spent, she slumped down, her face still in the mess.

'Like mother, like daughter, don't you think, Mr Spince?' Mrs Mabberley remarked.

'Like enough,' he agreed. 'D'you recall how Lias strung her up from the apple tree that time? Squealed like a stuck pig when she spent.'

'Always did, that one. Now come on, girl, you've had your fun, not that you deserved it, so finish up the floor and you can get dressed again.'

Catherine took one deep breath, poked her tongue out and once more began to lick the mess up from the floor.

'Not like that, you dirty tart!' Mrs Mabberley laughed. 'Use the rag, like before, and then a spot more polish. Imagine that, Mr Spince, just spent and still she wants her mouthful. Worse than her mother, I'd say.'

Spince merely chuckled, leaving Catherine to complete the cleaning up with her face scarlet with blushes. After tidying themselves, the two of them went back to their port, not speaking until Catherine was finished. She began to dress, only to be stopped with a hard swat of the spoon on her bottom.

'A moment,' Mrs Mabberley ordered. 'Stick it out. Rest your hands on your knees.'

Catherine dutifully presented her bottom, across which three hard smacks were laid.

'Hurts, doesn't it?' Mrs Mabberley asked as Catherine stood to rub at her sore cheek.

'Yes, Mrs Mabberley,' Catherine answered. 'Like anything.'

'I'm sure it does, but not next to a birch, it doesn't, nor half a dozen other things as might get used across a girl's bottom. So listen well, and here's the last thing. There's like to be some goings on in this house what might raise eyebrows elsewhere, not that it's none of their business. Do you understand?'

'Yes, Mrs Mabberley. Colonel St John has told me I must be discreet.'

'I dare say he has, and I dare say he'll put you out on your ear if you're not, but hear this. He's a good master, is the Colonel, Miss Bomefield the same for a mistress, and, if you breathe a word out of place, Mr Spince and I'll have the skin off that great fat arse, and that's a fact. Then you'll see what hurts.'

Summer 1922, Chelsea, London

Cicely – now Mrs Cyprian Yates, or even Mr George Yates to their closer friends – stood at the window of the house they had purchased in Oakley Street. For a variety of reasons she was feeling less than happy, and less than comfortable.

For one thing, being pregnant was very hard to reconcile with her self-image, while for clothing she had found herself obliged to buy garments designed for ever more obese men as her belly had expanded. Braces had become necessary, which tended to spread out to either side of her breasts, pushing them together and making them harder to conceal. They were also a great deal bigger than they had been, and the nipples had grown darker and larger, making a male identity ever harder to carry off. Looking at herself in the mirror, she realised that she no longer looked like an exceptionally pretty teenage boy, but more like a comic best boy from a pantomime.

Another irritation was her increasing taste for anal sex. Ever since Cyprian had first buggered her she had come to enjoy the sensation of having a cock pushed up her bottom hole more and more. Like being pregnant, it was a direct contradiction to the way she had always viewed herself. She wanted to take on not merely a male role, but a dominant male role. Cyprian was more than happy to wear nighties and even dresses occasionally, and for Cicely to bugger him, yet more and more often their sex sessions ended up with his cock wedged firmly up her bottom.

The third problem was that she was still desperately in love with Charlotte and didn't know what to do about it. Her last visit to Ashwood had ended in a blazing row. The Colonel had been furious over their decision to marry without consulting him, and to Cicely's surprise Cyprian had stood his ground, which had been the worst possible thing to do. They had left with Charlotte in tears, the Colonel red-faced with fury and Cyprian coldly silent. Since then it had been made plain that Cyprian was not welcome at Ashwood. Cicely had not gone, either, supposedly in support of her husband, but really because she felt horribly guilty at having left Charlotte with the prospect of bearing an illegitimate child, even if she had not done it intentionally. They had written to one another, but Charlotte's letters had seemed cool if civil and Cicely had not been able to find it in herself to reply other than in kind.

In addition to the major difficulties there were several minor ones, mainly involving Cyprian. They shared many tastes and generally got on well, although not in terms of aesthetic sense. Cyprian's preferences ran to an abundance of purple and lilac drapery set off with gold leaf and mahogany, Cicely's to simplicity and absolute chiaroscuro. Each had their own rooms, yet in decorating the major part of the house they had found it impossible to reach common ground. He had also refused to give up either meat or rent boys. There seemed to be nothing she could do about the meat and, unwilling to hire female heterosexual prostitutes for her own satisfaction, she had been forced to content herself with the vindictive pleasure of buggering Cyprian's paid lovers. To make matters worse, most of the lesbian women who had accepted her as one of them refused to acknowledge her rather more complicated true sexuality, leaving her frequently frustrated.

Turning abruptly from the window, she stubbed out her cigarette. It was raining outside, making a walk impractical, while if dressing as a man in public had provided an illicit thrill before, now that she was pregnant it was merely embarrassing. Briefly she considered masturbating, only to decide that she wasn't really in the mood and that irritating thoughts were bound to intrude and spoil whatever fantasy she worked up, as they had with increasing frequency. Cyprian was out, so it was impossible to take her ill feeling out on him, either verbally or with the combination of dildo and riding crop he most enjoyed. Besides that, she knew full well that she would just have ended up asking him to bugger her.

Lighting another cigarette, she tried to read the volume of Havelock Ellis's work *Sexual Inversion*, which she had purchased in order to try to understand herself. As always it managed to seem both simplistic and obscure at the same time. She was soon back at the window, staring out at the grey street while wishing she was back at Wiltonheath, where everything had seemed so beautifully simple.

Summer 1922, Ashwood House, Somerset

'Twelve pounds!' Colonel St John exclaimed. 'Good God!'

'Twelve pounds and four ounces, to be precise,' Charlotte answered. 'Mrs Mabberley measured her on the kitchen scales.'

'Good God,' the Colonel repeated. 'Damn, that's going to make it hard to bring this thing off, eh? How long d'you have?'

'Four months,' Charlotte answered.

'Four months, eh? Damn, and the excuses are already running pretty thin. Catherine's brat'll be ... God knows, sixteen, even twenty pounds by then. It'll look damn odd if we're to claim they're twins and one's three times the size of the other.'

'They need not be identical twins.'

'No, but still. Look, at the least I wish you'd eat properly. If you don't put some weight on you'll produce a damn midget.'

'I eat very well, thank you.'

'No, you don't, damn rabbit food. Not healthy, it's not, not in your condition. At the least you take a glass of milk now and then.'

'I'm sorry, but I must hold firm to my principles. I will not take from animals.'

'Stuff and nonsense! Still there's a way around that, you know. When I was out in India I came across a peculiar local habit, somewhere along the Khotri river it was, I think. Plenty enough of peculiar habits in India, and at the time it seemed no more than a curiosity. Typical heathen going on, in fact. The thing is, the women thereabouts used to keep their children at the breast for a remarkably long time. Often enough there'd be a fair bit over, which they'd give to their families.'

'Human milk?'

'The very same.'

'Are you implying that I should do the same?'

'Certainly I am. Supposed to be the best there is, and you can't say you're taking from animals.'

'True, but it hardly seems Christian.'

'Aha, but then you're an atheist, aren't you? Told me so yourself.'

'Well, yes . . .'

'You can't have it both ways, girl. Either you are or you aren't. If you are you needn't worry about whether it's Christian or not, damn it.'

'Well, no, but it doesn't seem right, somehow.'

'Doesn't seem right? Why the hell not?'

'Well, I . . . it . . . Surely it's immoral?'

'Immoral? Don't drivel, girl! You think it's wrong because a load of puritans like that Miss Mebbin of yours have filled your head with rubbish. They think anything to do with the human body's immoral, damn it, even taking a crap, you'd think. When a man's been abroad as long as I have, and seen as many things, he knows better, and so should you.'

'Well . . .'

'Not another word. If you insist on being a nut then fair enough, but either you're a nut or you're not. You can't have it both ways. Now tell me you'll drink the milk.'

'I suppose so, but –'

'I'll have no buts,' the Colonel finished and reached for the bell pull, summoning Spince, who appeared before Charlotte could order her thoughts to find any reasonable argument against what the Colonel was suggesting. Spince was sent to fetch Catherine, who appeared while Charlotte was still trying to think of any convincing reason why she should not drink human milk, or rather a reason that the Colonel would accept. To her the idea seemed frighteningly immoral, although she couldn't work out exactly why.

'Ah, Catherine, I understand that congratulations are in order, of a sort, anyway,' the Colonel said by way of greeting as Catherine bobbed a nervous curtsy. 'Are you fully recovered?'

'Yes, sir. It's been three days, sir,' Catherine answered.

'Splendid, splendid, and over twelve pounds, I hear.'

'Yes, sir.'

'Good for you. And what's the little tyke's name?'

'Hazel, sir, but Mrs Mabberley says she should be called Mary or Lucy.'

'Mrs Mabberley? What the hell has Mrs Mabberley got to do with it?'

'She says on account of them names being more suited to a maid's girl, sir.'

'You call her what you damn well please, my girl. Hazel, then, very pretty, very modern, too. There were no Hazels when I was a boy. Damn peculiar, in fact, calling your baby after a tree. Still, it's your choice, I suppose.'

'Yes, sir. Thank you, sir.'

'Good, quite. Now look here, Catherine, my dear, I've something important to say to you, and I'll come straight to the point. You can hardly have failed to notice that Miss Bomefield is in the same condition as you are or, rather, as you were, eh?'

'Yes, sir.'

'Good, good. Now the thing is, d'you see, it's awkward enough for you, but for someone of her

106

station it's *damned* awkward. As you know, we've had the house shut down all season, and Charlotte's supposed to have the scarlet fever, and who knows what besides.'

'Yes, sir.'

'Well you've played your part, and proved your discretion, but here you'll have to be more discreet than ever. Now, there are three things I need you to do. First off, when Lottie pups – that is, I mean to say, when Miss Bomefield has her baby – we want you to be the wet nurse. Plenty enough milk to go round, I dare say, eh?'

'Yes, sir. I'm sure, sir. An honour, sir,' Catherine stammered.

'Good, good,' he went on. 'Now, the other things are a bit delicate. The thing is, Lottie – Miss Bomefield – can hardly go out in society with a bastard . . . that is to say, with an illegitimate child. Now, for you it doesn't matter so much and, besides, you've one of your own. So, when the time comes, it's to be put about that Lottie's baby is your own. Got that?'

'Well, yes, sir. I suppose so, sir.'

'Good. Splendid in fact. Now, of course, the circumstances are hardly usual, but I'm sure we can all manage. The third matter also requires your discretion, and is to do with Miss Bomefield's health. Now how much milk are you making?'

'Beg pardon, sir?'

'How much milk are you making? I said.'

'I don't rightly know, sir. Plenty enough for baby and some over, I suppose,' Catherine answered as her cheeks flamed from pink to scarlet.

'Good, good. Now, I don't want you to deprive your child, not a bit of it, but once you've finished feeding her, I want you to squeeze out what you can, into a glass or something. When you've done it, put the glass on a tray, perhaps with a napkin over it, eh, and bring it to Miss Bomefield. Got it?'

Catherine gave Charlotte a nervous glance. Charlotte nodded in response, determined not to show her uncertainty in front of the maid.

'Yes, sir. I understand,' Catherine answered.

'Good girl. Now run along.'

Hurrying back to the kitchens, Catherine cast quickly around for Spince and Mrs Mabberley. Neither was visible, but the cellar door was open, suggesting that Spince at least could be accounted for. She was determined that neither should discover what she was about to do, both because of the intimacy it involved and because of the certainty that they would use it in some way to add to the humiliations and punishments they gave her almost daily.

Mrs Mabberley in particular she had come to dread. Spince was merely lewd, but the housekeeper took endless sadistic pleasure in Catherine's body, and was certain to find some cruel and amusing way to exploit the fact that Catherine was in milk if the idea was put into her head.

Going to the cupboards, she began to sort through the various containers, looking for a jug big enough to take one of her breasts so that she would spill none of the milk. They had always been big, but had swollen as her pregnancy advanced, until by the time she had come into milk each filled two hands, great, fat globes of girl flesh, topped by nipples that Spince had more than once compared to claret corks on occasions when they had made her work topless or nude.

The largest of the stock jugs seemed the best choice. She took it carefully down from the shelf and held it carefully in both hands so as not to risk dropping it and inviting the session with Mrs Mabberley's spoon that would undoubtedly follow. Taking the jug into the parlour, she quickly pulled one fat breast from her clothes. The flesh felt firm, despite Hazel having drunk her fill less than an hour before, and Catherine knew that milking herself was going to be a pleasant relief despite the embarrassment that was welling up inside her. Poising her breast over the jug, she squeezed, only to see the tiny jets of white fluid spurt out in several directions. Not all had gone in the jug, and she tried again, this time with her globe pressed to the mouth of the jug. The milk came again at the same pressure, squirting out in thin jets to patter down into the big jug. It felt lovely, even better than she had expected, with the same relief that came when Hazel fed, but also an added rudeness.

With her eyes closed in bliss, she began to milk herself, squeezing and massaging first one breast, then the other, until there was a good glassful in the jug. When she finally stopped there were runnels of milk on both breasts, while a good deal had soaked into her open dress and chemise. After lifting her breasts quickly to her mouth, she licked the excess off, only to find that it was still coming, with little beads of white fluid forming on her nipples even without squeezing. With a deliciously naughty feeling and a good deal of shame, she began to suckle herself, the milk now spurting out into her mouth, rich and oddly sharp.

She could feel the heat in her sex and was wondering if she dared sneak upstairs to masturbate when the sound of the cellar door closing put an abrupt stop to her dirty game. Stuffing her breasts back into her dress, she just managed to avoid being caught by Spince, who entered the room with a number of cobwebbed bottles.

'What are you about?' he demanded.

'Fetching milk for Miss Bomefield, begging your pardon, Mr Spince,' she answered quickly.

'Milk? For Miss Bomefield?' he demanded.

'Colonel's instructions, Mr Spince,' she said, hurrying to fetch a tray and a glass before his questions could become awkward.

'Good thing too, not that it's my concern,' Spince answered. 'Parcel of old crams, this vegetarian business. Now make sure you give the scoop a good clean, nothing worse than sour milk for smell.'

Catherine threw a glance to the row of unused scoops hanging behind the butler as she picked the tray up, wondering how to explain before deciding not to. Hurrying from the kitchen, she made her way to the library, where both the Colonel and Charlotte were still seated, the one reading a newspaper, the other a magazine.

'Your milk, miss, as was ordered,' Catherine said, placing the tray on a table beside Charlotte.

'Aha, splendid, and fast work,' the Colonel remarked. 'Pour some out, then, my dear. You should have it while it's nice and warm, Lottie.'

Catherine removed the cloth she had draped over the tray and poured the milk from jug to glass. The distinctive scent caught her nose and she saw Charlotte's wrinkle. She kept pouring, until the glass was full, which left a little milk still in the jug.

'Splendid,' the Colonel said, 'plenty to go around. You should be proud of yourself, Catherine, my girl. You make a damn fine cow.'

'Thank you, Catherine,' Charlotte added. 'Now, are you sure this is breast milk?'

'Certain sure, Miss Bomefield,' Catherine answered.

'Of course it's breast milk!' the Colonel exclaimed. 'Catherine's no liar, damn it!'

'There's an awful lot of it,' Charlotte said dubiously.

'Like I say, she makes a good cow. Damn it, I mean to say, look at the size of those udders!'

'It is my milk, I promise, Miss Bomefield,' Catherine said blushing. 'Every drop.'

Charlotte lifted the glass, then sniffed it before taking a cautious sip. Her frown quickly changed to a surprised smile, and back.

'It doesn't taste any different,' she said.

'How the hell would you know, when you haven't had any cow's milk in over a year?' the Colonel demanded. 'For goodness' sake, girl, just drink it.'

Still Charlotte hesitated, then suddenly put the glass to her lips and began to gulp it down, quickly draining it.

'More, Miss?' Catherine asked, holding out the jug. 'Shame to let it go to waste.'

'Yes, thank you,' Charlotte answered.

Catherine noticed that her mistress's lower lip was quivering as the glass was filled, but she paid no attention, standing patiently until Charlotte had drained the second glass.

'Thank you,' Charlotte said as she returned the glass to the tray. 'Very well, Francis, I shall take my milk, but only Catherine's milk. There are to be no tricks.'

'Absolutely not,' the Colonel answered. 'What do you take me for?'

Charlotte didn't answer, but dismissed Catherine, who returned to the kitchens. Her feelings were an odd mixture of shame and pride. It had felt strange to watch Charlotte drink the milk, provoking a desire to cuddle her mistress to her chest, to comfort her, even to feed her. She was blushing in confusion at her own feelings, but the urge to masturbate was stronger than ever, and when she found neither Spince nor Mrs Mabberley in the kitchen she quickly tidied up before running up to her room.

Hazel was asleep, the servants' passage quiet and still. Peering from a window she saw Mrs Mabberley in the kitchen garden, cutting flowers for the house. Spince was there, too, sitting on a bench, a glass in his hand. With growing excitement she moved back from the window, her hands going straight to her dress. The front came open easily, her breasts spilling out, fat and heavy in her hands. Her nipples were already hard, and wet with milk, which she sucked up eagerly, lifting one and then the other to her mouth.

No longer able to stop herself, she kicked off her shoes and pushed her dress quickly down over her hips, then stepped from the puddle of cloth. Her chemise followed, then her drawers, leaving her in nothing but stockings. She went to the bed; kneeling down, she put her hands straight to her breasts, catching the nipples and squeezing to send little fountains of milk into the air. Giggling at the sight, she did it again, watching the beads form before the milk spurted out to run down the pale flesh of her breasts.

Cupping them, she smeared the milk over their smooth surfaces, letting her fingers linger on the big nipples. It felt glorious, filling her with the urge to make more milk, to see it spray from her breasts, to fill her mouth with it and rub it into her skin. Lifting a breast to her mouth, she began to suckle herself, her eyes shut in bliss as her mouth filled with warm, rich milk and the blissful sensation filled her head. The second breast followed, squeezed and sucked until there was milk running from her lips and down her chin. She swallowed, revelling in the taste, abandoned to the idea of masturbating in her own milk.

Taking both huge breasts in her hands, she began to massage them, squirting the milk out so that it ran down her breasts and sprayed her thighs. Her legs came apart and she leaned back, opening her sex as she milked herself down over her midriff. The trickles ran to either side of her still swollen belly and she caught them, rubbing it over her stomach, over her breasts again. Her whole front was wet and the air was thick with the milky smell as she let her hands go lower.

Her vagina was still sore from childbirth, but she touched it, taking milk from her nipples and rubbing it gently over the smarting flesh. It felt soothing and she repeated the action, her pleasure rising and her inhibitions slipping away as she played with herself. A wet finger went down between her bottom cheeks, burrowing between them to find her anus and rub milk over the tiny hole. She began to tickle it, teasing herself as she found her clitoris with the ball of her thumb.

She began to masturbate, stroking her quim and bottom hole with her fingers as she dabbed at her clit with her thumb. It felt good, her pleasure rising and rising as with her other hand she squeezed and stroked her breasts, spraying the milk out over her body and rubbing it in. Soon her whole front was wet with it, while her sex was burning beneath her hand.

As her orgasm approached she was wishing she had more milk, enough to spray out in great fountains, enough to feed everyone in the house, enough to bathe in. One finger was up her bottom, two at the mouth of her vagina, her soreness turning to pleasure as the climax hit her. She went back, kicking out her legs, one hand snatching at her sex, the other pinching a breast hard, to squirt a fountain of milk into the air. With that she cried out in ecstasy, coming, her body soaked with her own milk, more dribbling from her nipples, her mouth full of the taste of it, one finger well up her wet bottom and her clitoris burning under her thumb.

Only at the very peak did her thoughts stray from the simple response of her own body. Completely out of control, at her most vulnerable moment, she thought of Charlotte drinking up the milk and imagined how it would have been if it had come direct from the breast.

Summer 1922, Somerset

Sitting in the study in Babcary Manor, which had been his father's study before him and his grandfather's before that, Toby St John found himself struggling to find the grief he felt was proper. The telephone stood on the desk in front of him and, only moments before, he had replaced the receiver after a call from the asylum. His father was dead, yet he felt no sorrow, only a curious detachment, and shock only at his own reaction in that the title that was now his, Lord Cary, kept running through his head.

It was impossible to remember his father as anything but a vague-eyed old man who had always seemed to look through him rather than at him. By reputation, Lord William Cary had been a man of considerable talent and achievement, and while Toby felt a certain pride in this, it was extremely difficult to relate his father's success to himself. Two words came primarily to mind, 'mad' and 'distant', neither of which prompted much in the way of grief.

He frowned, trying to think of the practicalities of the matter, the first of which was clearly to relay the news to his uncle and sister. The Colonel, he knew, would regard it as a merciful end. Cicely was harder to judge, but as she had been seven when their father was committed it seemed unlikely that her reaction would be any less muted than his own. He reached for the phone, only to stop, suddenly finding the prospect of delivering such news by telephone intensely distasteful. There was also a need to do something other than sit in his study, and he determined to telegraph Cicely and then drive to Ashwood and tell his uncle face to face.

As he walked to his car he was fully aware that wanting to talk to the Colonel in person was not his only reason for visiting Ashwood. Since the spring, both the Colonel and Charlotte had refused to allow him to visit, finding ever more ludicrous excuses to put him off. Beforehand he had felt that he was getting on rather well with Charlotte, and he was sure that for all her protestations his teasing and occasional deliberate provocation had not been unwelcome. After all, he had always done it, and she had certainly been giving him preference over her other suitors. Despite his natural instinct to take the rejection as personal, he knew that it wasn't. Charlotte had also refused to see Victor Cushat, or Reggie Thann, while to the best of his knowledge she had not left Ashwood all season. A more probable cause seemed to be that it had something to do with the marriage between Cicely and Cyprian Yates, yet it was impossible to see why that should involve him, or Charlotte's other friends and suitors. It was a puzzle, and one he now felt he had the perfect excuse to solve, despite a flush of guilt at using his father's death for the purpose.

In less than half an hour he was in Ashwood Village. The drive had cleared his head, and made him more determined than ever to find out why Charlotte wouldn't see him. Having stopped outside the post office, he spent a while in the careful wording of his telegram to Cicely and when he was finished asked after Charlotte, only to find that she had not been seen in the village either. More puzzled than ever, and even worried, he decided not to drive to the house but to walk, arriving without any warning whatever.

The lane that led to the back of the house was more convenient than the front drive, so he took it, and reached the point where it turned into the yard only to stop dead in his tracks. Charlotte was there, visible through the ironwork gate that led into the kitchen garden, bending as she cut a rose, in profile to him, with her normally tiny waist bulging in unmistakable pregnancy. For a moment he merely stood and stared as the solution to his perplexity sank in, with a dozen questions crowding behind. Deciding to delay the announcement of his father's death, he pushed open the gate. Charlotte turned at the squeak of the iron hinges, her mouth opening in shock as she saw him.

'Good afternoon, Lottie, old thing,' he addressed her, grinning.

'Toby . . . Mr St John . . .' she stammered. 'I didn't . . . I mean . . .'

'Didn't expect me, eh? No, I'll bet you didn't. So this is why you've been hiding away all season. Good Lord! Pregnant, eh?'

'Yes. I'm sorry. I mean I'm . . . Oh, my, what I am to do?'

'Oh, don't worry about me. I'm not shocked at all. I just wish it had been me who did the dirty deed. In fact, damn it, Lottie, I mean to say, you never would, and look here!'

'I'm sorry, Toby, I . . . it just happened.'

'Just happened! These things don't just happen, damn it! Come on, who had your drawers apart?'

'I'd rather not say.'

'Well, I'll guess then. Not Jerton, that's for sure. Cushat? No. Thann? Not Cyprian, surely?'

Charlotte's face immediately coloured.

'Cyprian Yates? Good Lord! What did you do, take a leaf out of Sissy's book and dress up as a boy? Slipped into the wrong hole, did he? Ha, ha!'

'Mr St John!'

'That's Lord Cary to you, my girl . . . Oh hell.'

'Lord Cary? How do you mean?'

'Yes, quite, sorry about that, bit of a slip, what? No, the thing is, you see, that's what I came over for. My father's dead, damn it, this morning, some kind of fit.'

'Oh, good gracious!'

'I er . . . wanted to tell Uncle Francis in person, you see, so I came straight over.'

'But of course, you must see Francis, of course, immediately. He'll be in the library.'

Late Summer 1922, Ashwood House, Somerset

Charlotte selected a rose, a beautiful deep-red flower just beginning to open properly, cutting the stem at a sharp angle before placing it in her trug with the others. She felt buoyant, better than at any time since the day she had realised that she was pregnant. The heat of the day, which had seemed merely stifling all summer, was now a glorious warmth, while she was humming a tune from a comic opera, happy and thoroughly at peace with the world. Even the prospect of having an illegitimate baby no longer seemed daunting. After all, with land, wealth and the prospect of more of both, what did the sneers of society matter?

Not that the reaction to her pregnancy had been as bad as she had expected, at least not among those few who knew. Cicely and Cyprian had maintained a discreet silence. Even the servants seemed to have managed to keep it to themselves, although with Catherine milking herself daily and the loyalty of the others always above question this was perhaps to be expected. More surprising to her, Toby St John had also kept quiet, when she had expected him to be uncompromisingly furious and to expose her. Instead, his sole objection seemed to be that it was Cyprian and not himself who had succeeded in seducing her, and even then there was more sorrow than anger in his reaction. He had even begun to visit again, quite frequently, and to tease her in much the way he had before, even trying to persuade her to lift her dress and show him her belly, with which he seemed oddly fascinated.

As she cut another rose she smiled to herself at the memory, and at how close she had come to doing it. Only the appearance of Spince to announce dinner had stopped her, and the exchange had left her uncomfortably wet between her thighs for the rest of the evening.

So frequent were his visits becoming that she had even begun to dare hope that he might still have an interest in marrying her. Certainly his behaviour was little different than before her disgrace, and in response she had taken to making more effort with her looks when he came.

A gentle thud drew her attention and she turned to see the Colonel pushing open the French windows that led from the drawing room out on to the lawn. She smiled at him, holding up the basket of roses. He stepped out, walking briskly towards her.

'Roses? Splendid,' he said. 'D'you remember how you and Sissy used to hate it when I asked you to wear them in your hair?'

'Yes,' she answered, 'and we would take them out as soon as we might.'

'Until I caught you doing it.' He laughed. 'I'll bet you remember me matching the petals against the flush on your cheeks as well, eh?'

'Yes, I do,' Charlotte admitted, smiling despite her best efforts to put a disapproving inflection into her voice.

'By God, you were in prime spanking condition in those days, the pair of you,' he went on, 'certainly a damn sight better than after you'd taken up on the vegetarian nonsense. Still, just now you're looking healthier than ever. Positively blooming, in fact.'

119

'I feel better, too,' Charlotte replied. 'I don't feel sick in the mornings any more, and that awful tiredness has gone.'

'Splendid, splendid. It's the milk, of course, does wonders.'

'I suppose it must be. Catherine says it's normal to be poorly at first, then to bloom, but that seems foolish. After all, surely if one feels ill because of something that grows, the illness is sure to grow with it.'

'Absolutely. Common sense. Full of old wives' tales, these village girls. No, it's the milk, mark my words. It was the same with the Indians I was telling you about. Big, healthy Johnnies they were, full of beans. Lived longer than most as well.'

'Were you with them for long?'

'A couple of months, that's all. They made no secret of it. I've seen grown men feeding from the teat, in fact, women too. Not usually though: in general they made a bit of a ritual of it, with special brass cups and whatnot; some sort of religious gobbledegook. They had a special name for the milk as well. It doesn't translate very well, I'm afraid: "fluid of life" is close enough, I suppose, or maybe "vital essence".'

' "Vital essence", how wonderful. Why did you keep this to yourself?'

'I didn't. We all knew, Captain Soames, myself, Broderick. Our sepoys knew, too, but they were Muslims and wouldn't touch it. We British thought it a load of tommyrot. So did I, until I saw the way it brought you around.'

'It has done wonders, certainly. I don't remember ever feeling quite so well.'

'And six months gone, to boot. When your mother was at that stage she was continuously faint. She had a maid who used to carry around a bottle of Epsom salts everywhere they went.'

'Which it seems that I am to be spared. There is wisdom in these primitive cultures, I always think. At school the mistresses would always point to the advantages we enjoy as civilised people and as Christians, comparing our lives with those of less advanced peoples, such as the Hottentots and the Esquimaux. I always felt that they were wrong in a way, and that there was much to be said for the simple life, without the clutter and burden of our society. The story you tell would seem to bear that out.'

'Absolutely, yes. Clever fellows, these Indian Johnnies. Our lot were still running around in skins when they were building cities, you know. Mark you, we've caught up since, but all the same. No, no, Catherine's milk is the thing for you, and don't let anybody tell you otherwise.'

'Oh, I am quite sure of it, but you must tell me more. How much they drank, everything.'

'I dare say they drank as much as they could get. Look, what I came out to say was that young Toby's motoring over for tea.'

'He is? Why didn't you tell me? He'll be here any moment. I must change, and my hair will never do like this. Oh dear, perhaps if you could have Catherine sent up?'

'By all means. I'll tell Mrs Mabberley to serve on the lawn, shall I?'

'Yes, absolutely.'

Charlotte ran for the house, abandoning her roses, and went up to her room. Stripping quickly, she made as extensive a toilet as she dared, and had begun to select her clothes when Catherine appeared. The maid curtsied, apparently oblivious to Charlotte's nudity.

'You sent for me, Miss Bomefield.'

'Ah, Catherine, yes. A little help with my hair, if you would, and just be there – I may need you for all sorts of things.'

'Yes, Miss Bomefield.'

'Oh, dear, my complexion. Do I look sallow, do you think?'

'Not at all, Miss Bomefield.'

'I do, dreadfully. Oh, heavens! I must have some milk. Look, I wish you would make some.'

'Certainly, Miss Bomefield.'

'No, no, don't go down to the kitchens; there's no time.'

'But what should I put the milk in, Miss Bomefield?'

'I don't know, girl! Try to think for yourself for once. There must be something. No, not the chamberpot.'

'I'll fetch a glass, miss, or . . . well, I could feed you, if you've a mind.'

'Feed me?'

'From the teat, miss, as Hazel does.'

'I couldn't possibly . . . oh, very well, quickly then, girl, take them out.'

Catherine hastily adjusted her dress, opening the front to produce two melon-sized breasts with the huge, dark nipples poking up from the tips. Charlotte swallowed, thinking of how she and Cicely had so often suckled each other with a sudden rush of arousal.

'How should I go?' she asked, struggling to keep her voice steady.

'Across my lap, I suppose, miss,' Catherine answered, sitting down on the bed. 'That's the usual way.'

Charlotte climbed on to the bed and laid herself into Catherine's arms, suddenly acutely aware of the fact that she was stark-naked while her maid had only her breasts bare and was about to feed her. Trying hard to fight down her feelings, she opened her mouth as Catherine cradled her head, allowing one long, firm nipple to be fed into it. She tasted the milk immediately, sweet and sharp, and began to suckle. Warm, rich milk flowed into her mouth and with it came a glorious feeling of wellbeing and security.

Snuggling closer into Catherine, Charlotte began to suck properly, mouthing at the big teat. It was blissful and she found her arms going around the maid's body, simply by instinct, holding on tightly as she fed. Catherine gave a gentle sigh and adjusted her hands to cradle Charlotte's head closer still. Charlotte closed her eyes, lost in the sensual delight of suckling at Catherine's breast. Being nude felt right, exactly right, cradled bare in Catherine's strong arms, her mouth full of warm, firm nipple, the milk filling her senses. Catherine had begun to stroke Charlotte's hair, and to whisper soothing words as gentle as her touch. Charlotte nuzzled into the breast, lost to everything but her pleasure as her thighs came slowly apart.

As the blare of a motor horn sounded from beyond the window the two girls broke apart. Charlotte scrambled to her feet, red with blushes. Feeling thoroughly confused, she threw a hurried glance to the window, where Toby's car was pulling to a halt.

'Quickly, girl, we're wasting time!' she snapped. 'My clothes. Where are those new drawers you found for me in Bridgwater? And a chemise.'

Catherine hurried to help, her face also pink with blushes. The drawers were found, small ones in the new fashion, split at the back but high at the sides, allowing them to be opened in the old-fashioned manner or pulled down according to choice. Charlotte hurried into them, a matching chemise, stockings, garters of mauve ribbon, silk slippers and finally a primrose-coloured dress, which she knew allowed a hint of her figure to show beneath.

Despite her best efforts, tea was ready by the time she came out on to the lawn. Mrs Mabberley was serving, and the fat housekeeper's normally placid features showed a brief scowl as Catherine came out behind Charlotte. The roses had been placed on the table in a tall vase and Toby was sniffing one as he prepared to take his seat.

With the usual flush of shame for the state of her belly, Charlotte greeted him and took her own place.

Toby replied with a nod and a smile, his expression open and friendly, but with a subtle hint of a leer, even of mockery.

'You're quite the fashion, I see,' he remarked. 'How do you manage?'

'Cicely sends me down magazines,' Charlotte replied, 'and we send the maid or the housekeeper into Bridgwater for what we need, sometimes even Bristol.'

'And a very pretty maid you have,' he said, glancing at Catherine but speaking as if she was not there. 'A little clumsy, perhaps, but pretty. Get her from the village, did you?'

'Yes, she comes from a local family.'

'A large one, I expect. Girls are easy, of course, but it's hard to get a decent manservant these days.'

'These days?' the Colonel snorted. 'You were what, eleven, when the war started?'

'Twelve,' Toby replied, 'but I remember well enough. 'Two footmen you had, Spince, of course, your Indian servant, a boots, and that was just indoors.'

'Quite, and lying dead in France, more than half of them,' the Colonel answered. 'Let us choose a more pleasant topic. Been to Lord's much this season?'

Charlotte's interest drifted away as they began to discuss cricket. She sipped at her tea, admiring the garden and trying not to think of how it had felt to feed at Catherine's breast. It had provided a sense of comfort and security she had not felt since the last time she had slept with Cicely, and in ways it had been stronger still.

Only when Catherine began to clear the tea things away and Toby suggested a walk did her mind return to what she was doing. She accepted hastily, leaving the Colonel in a light doze in his chair. Toby had taken a rose from the vase, and as he steered her in the direction of the yew garden she found her heart beating faster and a strong sense of anticipation rising in her throat. His manner was familiar, as it always was, but somehow more intimate, more caring.

He had taken her arm as they crossed the lawn, and he transferred it to her waist as soon as they had reached the shelter of the yew hedges. They had seen nobody, so when Toby took her into his arms she felt more excitement than worry for their exposure. He kissed her, his hands going lower, but not to her bottom as she had expected, but to the swell of her belly, holding it as he might have held a ball.

'Beautiful,' he said. 'I could only wish it were mine.'

'I know,' she answered softly. 'I wish it too.'

Again he kissed her, with more passion than before, and as he pressed to her she felt the hardness of his cock beneath his trousers. She giggled nervously, wondering if he was simply going to put her on the ground and fuck her, something she knew would be easy from the warm, wet feeling between her thighs.

'I want you, Lottie,' he said.

She nodded, trembling in anticipation of being pushed down and entered where she lay. He had always made it plain that he wanted her, and now she was pregnant, disgraced, with whatever social barriers had held him back from simply having her when he pleased no longer in place.

'I've always wanted you so much,' he went on.

'Yes,' she answered.

'I mean, really wanted you, for myself, you know I have.'

'Yes,' she said again, sudden new hope rising within her.

'I mean to say, I want you to be my wife, Lottie. Marry me.'

'I will,' she sobbed, 'oh, of course I will.'

'Splendid, then how about sealing it, eh?'

'Sealing it?'

'Yes, why not? After all, it's not as if you're going to get pregnant, is it?'

She gave a squeak of protest as she realised what he meant, but he shut her mouth with his and he had already started to pull her dress up at the back. A moment later her expensive new drawers were on show for his hands to close on, squeezing her cheeks, then pulling them wide.

As she felt her bottom hole stretched open to the breeze she gave up her half-hearted attempts to break free. Toby relaxed, pulling back but keeping hold of her dress.

'Really, I –' she began.

'Oh do shut up,' he said, cutting her off. 'I've wanted to fuck you for as long as I can remember, and now I'm going to, so no protests.'

'Toby!'

'No protests, I said. Now off with it, I said, all of it. I want you nude!'

'Nude! What if somebody should come? I wouldn't be able to cover up!'

'The Colonel's probably asleep by now, and the maids doubtless about their business. Come on. I have never seen you nude, Charlotte, darling, though I've imagined it often enough.'

'I'm sure you have. Well, if you really insist, but you must be, too.'

'Me? Not a bit of it. Think of it as your punishment if you like, for letting Cyprian have you. You'll be starkers and all I'll have out is my cock, and that inside you.'

'You are so terribly rude!'

'Which you love me for. Don't think I don't know the sort of state you get into when I speak about your body and what I'd enjoy doing to you. I do speak to my sister, you know.'

'She wouldn't tell you!'

'Ah, but there you are wrong. With a little prompting, she has told me plenty. She's two years my junior, remember, and I don't think she ever quite got over those worms. In particular, she told me how you hate the word "cunt", and what it does to you.'

126

'No, really, that's not true at all. It's just a word, rude or otherwise.'

'Then you won't mind if I suggest that you show me your cunt, that you open your cunt for me, that you let me fuck your cunt.'

'Toby!'

'Then strip. I'll watch you, and as I watch I'll show you what's going to be put inside your body.'

Charlotte answered with a low moan and a nod, stepping back as he released her. She was shaking as her hands went to the neck of her dress, finding the button that held it closed and tweaking it loose. The second followed, and the third, her dress coming slowly open until her chemise was showing, then the skin of her swollen belly below. Toby had pulled his cock out of his trousers, a great pale thing, already starting to swell. As he watched her strip he stroked himself, building it quickly to an erection of impressive size. Shyly, she opened her chemise and let it fall apart, exposing her breasts, already starting to swell towards the approach of childbirth. He grinned at the sight, then more broadly as her dress fell from her hips to reveal her new drawers.

'Pretty,' he remarked. 'Don't cover a great deal, do they? Turn around, show me your rear.'

She swallowed hard, but turned, looking back over her shoulder. His eyes were fixed to her bottom, which she knew was barely covered, with no more than a scrap of material pulled taut against each cheek and narrow frills at the hems and slit.

'Glorious,' he said. 'Now undo the button. Open them, but don't take them off.'

Reaching behind her, Charlotte obeyed. The button came open and she peeled the flaps wide, exposing her bare bottom with a knot tightening in her stomach.

'Now the stockings,' he said.

She tried, but as she bent her drawers fell down, leaving her hopping on one leg for a moment, off balance until she managed to kick them free. Toby chuckled at the sight, bracing his legs apart as he began to tug more firmly at his cock. Charlotte finished her strip by removing her shoes and peeling off her stockings to go stark-naked.

'Truly beautiful,' he said, 'apples for titties, a bottom like a ripe peach. You're better than I had dared imagine. Now get on to the ground – you're about to be fucked.'

He stepped forward, putting his hands on her shoulders and pressing her down. She went with the pressure, on to all fours, her swollen belly hanging heavy, her little fat breasts swinging beneath her chest as she moved. He remained standing, looking down at her as he nursed his erection.

'You are so beautiful,' he said. 'D'you know, I've a mind to keep you this way when we're married. Bare, pregnant too, and on all fours as often as not, even in front of the servants. Wouldn't you just hate that?'

Charlotte nodded miserably.

'I shall do it,' he went on, still nursing his cock. 'I shall make you go quite bare around the house, even when I've had to spank you. In fact, I shall do it in front of the servants. Yes, magnificent. I'd line them up and have them watch, with you stark-naked across my knee and your little sweet cunt showing behind. Your arsehole shows, too, because you're so pert. I can see it now. You know that, don't you?'

Again she nodded, feeling the blood rush to her cheeks at the sheer dirty intimacy of his comments. Toby chuckled.

'Yes, Lottie, darling,' he said. 'Your arsehole, your cunt and your arsehole, two rude little entrances in your body. Two dirty little holes for men to stick their cocks in, for me to stick my cock in. How must it feel, darling, knowing that they're always there? How does it feel, darling, knowing you can always be invaded, fucked in your cunt, fucked in your dirty arsehole?'

'Please, no,' Charlotte answered drawing a fresh chuckle from Toby.

'Well, it's going to happen, my dear,' he rasped. 'My Lord, but you don't know how many times I've imagined this sight. And now you're mine, and I'm going to fuck you, long and slow, and put my cock in every hole in your body.'

'You may, Toby, you may, just not –'

'I will, be sure of it, that sweet little cunt and your mouth too, not to mention that darling little bottom.'

'Not my bottom, no!'

'Oh, yes, Lottie, your bottom. D'you think I could resist that little rosebud arsehole? Not for a second.'

'But I've never . . .'

'What? D'you mean to say Cyprian didn't?'

'No. I was drunk. I hardly knew he had had me.'

'And he didn't bugger you, a bottom like yours? I'm amazed!'

'Not mine, George's . . . Cicely's, while I watched.'

'Cyprian buggered my sister? Good God, and then fucked her, I suppose, and you besides. Christ, what a thought! I'm not waiting, Charlotte: this is going in your mouth, right now, then up your arse.'

As he spoke he flourished his cock at her. After dropping to his knees, he took her by the hair, stuffing the full length of his erection into her mouth. With his eyes closed and his mouth open in bliss, he began to fuck her head, controlling her with one hand and feeding his cock in and out with the other. Charlotte did her best to suck, scared of the threatened invasion of her bottom and hoping to make him come before he could do it.

'Oh no you don't, my darling,' he said suddenly and at the same time pulled her head off his penis. 'You don't escape that easily. Now stick it up, good and high, so that I can see the target.'

Shaking hard, Charlotte lowered her face to the ground in shame and submission, lifting her bottom at the same time. Her cheeks were well apart, and as he crawled quickly behind her she knew that the little brownish star of her bottom hole would be on plain view, just as her sex was.

'Right,' he said, 'just hold still. There's an art to this. How does it go? Yes, that's it . . .

Butter for a rich girl, dripping for a poor,
Nothing for a dirty girl, spittle for a whore.

Well I'm damned if I'm going back to ask the Colonel for some butter, and you're not at all dirty, really, so you'll have to be my whore, I'm afraid. I trust you don't mind?'

He finished speaking and something wet landed between Charlotte's buttocks, and she realised that he had spat on her even as it trickled down into her anus. She made to protest, only to stop as his finger found her bumhole, rubbing the spit in. Her ring began to open and she sighed as the tip of his finger invaded her, sliding up with no great difficulty.

'Tight, but not that tight,' he remarked. 'Are you sure you're a virgin, anally, I mean?'

'Yes, I promise,' Charlotte gasped.

'Well I've taken more than one in my time, and yours is the loosest. For a virgin, that is.'

'I . . . I use my fingers,' Charlotte admitted, with an agonising burst of shame.

'Filthy . . . dirty . . . slut . . .' Toby said, punctuating the words with gentle slaps to her upraised bottom. 'What are you?'

'A slut,' Charlotte mumbled.

'Louder.'

'A slut.'

'That's not what I said.'

'A filthy, dirty slut. I know I am, Toby. I can't help myself.'

'Well, I'd say you'd managed well enough, splitting your drawers for Cyprian, and there's Sissy, of course.

130

Fair enough, you're a slut. Relax, will you? You'll hurt yourself.'

'I'm sorry. I'm trying.'

'I know, darling. The first is never easy. Right, you're ready, I imagine. Your arsehole's nice and sloppy, anyway, so I'm going to bugger you now.'

As they had spoken he had been first delving deeper into her bottom and then wiggling his finger inside her rectum, before twice pulling out to rub slime on to her ring. As his finger came out once more she shut her eyes, bracing her legs apart and trying to fight down her rising apprehension. His cock was big, not so much in length, but very thick, with a meaty glans and a broad shaft. The idea of his putting it up her bottom was both terrifying and compelling, not that it mattered what she thought, because he had taken her by her hips and the great, fat, obscene thing was resting between her bottom cheeks.

He pressed himself to her, squashing his balls against her sex and rubbing, with his hard shaft moving up and down in her crease. His knuckles touched her skin and she felt his cock, the big head sliding down the length of her bottom crease. Her stomach was knotting, and as he reached her anus and pushed at the entrance she gasped in anticipated pain. None came, his cock continuing down, to the mouth of her vagina, which he filled.

'A little cunt cream will help, I dare say,' he remarked, wiggling his cock in the mouth of her sex. 'There we are, nice and slimy, just like an excited cunt should be. Invert, indeed. Nothing like a nice, big cock when it comes down to it, is there?'

Charlotte could only manage a choking sob in reply. Toby chuckled and pulled out, the air escaping from her vagina with a rude noise as he once more prodded at her anus. She winced, trying desperately to relax, at once eager and terrified. He pushed and she felt her ring start to stretch, her mouth coming open even as her bottom

131

hole did. There came a sharp stab of pain as her muscle pushed in, straining against the invading cock. It wasn't going to go: her anus was too small, too tight; she would split and he'd probably just laugh as he buggered her in her own blood.

'No, please, stop, I can't take it,' she gasped.

'You already have,' he answered. 'My cockhead is in your arsehole, only up to the neck, but in. Ah, but you've no idea how good you look with your ring punctured. Now just relax and it will soon be all up, there's a good girl.'

Charlotte nodded. Her anus was stretched agonisingly wide on its load, but the pain was dying, to be replaced by a hot, helpless feeling, as if something was coming out rather than going in. With that thought came the full realisation of just how dirty an act she was performing, and willingly, without even putting up a proper fight.

He had begun to push, and her mouth hung slack as his cock was forced slowly up her reluctant bottom hole, spittle dribbling from one corner of her lower lip as inch after inch went up. Bit by bit it was jammed in, Toby grunting with the effort, Charlotte gasping and panting as for the first time in her life her rectum filled with penis.

At last it was all up her. She was being buggered, her anal virginity was gone, and she was gasping and clutching at the grass in pained ecstasy as he began to move in her bowels.

Toby St John drew in a long, deep breath. His cock was in Charlotte Bomefield's body, something he had come over more times than he could count. Not only that, but it was up her bottom, deep in the hot, wet cavity of her rectum with her on her knees, stark naked before him and utterly surrendered.

Reaching down, he spread her bottom cheeks with his thumbs, admiring the straining ring of her anus. It was

132

a picture he'd imagined so often, little Charlotte with her bottom hole stretched taut around his cock, an image he had masturbated over until he was sore, time and time again, only marginally less often than he'd done it over the thought of fucking her, and that was his to take as well, at leisure.

Once more he began to move, watching her anal ring pull in and out as he buggered her. The feel of her slimy rectal flesh against his cock was making him want to come, to finish off with a series of hard thrusts and spunk up her bottom. It was hard to resist, but his head was telling him the opposite, to draw out the moment, feeding his cock in and out of her bottom, and revelling in the knowledge that he was up her.

She was panting and giving occasional pained grunts and squeaks, reactions that delighted him, appealing to his sense of cruelty. It was good to see her on her knees. It was good to see her nude. Most of all, it was good to see her with his penis up her bottom. It made up for all the years of yearning, of wanting her so badly it hurt, of fighting down the desire simply to fuck her anyway and damn the consequences.

He slowed yet further, concentrating his whole mind on the feel of his cock in her back passage, on the hot, wet, slimy girl flesh enveloping his penis. Her panting slowed in reaction, changing to deep, even breaths. He slapped her bottom, hoping to make her squeak again, only to gasp in sudden pleasure as her ring tightened on his cock. She giggled at his reaction and squeezed again.

'Oh, you are a slut, aren't you?' he said in delight. 'Yes, squeeze it on me, like that. Lovely, you bugger like an angel. You never learned that trick from Miss Mebbin. Someone's taught you to use your arsehole, I swear it. Are you sure Cyprian didn't bugger you?'

'No,' Charlotte panted. 'I swear. It is only what Cicely does, on my tongue.'

'Cicely? On your tongue? She makes you lick her arsehole?'

'Yes.'

'By God, but you're a pair of dirty bitches! Christ, but I'd like to see that! Come on, tell me, you little bitch, tell me about it while I bugger you. That's good, you're so hot inside. Keep doing that and tell me.'

'I . . . I . . .' she gasped.

'Tell me!' he grated, ramming his cock home to make her squeal in sudden shock.

'She . . . Cicely, she likes it,' Charlotte stammered. 'She likes her bottom kissed. She likes to sit on my face and make me put my tongue in her, in . . . you know . . .'

'Say it, say what you mean, damn you!'

'In her . . . in her cunt, you pig! In her cunt and in her arsehole, right in, so I can taste her, and I have to push my tongue right up and I have to lick her clean and I have to make her come and she tightens herself on my tongue. She tightens her hole on my tongue, her bumhole, her arsehole. Yes, Toby, you pig, do it, harder, bugger me, make it hurt, come up me, please, up my bottom, in my dirt, come up me . . .'

'Stop it!' he ordered. 'You're going to make me come, you dirty bitch. Enough, I've got to stop.'

'Do it. I don't care. I want it.'

'No, I want to remember this. I said all your holes and I'll have them.'

He grunted as he began to pull his cock out. Charlotte winced, gritting her teeth at the pain and the awful, helpless feeling as the length of his erection was pulled slowly from her bottom hole. It hurt as much as it had going up, and her anus was left gaping and sore, to close with a long fart. She shut her eyes in shame but Toby merely laughed.

'That happens, I'm afraid,' he said merrily. 'Right, if you want it clean for your cunt you'd better suck on it.'

Charlotte nodded, dizzy with pleasure from her buggery, opening her mouth for the added degradation of sucking his cock clean. after crawling round on his knees, he pushed his hips out, sticking his cock towards her face. For one moment she hesitated, part of her appalled by what she was about to do, and then she had done it, leaning forward to take the fat, slimy cock in her mouth and starting to suck.

She caught the taste of herself, remembering how it had felt to be made to lick Cicely's bottom as she sucked on the cock that had just been up her own. It seemed so right for her, something she ought to be made to do, even though she didn't understand why. *Why* didn't matter, just that Toby, like his sister, had the mastery and cruelty to make her do it.

He let her have a good, long suck, her tongue licking at every part of his erection, before he pulled reluctantly out. Charlotte stuck up her bottom and set her knees wide apart, once more offering herself for entry.

Toby crawled back behind Charlotte, cock in hand, pausing to admire her rear view. She looked glorious, an ideal target for his cock. Her pregnant belly hung low between her open thighs, touching the grass. Her bottom was high and wide, her cheeks pink and glossy with sweat. Her anus was a wet mush of glistening flesh, still not fully closed and quite clearly freshly buggered. Best of all, at the centre, her neat, furry quim, stretched wide in her pregnancy, the lips and clitoris pink and moist, the hole open and dribbling white juice in ready invitation for his erection.

He moved in close behind her, then pressed his cock to the beautiful, moist quim. Looking down, he watched the head, holding it against her flesh before slipping into the dark interior of her body, as he had imagined so many times. She gave a long, pleased moan as her vagina filled with cock. It was right in, his front pressed to the soft flesh of her neat bottom, making the cheeks wobble as he began to fuck her.

As he had when he buggered her, he took his time, enjoying the sight of her naked body and the feel of his erection inside her. Her vagina was hot and wet, less tight than her bottom hole and easier to fuck, yet not so very different if he didn't look down to see what he was doing. What was different was her reaction, moans and sighs of ecstasy, the occasional grunt, but not of pain. She was panting, but it was more urgent, more needful than before.

Even kneeling, her pregnancy was obvious, her swollen middle bulging out to either side. Fascinated by it, he took her bulge in his hands, supporting it and stroking her skin as he fucked her, feeling her swollen flesh as his cock moved in her hole. In response she gave a little sob, as if she was ashamed of herself, giving him a fresh pang of cruel pleasure. He began to fuck faster, jabbing his cock into her with short, hard thrusts as he curled one hand lower.

'By God, I wish it had been me who got you this way,' he sighed, 'and by God it will be, in future, again and again. You'll be pregnant, Lottie, pregnant and nude, with your great fat belly bare for all to see, to show what I've done to you, what I've done in you.'

He gave another sob, then a gasp as his fingers found her clitoris. Gritting his teeth, he began to masturbate her as he fucked her, determined to make her come despite the awkwardness of the position. His other hand was still under her belly, wobbling the big, rotund bulge, his fingers stroking the smooth lines where her skin had stretched.

'Oh, yes, so beautiful,' he breathed. 'Oh, you are lovely, Lottie, and I do love you, for all that I want to shame you and abuse your body. You look so sweet; you look so innocent, and yet you're so dirty, taking cocks inside you, licking my sister's bottom clean, letting me up your arse, oh, you lovely, dirty, filthy little whore!'

Charlotte gasped, screamed, screamed again and then she was calling his name over and over again as her vagina went into a series of frantic contractions on his cock. Her whole body seemed to lurch, in a way he had never felt before, and for one awful moment he thought she was going to have the baby, then and there. It was too late to stop anyway, her climax running beyond control. His cock jerked in sympathy to her orgasm and his own began, deep up her as her contractions slowly faded, and even as his come erupted in her vagina her knees were slipping apart. Spent, he slowly withdrew, leaving her to sink down into the warm grass with a sigh of pure, unalloyed bliss.

Autumn 1922, Ashwood House, Somerset

Charlotte took the Colonel's arm, allowing him to support her as they crossed the lawn. At eight months from the day she had conceived, her belly was huge, a great, round bulge of taut flesh that wobbled as she walked. Because she was so slim, concealment had become impossible very quickly, but now her pregnancy was not merely obvious but blatant, embarrassingly so. Even the loosest of gowns stretched taut over her belly, at the centre of which her navel made an annoyingly conspicuous feature. It had everted, and now stuck out like a tiny cock, making a bump in her clothes, which she found acutely indecent. Worse still, the Colonel found it humorous, while Toby liked to suck it, which tickled dreadfully, a discovery that had made him keener still. He had become a frequent visitor, with their engagement due to be announced as soon as Charlotte could reasonably be mistaken for a virgin.

'Less than a month to go now, eh?' the Colonel remarked, glancing down to her belly.

'Yes,' Charlotte answered, with the now familiar anxiety the thought of childbirth brought on.

'D'you know, I think we're going to get away with it,' he went on, ignoring the tone of her voice. 'We'll have to tell Mrs Mullins, of course, as she's actually going to be there, and it'll be damn hard to stop it getting out in the village. Other than that, I think we're pretty damn safe. Then you can marry Toby and it'll be happily ever after, eh?'

'I suppose so,' Charlotte said doubtfully.

'It will be, mark my words,' he said. 'Chin up, old thing.'

Charlotte managed a wry grin, wondering how she was going to cope with the pretence that her child was Catherine's, a factor the Colonel seemed to be entirely unaware of. It was not going to be easy, yet since the day she had fed at Catherine's breast they had become closer, still mistress and maid, but with a great deal of intimacy. Twice more she had suckled, and both times it had made her want sex, only her sense of social place holding her back.

What there had been was plenty of sex with Toby, who took endless pleasure in her body, enjoying her at every opportunity, and as often as not up her bottom. In contrast her after-dinner sessions with a book and the Colonel's cock had become rarer. She had always regarded masturbating him as an embarrassing duty and thoroughly indecent, but as an engaged woman she found it even less proper than before.

For a while neither of them spoke, as they walked across the width of the lawn and through the yew garden. The Colonel seemed preoccupied, his brow furrowed and his lips set in a frown. They had reached a stile, separating the gardens from a poplar grove through which the gentle breeze hissed and rattled.

'Splendid weather,' the Colonel remarked, seating himself on the stile. 'Warm enough, but bracing.'

'Yes,' Charlotte answered vaguely.

'How's the milk going?' he asked.

'Well enough, thank you. Catherine always seems to have plenty. Indeed, it is often a relief to her.'

'Well, you look good on it, I must say. You mentioned you wanted to know more about those Indian fellows.'

'Yes.'

'Well, there was something else, something which . . . well, which it didn't really seem the done thing to mention.'

'Which was?'

'The stuff, you see, the vital essence. Well, it wasn't pure milk.'

'No? I had guessed that might be so. What was added? A spice, some secret herb?'

'No, not at all. Nothing exotic at all, in fact.'

'What then?'

'Jism, that's what. Just good old jism.'

'You mean . . . the white matter that comes out . . . you know, when . . .?'

'The very same. Makes sense, you know, when you think about it. After all, what could be more life-giving than the very stuff that creates life.'

'Surely not, it seems so . . . so unnecessarily rude!'

'To us, maybe. They're not Christians, remember. Heathens like that don't understand our morals, not at all. Anyway, look at the benefits: better health, longer life.'

'Longer life?'

'Absolutely. Works best mixed with the milk, but even pure you can see the good it does all around you. Think about it. You know that women live longer than men, on the whole, don't you? Well that's why, plenty of jism in their diets.'

'What a disgraceful thing to say! As if any decent woman –'

'Nonsense. You've drunk enough, damn it, at our little reading sessions, yet I'll bet your admirers would never have dreamed it of you. Don't be fooled by outward appearances, my girl. Why, I'll warrant there isn't one woman in a hundred who hasn't sucked at least a dozen cocks in her time, and swallowed what comes out to boot.'

'Francis!'

'No need to be coy, my girl. Don't forget, I've seen you with mine in your mouth and two fingers up your own twat.'

'Francis, really! One may do these things when overcome, but one does not speak of them.'

'My point exactly. Now these Indian Johnnies, they had no such scruples. Why, I've seen one young fellow do his porridge in his sister's milk and then drink it together. They even offered me some.'

'Did you drink it?'

'Naturally. They'd have been mortally offended if I hadn't. Best way I know to get a spear in the guts, abroad, that is, to refuse a gift well meant. Anyway, I think you should take some too, together or separately, I don't suppose it makes much difference, but as a regular dose.'

'And whose might I be expected to take, pray?'

'Well, mine, naturally.'

'I thought as much. This is just a trick to make me give you relief as often as I used to.'

'Not at all, though I won't pretend I don't think you're being damn unreasonable about it. As it goes, all this talk is making me as stiff as a lance. Come, girl, for old times' sake?'

'Francis! Really!'

'Oh, for goodness' sake! Stop being so damn mawkish! All I want is my penis sucked, for God's sake. Anybody would think I was asking something difficult.'

'No.'

'By God, Lottie, if you're weren't so damn far gone I'd put you across my knee here and now. We'd soon see if you were so damn fussy after a good spanking, wouldn't we?'

'It would make no difference.'

'You know damn well what difference it would make, my girl. Now come on, down on the ground with you, this moment.'

141

'No! I said no and I meant it. I will help you after dinner tonight if you really insist, yes, but I will not be used as your strumpet. I am an engaged woman now! Besides, we can hardly do it here, someone might see.'

'I don't see why you have to make such a fuss about being engaged. Come on, girl, think of the good it'll do you.'

'Perhaps, if what you say is true.'

'Oh, it's true, you may count on that. Why do you think I made you take it in your mouth after dinner so often?'

'For your pleasure, no doubt.'

'Not at all. If that was all I'd had in mind I'd have had you up your bottom, count on it.'

'Francis! How can you be so disgusting!'

'Nothing disgusting about going up a girl's bottom. Bit messy, perhaps, now and again, but hardly disgusting. After all, you wouldn't be in trouble if you'd had the sense to take that blighter Yates in your arsehole, would you?'

'Francis!'

'Well, it's true, damn it, and besides you've read me enough pieces where the girl gets buggered. It never seems to bother you.'

'The reality is a very different thing.'

'Nonsense, and haven't I had a finger up your arse often enough?'

'That's different, a cock hurts ever so much more!'

'So you've had it, have you? I might have known, wanton little tart that you are. Who was it, eh? Yates? Toby? Toby, eh, the sod! I might have known.'

Charlotte had nodded, blushing so furiously that she was unable to speak. She knew she was lost. As always, the dirty words were getting to her, while his sheer confidence was difficult to resist. With a last despairing effort, she tried at least to put off the inevitable.

'Well, maybe,' she snapped, 'but not here! I shall do it after dinner, I promise. Perhaps I will even read from

"The Romance of Lust". That is your favourite, is it not?'

'Fine, but dinner's not for hours. Come on, girl, down with you, and you can get that trim little behind out while you do it.'

'Oh, very well! But you are to be quick. Really, you are nothing but an old goat, and I don't believe a word about the jism!'

'It's true, every word. Believe it as you will.'

Now smiling, he sat back on the stile, opening his legs as wide as his trousers would permit. Charlotte arranged herself on the ground, kneeling in the warm grass before lifting her dress and tucking it up into her waistband. With her bottom stuck well out, she split the rear of her drawers, exposing herself so that her trim cheeks were wide and she could feel the air on her quim and anus. Her pregnant belly was resting on her thighs, and had spread a little to either side, making it seem bigger still.

Despite the resentment she felt, she was wet and felt ready, her vagina gaping for entry. For a moment she considered asking the Colonel if he would like to fuck her, only for a pang of guilt to choke back the words before she could say them. He had freed his cock as she got ready, and she took it quickly in her mouth to stop herself from asking for what her body needed. He gave a contented sigh as she began to suck, leaning back against the top bar of the stile to get his belly out of the way of her face. She took him as deep as possible, remembered his trick of making her choke on his cock, and pulled back, mouthing at the sensitive head. Again he sighed and she closed her eyes, concentrating on making him come and trying to forget that she was bare-bottomed in the grounds where anyone might see.

'So young Toby buggered you, did he?' the Colonel said suddenly. 'The young scamp. I'd make you tell me about it if you didn't have your mouth full.'

Charlotte continued to suck, thinking of how she felt with Toby's cock up her bottom. He had had her several times, and always talked to her as she was buggered, using the rude words that had always had so powerful an effect on her feelings. He made her feel dirty, and subservient, as if her dignity and modesty were inconsequential. With the Colonel's erect penis in her mouth and her bare bottom stuck out behind, it was getting harder not to feel the same way.

'I know you fuck, naturally,' he went on, 'but up the arse, eh? Still, I'm sure it does you good. Ah, wonderful, that's my girl, Lottie, nice and slow.'

She had shut her eyes, sucking slowly and trying to resist the urge to play with herself. Not that masturbating would be easy, with her huge belly in the way, but the need to come was rising to push aside her bitterness at being made to suck his penis. Already she had decided to have a long suck instead of hurrying, while having her rear view bare had become exciting rather than worrying.

'One day,' he continued, 'maybe I'll bugger you myself. Perhaps as a wedding present. For now I am content to feed you jism. Three days you've refused me, so you can expect plenty, my dear. Yes, I think I shall bugger you. You may sit on my lap, with that divine little bottom quite bare and spitted on my erection.'

In Charlotte's mind she was already being buggered, not by the Colonel, but by Toby, lying sideways on her bed, as she had the last time he did it. He had made her come, under his fingers, so that her bottom hole went into spasm on his cock, which had felt gloriously dirty and had made him come in her rectum.

Setting her legs as wide as they would go, she let her belly hang down on to the grass. Reaching back, she struggled to get comfortable, to allow herself to masturbate while the Colonel was still in her mouth. She succeeded, finding the soft, fat lips of her sex, well splayed. Her other hand went to his cock, tugging at the base of his shaft as she sucked on the head, intent on a mouthful of come at the moment of her own orgasm. He groaned, pushing himself up into her mouth as he took her firmly by the hair, and she was starting to come.

'Your milk, Miss Bomefield,' Catherine announced, placing the discreetly covered tray on Charlotte's dressing table.

'Thank you, Catherine,' Charlotte answered, 'and you needn't be quite so formal. Miss Charlotte will do very well. Lottie, even, if we happen to be alone.'

'Very well, Miss . . . Miss Charlotte,' Catherine said, removing the napkin.

Charlotte took the glass, draining the sweet breast milk down her throat in one. As always, even the act of drinking it gave her a feeling of wellbeing, and she was smiling as she set the glass down.

'My, you are thirsty,' Catherine said. 'Perhaps, miss, if you'd care to . . .?'

As she spoke she gave a meaningful glance downwards to the swell of her ample bosom, now more prominent than ever with her waist once more returned to a normal size.

'I might, in fact,' Charlotte answered, trying not to sound overeager. 'Are they sore?'

'A little, yes, thank you, miss,' Catherine said. 'They often are now that Hazel's on pap, and they do get so terribly hard.'

'Oh, you poor thing. Of course I shall help you. Come, sit on the bed beside me.'

Catherine sat down, immediately opening her dress and chemise to pull out her huge breasts. They looked swollen, the skin glossy and smooth, the nipples hard, as they always seemed to be, and damp with milk, as was the material of the chemise.

'Oh, you poor thing,' Charlotte repeated. 'Never mind now, I shall make you better.'

She went into Catherine's arms, cradled, with the feelings of comfort and security that suckling always gave already rising. Catherine's flesh smelled milky, feminine as well, and as her head was taken gently into the crook of the maid's arm her mouth came open immediately. Catherine fed the nipple in and Charlotte began to suckle, mouthing on the big teat as she relaxed into a state of contentment, body and mind. Pressing close, she snuggled against Catherine's body, feeling the warm flesh of the maid's breasts, and the softness of her body through their clothes.

Catherine's breasts felt hard, swollen with milk, particularly the one Charlotte was suckling. It was flowing into her mouth, filling her senses with the sweet sharp taste until she was dizzy with pleasure. Catherine began to stroke her hair, as she usually did, and to make small, contented noises as the pressure in her breast slowly eased. For Charlotte, nude beneath her nightie, the feelings were becoming increasingly sexual, with the urge to be masturbated by Catherine almost as strong as the urge to be mothered by her. For a while she tried to fight it, still conscious of the impropriety of showing too much affection for her maid, never mind erotic feelings. She held on around Catherine's waist, very aware of the soft flesh through the maid's dress, until finally it was too much and she took the fat, heavy breast into her mouth and held it as she suckled. In response Catherine moaned and her stroking became firmer and more deliberate.

When the maid's breast had started to soften, Charlotte stopped, eager for the second. She was also doubtful whether she would be able to hold back, as she always had before, and whether she wanted to.

'Thank you, miss, I do feel ever so much better,' Catherine sighed. 'Could you manage the other?'

'Certainly,' Charlotte answered, 'but I think I shall take off my nightie. It feels more natural naked. You don't mind, do you?'

'Not at all, miss,' Catherine answered.

'It is a natural thing to do, isn't it?' Charlotte went on as she sat up. 'I mean to say, when it feels so natural it must be, don't you think so, Catherine?'

'I wouldn't rightly know, miss,' Catherine answered as Charlotte peeled the nightie high over her head.

'Of course you wouldn't, you poor thing,' Charlotte said as she let the nightie drop. 'There, that feels better. Oh, I do like being naked with you. It is natural; it must be.'

'It's very nice, I'm sure,' Catherine said quietly. 'Now you come into my arms, miss, and never mind all that thinking.'

'You're so right,' Charlotte answered. 'You are really quite wise, sometimes, Catherine, for a country girl. Now, I'm going to suckle and suckle, so you'll have to tell me when to stop, or there won't be any for poor Hazel.'

'There's plenty to go around,' Catherine said, cupping the unsuckled breast for Charlotte's mouth.

Now nude, Charlotte curled herself back into Catherine's arms, suckling more eagerly than ever. Catherine began to stroke her hair once more, then her back. Charlotte began to purr, deep in her throat, utterly content as she sucked and swallowed. The soothing feelings were growing rapidly more sexual, the urge to spread her thighs stronger. Catherine's hand was going lower, to the middle of Charlotte's back, then lower still, stroking and patting in turn. It was soothing, and too arousing to be resisted, Charlotte's inhibitions slipping with each gentle touch until finally she could resist no more and pulled back from the nipple.

'I wish you would stroke my bottom,' she said. 'I should enjoy that.'

147

Catherine didn't answer but, as Charlotte's mouth once more closed on the firm, milk-wet nipple, her hand went lower, following the curve of her mistress's spine and on, over the gentle rising swell of her bare bottom. Charlotte purred, nuzzling at Catherine's breast. Catherine giggled, plainly fully aware of what she was doing as she cupped one of Charlotte's buttocks and gave it a playful squeeze. Purring, Charlotte stuck out her bottom. The caressing went on, Catherine's hand moving slowly across Charlotte's bottom flesh, stroking each cheek, the fingers occasionally grazing the yet more sensitive flesh in the crease.

'Is that better, miss?' Catherine asked. 'Like this?'

Charlotte nodded around her mouthful of nipple and pushed her bottom against Catherine's hand. Immediately the exploring fingers went deeper, opening Charlotte's cheeks. A fingernail touched her anus, just briefly, but enough to send a shiver through her and put a catch in her throat. Catherine giggled in response, squeezing more firmly, then she spoke.

'I know what you need, miss. Something I don't suppose a well-brought-up girl like you would know anything about.'

Thinking that Catherine meant to punish her, Charlotte turned herself to make her bottom more easily accessible for spanking. As it always had, the prospect filled her with both fear and delight, while it also seemed entirely appropriate.

'Other way up, I think, miss,' Catherine said.

Immediately realising her mistake, Charlotte rolled over, the joy of realising she was to be masturbated pushing down the disappointment at missing her spanking. Her thighs came apart, an open, luxurious gesture as she spread herself for Catherine to work on. Sucking harder, she filled her mouth with milk, swallowing as the maid's hand went lower.

'My, you are urgent,' Catherine said, and her fingers found the wet, sensitive mush of Charlotte's quim.

148

Huge belly turned up, thighs cocked wide in open admission of her need, Charlotte surrendered herself to being masturbated as she suckled. She felt perfect, content and aroused under Catherine's ministrations, with her body's needs tended to so well, and so intimately. She was nude and Catherine was dressed; she was being fed and she was being stroked towards her climax, a condition she felt perfect for her, vulnerable, subservient, but at the same time protected and cosseted.

The orgasm came slowly, Charlotte having to fight down the regret that her bottom hadn't been warmed and concentrate on what was happening. When it did come, it was from pure physical ecstasy, with her whole mind concentrated on the nipple in her mouth, the fat breast against her face, Catherine's fluttering fingers and her own total nudity. As it came, so it lasted, long and high, a plateau of sheer bliss with Catherine all the while mumbling soothing words. Charlotte's clitoris was burning, her back arched, her belly stuck up, and as her vagina spasmed to the rhythm of Catherine's stroking, so she felt a new sensation, the firm, powerful contraction of her uterus. She gasped, the nipple slipping from her mouth so that a spray of milk splashed across her face, her orgasm breaking in sudden shock.

'Stop, stop,' she begged. 'I . . . my baby. Oh, that was odd, so odd. My whole belly just squeezed in.'

'That's how it starts, miss,' Catherine said. 'Don't mind it for now. There, was that nice?'

Charlotte paused, letting the strange feeling in her insides settle before she spoke.

'Beautiful, wonderful. Thank you, Catherine, you are very good to me.'

'There are some things us country girls know, miss,' Catherine replied.

'Oh, I've been touched off before,' Charlotte answered happily. 'Not quite like that, maybe, but still.

149

Oh dear, maybe I've been thoughtless saying such things. Well, if I behave so again, you must smack me on my bottom.'

'Smack your bottom, miss?'

'Why, yes, if I have said something to upset you, you should punish me, and what better way to go about it?'

'I'm not sure, miss. It wouldn't seem right, miss.'

'Oh, nonsense. From now on, any time I'm naughty you're to give me a good, firm spanking, just as if you were my mother. And it is to be done properly, with my dress turned up and my drawers apart so that there is no modesty left to me. Now, will you do that?'

'I suppose so, miss, but –'

'No buts, Catherine, darling. I'm sure I'm impertinent very often, and the next time you're to put me straight across your knee. If you wish, you may do it now. Haven't I been very rude to you?'

'Not *so* very rude, miss.'

'Oh, nonsense, of course I have, many times. Just now. And didn't I call you clumsy the other day, and stupid, too? I'm sure. And do you know, I can't even remember why? Now wasn't that rude of me?'

'It was a little hurtful, miss. I had only put the grey cushion on the blue chair.'

'Then you shall spank me for it, and both of us will feel the better for it. Come, I am ready.'

She was trembling, desperate for the punishment yet scared of the pain it would bring. Without waiting for a reply, she crawled across Catherine's lap, her swollen belly leaving her bottom stuck well up. Modesty was the last thing she wanted, and she left her legs well apart, her quim and bottom spread to the air.

Without saying a word, Catherine began to spank gently, hesitantly, patting Charlotte's bottom with her fingertips. The effect on Charlotte was immediate, not in her body, but in her mind, a blissful, glorious sense of subservience. Not only was she naked across another woman's knee, not only was she having her bare bottom smacked in punishment, but it was her maid who was doing it.

Catherine's confidence grew quickly at Charlotte's open, grovelling submission. The pats turned to smacks, firm and precise, delivered to the crest of each buttock. At one, Charlotte gave a little squeak, a response that further increased the maid's determination. The smacks became firmer, more purposeful, until Charlotte began to feel that she was genuinely being punished. It had begun to hurt a little, and she could feel the slaps through her pregnant belly, her flesh rippling in response.

'I do need this,' she sighed. 'It is right. It is just. Harder, Catherine, punish me. Make me sorry.'

'I shall,' Catherine answered. 'I shall make you very sorry indeed, Miss Charlotte.'

Suddenly the spanking was no longer playful. Charlotte squealed in shock as her arm was taken and twisted hard into the small of her back even as Catherine's hand came down across her bottom with enough force to knock the breath from her lungs. An instant later Charlotte was bucking and kicking, wiggling her bottom about in frantic efforts to evade the smacks and wondering how she had ever let herself get into so stupid a position.

Catherine was a hard spanker, harder than Cicely, bigger and stronger, her muscular arms ideal for both holding Charlotte down and applying the spanking. In no time Charlotte was howling with shock and pain, kicking her legs high and wide, thumping her free arm on the bed in futile protest and writhing her bloated belly on Catherine's legs.

Catherine was enjoying herself immensely, spanking away at her mistress's bottom as she took out every slight and every discomfort of her work, not just those from Charlotte, but also from the Colonel, Spince and Mrs Mabberley. At first she had been scared to do it, sure that the consequences would be dreadful, despite Charlotte's apparent eagerness. Only when Charlotte had begged to be made sorry had she let go, turning the playful slapping into a full-blooded spanking.

Charlotte was crying, really bawling, in floods of tears as her little buttocks turned from pink to red. Yet there was no anger, no threat, only a jumble of words of apology and self-effacement. Catherine found herself grinning and thinking of all that she had been made to put up with as a maid, the little slights and injustices, the indifference, the Colonel pawing her bottom, Spince making her kneel to fuck her from the rear, having to lick Mrs Mabberley's quim.

Just that morning she had been beaten. Upended over the housekeeper's lap, in full view of the butler, her bottom had been exposed and she had been spanked, hard, with Mrs Mabberley's awful wooden spoon. Once punished, she had been made to kiss the housekeeper's huge white buttocks, then to use her mouth to bring them both to orgasm, swallowing what was done inside it. She had come herself, when ordered to masturbate, but that did nothing to dilute the pain and humiliation of the incident.

With the memory of how much her own beating had hurt, she felt suddenly guilty and stopped. Charlotte was really blubbering, gasping too, a broken, disconsolate sound little different from the fuss Catherine herself had made. She was also completely defeated, her bottom a blazing crimson ball, goose-pimpled all over and wet with sweat, the cheeks wide and her bumhole pulsing in her pain. Catherine knew she had looked the same across Mrs Mabberley's knee, although perhaps a fraction less obscene, with her fatter bottom going some way to hide the rudest details of quim and bottom crease.

'There, that is quite enough, I think,' she said, trying to sound soothing. 'I hope you feel better for it.'

'I do, Catherine, I do,' Charlotte answered tearfully. 'Now, hold me, cuddle me.'

Charlotte turned, still crying softly as she pulled herself into Catherine's arms. Taking a nipple into her mouth, she began to suckle more urgently even than when she had been coming.

'There, there,' Catherine said. 'That's right, you have a good suck, until you feel better. I'm sorry I was so stern with you.'

Charlotte shook her head.

'Would you like me to rub you again?' Catherine asked. 'Would that make you better?'

'No,' Charlotte gasped, pulling suddenly back to leave a wet, milky ring around her mouth. 'I want to do it to you, to lick and lick and lick, until you spend in my face. From behind is best, and I do so want to see your bottom. Come, let me open your drawers.'

'My bottom?' Catherine asked, suddenly mindful of the bruises that marked both her lower cheeks.

'Yes, your bottom,' Charlotte answered. 'You have a lovely bottom, so ripe and round. I should love to see it.'

'I'm not sure, miss . . .'

'Come, now, Catherine, I am naked, and I do so want to return the favour you paid me. Please?'

Catherine's embarrassment at what had been done to her struggled against her lust for what was being offered. Charlotte had got up into a kneeling position and was smiling hopefully, with a trickle of Catherine's milk still on her chin.

'I . . . I've been spanked myself,' she said in hesitation.

'You have? Who by?'

'Mrs Mabberley, miss.'

'I bet she was stern with you! She is such a tyrant. Are you still all pink?'

'Worse than pink, miss.'

'You are? You must show me. Come on, Catherine. Don't be so bashful. Look at me: I'm quite naked, and my bottom is ever so red. Now come on.'

Catherine gave a wry smile but turned on to all fours. Charlotte's hands went straight to her dress, hoisting it up, then to her drawers, splitting them wide to expose the well-smacked flesh of her bottom.

'Good heavens, Catherine!' Charlotte exclaimed. 'Oh, you poor thing! How it must have hurt!'

'It did,' Catherine assured her.

'And Mrs Mabberley did this, did she? Well, I won't have it. Discipline is one thing and to be approved of. A spanking, perhaps, when you need it, but not this. This is sheer cruelty! Why was she so stern with you?'

'I broke a cream jug, miss.'

'A cream jug? That's hardly reason for this! You poor thing. Anyway, at the least I shall kiss you better.'

'On my bottom?'

'Naturally on your bottom, silly girl. I want to make you feel better, and that's the hurt part, is it not? Besides, you've spanked me, and I should be made to kiss your bottom.'

Catherine giggled and shyly pushed out her bottom, which emerged fully from her open drawers, a great, plump globe of girl flesh, deeply divided at the centre in a musky cleft thickly grown with hair. Catching the scent of Catherine's sex, Charlotte swallowed. Her hands went to the fat peach in front of her, feeling the weight of Catherine's buttocks, pressing them together then letting them go once more to wobble back into position.

She puckered her lips, waited one delicious moment and planted a gentle kiss on the crown of one bruised buttock, then the other. There was shock at the apparent severity of Catherine's beating, but pleasure, too, at her own punishment. Before she really knew what she was doing she was burrowing her face in between the fleshy bottom cheeks, delving for the maid's anus with her tongue.

'Not there, miss, oh, you mustn't! Miss!' Catherine squealed.

The half-hearted protest trailed off into a long, happy sigh as Charlotte's tongue tip found Catherine's bottom hole. It went up, Catherine's anus moist and receptive, Charlotte's mouth filling with the thick, earthy flavour. She could feel the heat in her own rear, the smarting flesh of her cheeks and the warmth of her ready sex.

'You dirty, dirty girl!' Catherine exclaimed, but made no move to escape as Charlotte pushed in as much of her tongue as would go.

Charlotte was in heaven, her smacked bottom stuck out behind, her mouth full of the taste of the woman who had punished her, fed her from the teat, soothed her and smacked her, masturbated her and punished her, and at last permitted her to lick clean her bottom. Her hands went back to her sex, and she continued to feed greedily on Catherine's bumhole as she found the soft, wet lips and the hard bud of her clitoris.

She needed to come again badly, but she also needed to give the same pleasure, and to place Catherine's needs above her own. Fighting down her urgency, she pressed her face firmly into the maid's big, fleshy bottom. As she lowered her head, her nose pushed into Catherine's anus, the wet hole spreading around it. Her tongue found Catherine's clitoris, bigger than her own, a firm bump of flesh, only a fraction above the vaginal opening. Licking hard, Charlotte continued to masturbate, listening for the change in the tone of Catherine's sighs and moans that would signal the onset of orgasm.

It came quickly, the maid calling out in ecstasy and grinding her bottom into Charlotte's face. Charlotte let it happen, licking full on Catherine's clitoris and wiggling her nose at the same time. All the while she was holding herself on the edge of her own climax, until at last the maid's orgasm began to tail off.

Turning her attention back to Catherine's bumhole, she burrowed her tongue in deep. Her whole face was wet with juice and her own saliva, her body hot and sensitive, the feel of smacked bottom, open vagina, pregnant belly and dangling breasts all acute, with her clitoris at the centre of it all. She was coming, in heaven as she licked and slurped at Catherine's sopping, open bumhole, her mouth full of the taste of girl and earthy, rank bottom as everything came together in one blinding, dizzying climax.

Catherine collapsed on to the bed as soon as Charlotte did, before the two girls crawled together. For a long while they lay still, Charlotte's head rested against Catherine's leg. At first Charlotte felt only contentment, a happy, drowsy sensation, with nothing really seeming to matter at all. Only when she gave Catherine's still naked bottom a playful pat and the maid winced in response did Charlotte once more think of Mrs Mabberley. Not only did it seem that the housekeeper had been unfair, but Charlotte urgently wanted to be in Catherine's good books. Unfortunately it was impossible to sack the housekeeper, who knew far too much to be given an excuse for resentment.

'I would give Mrs Mabberley her notice at your word,' Charlotte remarked, 'yet, as you know, in the circumstances it is hardly practical. Besides, until I am twenty-one it is the Colonel's responsibility rather than my own. Still, I shall speak to her, really quite severely.'

'You might, miss,' Catherine answered, 'or if it pleases you, miss, you might give her a dose of her own medicine.'

'By punishing her? In what way?'

'Same way as I got it, miss, across the backside with a spoon.'

'To Mrs Mabberley? I couldn't!'

'A cane then, if that's more proper.'

'Not anything! I simply couldn't!'

'You could that, miss, if you'd a mind. You are the lady of the house.'

'I may be, Catherine, but Mrs Mabberley! I have known her all my life. I could never do it. It would seem such an outrage! Heaven knows what Francis would say. He'd have to know, of course, and why. Besides, she knows of my condition and is likely to be piqued enough to make sure it becomes common knowledge, and I don't just mean in the village. No, Catherine, I am sorry for you, naturally, and I shall speak to Mrs Mabberley, but that is all I can do.'

Catherine gave no reply, but Charlotte instantly sensed a withdrawal of the warmth that had been building up between the two of them. A sense of loneliness struck her, becoming more intense as Catherine sat up and began to tidy her clothes. Feeling suddenly weak and very sorry for herself, Charlotte reached for her nightie.

'I am sorry I spoke out of turn, Miss Bomefield,' Catherine said, with all the playful intimacy gone from her voice. 'It was wrong of me.'

'No,' Charlotte answered, 'it wasn't, not wrong at all. No, Catherine, don't be cross. Don't be cold, please?'

Catherine said nothing and Charlotte also went quiet, feeling utterly wretched and also ineffectual. She thought of Mrs Mabberley, the stern, no-nonsense woman she had known all her life. Within the servants' quarters she had been a tyrant, second to Spince in theory, but without the butler's kindly manner. To her, as a child, the kitchens had seemed another world, and one in which she and her brothers were definitely intruders. As for the two rooms the housekeeper called her own, they had been an inner sanctum, untouchable. Only Cicely had ever dared invade them, one hot afternoon when both families were at Ashwood and the housekeeper had been in the village.

Cicely, Charlotte knew, would not have been so timid. If Mrs Mabberley had tyrannised them as children, then the same was doubly true for Miss Mebbin, and Cicely had stood up to the headmistress and more.

Catherine had finished adjusting herself and was about to leave, a departure that Charlotte was sure would mark the end of an intimacy that had been growing increasingly important to her for months. It was too much to lose.

'I shall do it!' she declared suddenly. 'You are right, Catherine. I am to be the lady of the house, and I will not allow injustice. Come with me. We shall see the Colonel immediately.'

Colonel St John sat foursquare in his favourite library chair, trying to look stern but feeling thoroughly pleased with himself. In front of him stood Charlotte, Mrs Mabberley and Catherine. None looked particularly happy, the maid least of all, who had her back to him, her dress up and her drawers held wide apart to show the bruised cheeks of her ample bottom.

Each had explained her position, to which he had listened with a mock gravity while secretly delighted by the thought of Catherine being made to strip and then spanked with a spoon. At the end he had felt it safe to order the maid to display the evidence, which she had done, exposing her bottom with a very satisfactory level of embarrassment. Her naked, bruised glory had proved such a satisfying sight that he had made her keep it on display, an obviously improper choice but more than he could resist.

Now, sipping a glass of old Bual, he was taking his time over reaching a decision. There seemed to be three main choices, among which two seemed worthwhile.

158

The dull one was to smooth over the whole thing, tell Mrs Mabberley not to be so strict in future and let them all get on with it. He had already dismissed it.

The second choice was to take the side of the housekeeper. Mrs Mabberley had not only stoutly defended her right to discipline Catherine but suggested that the maid now deserved a fresh punishment for the sheer impudence of bringing the matter to his and Charlotte's attention. The prospect of punishing Catherine was enticing, yet there was very little he could do to her bottom that hadn't already been done. More importantly, he could see that in the long term he might gain more pleasure from supporting Catherine than could be gained from thrashing her.

That left the third choice, which was to do as Charlotte demanded and have Mrs Mabberley caned. At first it had lacked appeal, yet on closer study it had advantages. Her loyalty aside, she was too intelligent to sacrifice a career that relied entirely on his own good references, besides which, if she threatened to give notice, he could hastily retreat from his decision.

If he did it, Catherine would be grateful to him, Charlotte also. Then there was also the question of how each woman would react to corporal punishment. Catherine seemed likely to accept it with resigned misery. That was hardly appealing. Mrs Mabberley, on the other hand, was clearly going to be outraged, which he found far more satisfying. For years she had behaved more as if she was the mistress of the house than a servant, yet her worth had always far outweighed any temptation to get rid of her. He now had an ideal opportunity to put her in her place.

The decision was clear, but there seemed no reason to dilute his pleasure by hurrying. Letting his eyes wander from the magnificence of Catherine's bottom, to Charlotte's determined face, to Mrs Mabberley's haughty one and back, he sipped his Bual. At length he replaced the glass on the table by his side, steepled his fingers and set his face into an expression of stern authority.

'Very well,' he said, 'I have reached a decision. Do cover yourself, girl. Whatever are you doing?'

Catherine let her drawers close and dropped her skirt back into place, blushing furiously.

'That's better,' he went on. 'Now, as you know, I value discipline, and I see no reason why a maid should not be thrashed now and again. Does 'em a power of good in fact, be sure of it. Nor do I see any reason why such matters should be brought before Miss Bomefield and myself. After all, I hardly see why we should be troubled with issues of domestic discipline among the servants. Quite trivial, eh?'

Mrs Mabberley had began to smirk.

'On the other hand,' he continued. 'The punishment must fit the crime, and in this case I fear it has far exceeded it. Not only that, but I've seen a few smacked backsides in my time and it's damn plain to see this isn't the first time, as Catherine says, while I for one have been very pleased with her conduct. I fear that you have been exceeding your authority, Mrs Mabberley. Bullying, I might even call it, which is something I detest.'

'Begging your pardon, sir –' Mrs Mabberley began, only to be silenced by a gesture from the Colonel.

'My decision,' he said, 'is this. If you wish to keep my high opinion, Mrs Mabberley, you will accept a dozen strokes with a rattan from your victim, in the yard, barracks style.'

Grinning openly, Catherine flexed the rattan cane in her hands. It was old, with the blackening on the crooked handle and near the tip suggesting plenty of use. It was also heavy, certainly as heavy as Mrs Mabberley's terrifying spoon, and a good deal longer. From Charlotte's reaction when she had fetched it from the lumber room, Catherine could guess at least one of the people it had been used on.

Charlotte now sat on one of the chairs a stony-faced Spince had brought out to the yard. The Colonel occupied the other, with the butler standing behind him. Mrs Mabberley was in a far less comfortable position, and also a far less dignified one. After a great deal of fuss she had accepted her punishment and immediately been sent to fetch a trestle from the stables. She was now bent over it, her huge bottom rounding out her dress at the back and her face set in furious consternation at the front.

Feeling immensely pleased with herself, Catherine stepped forward. As she did so she saw the Colonel's mouth twitch up briefly into a smile before returning to the stern expression he had worn since they had come to him. Charlotte was making less effort to hide her feelings and had a faint but definite smile on her face. Spince simply looked worried, to Catherine's yet greater satisfaction.

She stepped in, beginning her task in a brisk, no-nonsense fashion. The dress came up and the drawers apart, exposing Mrs Mabberley's enormous white bottom. At the sight of the two great, fat orbs of flesh the Colonel gave up his attempts to look serious, grinning as he settled back to watch the show. Catherine was grinning, too, as she gave the cane a last experimental swish through the air, lifted it high and brought it down across the full width of Mrs Mabberley's bottom.

The housekeeper cried out in shock and pain as the cane hit, bouncing back to leave a long pale line across her buttocks. Even as Catherine lifted the cane once more her victim's skin flared from white to red and as she struck again her pleasure was becoming a savage, vengeful joy.

Eight times the cane bit into Mrs Mabberley's bottom, leaving a crisscross of double scarlet lines, each terminating in a darker blotch. Catherine's teeth were gritted, her eyes blazing as she lifted the cane for the ninth, only to stop at the sound of a motorcar. Hesitating, she threw a worried glance at the Colonel.

'My nephew, Lord Cary, no doubt,' the Colonel supplied. 'Don't mind it: this is a sight he'll enjoy immensely. Carry on, that girl.'

'Thank you, sir. I will, sir,' Catherine answered and landed another vicious cut across the housekeeper's bottom.

With three strokes left to her, she determined to put all her force into each. Mrs Mabberley had squealed in the most satisfying way with each cane cut, a noise that reminded Catherine of an angry sow, which she felt the housekeeper resembled in other ways as well. What she hadn't done was break down, and as Catherine measured up for the tenth stroke it was aimed deliberately low, across the top of the housekeeper's fat thighs.

The result was a squeal that would have put any sow to shame, and drew an amused chuckle from the Colonel. By then the engine had stopped, and Catherine waited, the cane poised over Mrs Mabberley's naked, thrashed bottom, keen that one more audience member be present to add to the housekeeper's humiliation.

Boots crunched on gravel behind her and Catherine braced her arm, intent on making it seem that Lord Cary's presence was of no particular importance one way or the other. The cane came down, Mrs Mabberley squealed louder still and Catherine stopped, aware that Charlotte was staring at something in open-mouthed horror.

The scene froze, Catherine with the cane half raised, Mrs Mabberley with her bottom bare and well decorated, the Colonel and Spince looking surprised, Charlotte with her mouth open and her hands folded over her pregnant belly in a completely useless attempt to hide her condition, and all of them in full view of Victor Cushat.

* * *

'For goodness' sake, Lottie, stop moping,' Toby declared.

'How can I not mope?' Charlotte answered. 'I'll never be able to show my face in London again.'

'Nonsense, nonsense,' he replied. 'Victor's a bit stuffy, yes, but he's a gentleman, after a fashion. He'll keep it to himself.'

'You didn't see him. He's a self-righteous prig, and jealous as well. He's sure to tell everybody I know.'

'No, he won't, not a bit of it. I'll soon make him see it's in his best interests to keep quiet. The fellow's a politician after all. Now cheer up and let's get that dress off. You know how the sight of that fat belly makes me.'

'Toby! Do you ever think of anything but fornication?'

'Yes. Shooting, hunting, cards perhaps. Food, wine, plenty of things, in fact, but not when I'm with you. Then the only thing I can think of is getting your sweet little body naked for a spot of cock exercise.'

'Well, you are not going to get any, not now.'

'Oh no? What if I tie your hands to the bedposts and simply have my wicked way with you?'

'Then you would be a horrid beast and I shouldn't speak to you for days.'

'Well, that's fine, then. If I'm going up to London to beard Victor in his lair then you won't have to speak to me. Hmm, now let me see: belly up or arse up? Which makes the best show of your pretty cunt?'

'Toby!'

'Belly up, I suppose, as you're so close to popping. Speaking of which, in your condition I'm sure all the quacks would advise against putting up a fight.'

'Oh, do stop teasing, Toby. I'm being serious.'

'I know, too damn serious by half. What you need is a good hard fucking. You'll thank me for it afterwards, you know you will.'

'If you tie me I shall scream.'

163

'Splendid, then Uncle Francis can come and watch. I'm sure he'd enjoy the sight, if it didn't give him apoplexy.'

'Oh, do stop it! What are you doing?'

'Looking for something to tie you up with. Where do you keep your stockings?'

'Will you just behave yourself! No, not in that drawer.'

'No? This one then? Aha!'

'Oh, no, Toby, come on now, really!' Charlotte protested as he pulled a handful of her stockings from the drawer.

He took no notice, turning towards her with a comic grin, giving his best imitation of a dramatic villain. Charlotte put her hand to her mouth, trying to suppress a giggle but failing.

'Now I have you in my clutches!' Toby declared. 'The noble Sir John Thoroughgood lies drowned in Whortleberry Bog and you are mine, all mine! Prepare to be ravished!'

'Toby, stop it!' Charlotte laughed. 'What if Francis came up?'

'My uncle won't save you!' Toby exclaimed. 'Don't you realise, you poor fool? He is my hunchbacked henchman!'

As he spoke he leaped on to the bed, grappling for her. Charlotte tried to roll away but was caught by the hands and pinned down. Toby was cackling dementedly, trying to get the stockings around her wrists and hold her down at the same time.

Charlotte was laughing too much to fight and her wrists were soon strapped securely together and tied off on to the head of the bed. Toby kneeled over her, rubbing his hands in glee.

'I have you where I want you!' he announced. 'Say goodbye to your precious maidenhead!'

'I already have, silly.' She laughed. 'Can't you see?'

'Don't think to put me off with such petty details,' he answered. 'You are tied and helpless, about to be raped. At least struggle a bit.'

'Untie me, you fiend!' she answered half-heartedly. 'You shall never have me!'

'Who will stop me?' he demanded. 'And what of this?'

As he spoke he had opened his trousers, pulling out his cock, already heavy with blood. Charlotte managed a theatrical gasp, only to have her mouth stopped.

'Suck on my cock!' he ordered. 'Debase yourself! Make yourself my whore!'

Charlotte sucked, feeling him stiffen in her mouth. He stopped laughing quickly, his humorous grin changing to a look of glazed pleasure, which held until his erection was rock-hard in her mouth.

'Good, and now for your cunt,' he declared, pulling back.

'Not that, anything but that!' Charlotte managed as he grabbed her by the legs and hauled them up.

Her dress fell away as her thighs were pushed up to either side of her swollen belly, wide, to leave her sex and bottom stretched open. Grinning once more, Toby wrenched her drawers off her hips and threw them aside, then put his cock to her hole. Charlotte gasped as it went up, sliding straight into her vagina, which seemed to juice more easily than ever. He took her ankles, holding her by them as he started to fuck her.

'Glorious,' he said, 'simply glorious. I look forward to plenty of this, Lottie, and I shall always enjoy it best while you're pregnant. In fact, let's have that fat belly out of your clothes. I do adore the way your button wobbles as I fuck you, your titties too.'

He reached down, tugging the front of her pregnancy gown up, first over her belly and then higher, taking her chemise with it, to expose her breasts. As she once more settled into his rhythm she had begun to pull against her bonds, enjoying the helpless sensation despite herself as her sexual feelings gradually overcame her shame and anger at having been caught by Victor Cushat.

Toby's eyes were fixed to her everted bellybutton, which looked more cocklike than ever as it wobbled gently in time to his fucking. He was grinning, obviously enjoying himself immensely, and as much from the cruelty of having her tied as the pleasure of having his cock in her body.

'No rush,' he declared suddenly. 'In fact, I think you're having rather an easy time of this, my dear.'

He pulled out, easing his slimy cock from her hole then wiping it on the inside of her thigh.

'What are you going to do?' Charlotte queried, already sure of the answer.

Toby moved back on his knees, his eyes fixed firmly on her straining belly, his grin more manic than ever. Charlotte felt her belly twitch, her skin crawling at the prospect of the agonising tickling sensations she was about to be subjected to.

'No!' she pleaded. 'Come on, Toby, not that!'

He merely chuckled and began to lean forward, his lips puckered, his eyes bright with pleasure at her discomfort. She felt his breath on her belly and her muscles began to jump and twitch, the little protrusion of flesh that was his target waving frantically in the air. His lips touched, in the lightest of kisses, but one that sent a jolt through her whole abdomen, making her cry out in shock. Toby chuckled.

'No, Toby, no, please,' she begged. 'Don't suck it, not that! No! Do anything, put it . . . you know where . . .'

'Say it and I'll take mercy on you,' he said, stopping with his mouth an inch from her bellybutton.

'Put . . . put your cock up my bottom. Please, Toby,' she answered.

'Properly now, Lottie, you know what I mean.'

'Beast! Oh, very well: sodomise me, please, Toby; bugger my bottom hole and make me suck your cock when it's been up there. Satisfied? Now please?'

166

'Dirty little girl. How disgusting, asking to be sodomised. Well, there's only one thing to be done about that.'

His head came forward, his mouth opened, his lips touching the flesh of her belly, wide around her bellybutton.

'No!' she squeaked. 'No! You said you wouldn't!'

'I lied,' Toby mumbled.

'Beast! Utter, utter beast!' Charlotte screamed.

Her last, despairing word became a high-pitched squeal as his lips closed on her bellybutton and it was sucked suddenly into his mouth. Thrashing her body, she broke free, only for him to take a firm grip on her swollen belly and once more take the little teat-like nubbin of flesh into his mouth. As he started to tickle it with his tongue she was in convulsions, thrashing and writhing on the bed, screaming, laughing and choking in helpless response to the unbearable tickling sensation. He took no notice until she screamed louder still, kicking out at him in sudden fright.

'Stop it! Stop it!' she yelled in panic. 'You'll make the baby come!'

'Nonsense!' Toby laughed as he pulled back. 'You've what? Three weeks to go, at the least. What a fuss, really!'

'It tickles so!' she answered. 'I can't help it.'

'You are nothing but a big baby,' he replied. 'However, I have decided to be merciful, or at any rate I want to spend now so you get off lightly. Now let me see, what shall I do or, rather, where shall I do it? In your mouth, perhaps, and make you swallow it? That is always satisfying, and I simply adore the faces you pull. It must taste perfectly horrid! Across your face is fun, too, of course, and you do make such a fuss if it goes in your eyes.'

'Not in my face, please!' Charlotte begged.

'No? Then maybe I should take mercy and just do it up your cunt, or perhaps I should bugger you. After all, you did ask, and very sweetly, too. That might be best, actually. You like it too much, really, but it might be fun, if only to watch your bottom hole when I pull out, especially if you fart and make bubbles. I adore that, your face always goes such a pretty shade of pink.'

'Beast! Pig!'

'Such language for a girl with her hands tied and no clothes on. Anyway, don't worry, I have a better idea.'

'What's that?'

'I shall spunk on your belly!' He laughed. 'All over the top, like icing on a great, fat Christmas cake. Wonderful, think how outraged Cyprian would be, if only he knew!'

'No, Toby, not that. Come on, have you no modesty at all? Is nothing sacred? Do it in me by all means, or across my face if you must be cruel, but not that.'

He merely chuckled and edged forward, pointing his erection over her upturned belly. She closed her eyes, resigned to the burning shame in her head, but opened them with a start as his weight shifted on the bed and something touched her bellybutton. Toby had one leg cocked over her, his cock touching her protruding navel as he masturbated.

'All over it, Lottie!' he crowed. 'I'm going to do simply the biggest dollop of jism you've ever seen, all over your fat belly, and especially over that tickly little tummy button. Ready for it?'

'No! Toby!' she squealed as his cock once more touched the little nub.

He went on masturbating, moving to let his knuckles rub over and over on her bellybutton. Her muscles started to jump again, making her pant, then gasp and her uterus squeezed.

'No! Stop it!' she yelled.

'I can't!' Toby rasped and came all over her belly.

She saw the sperm erupt from his cock, catching her bellybutton full on and she screamed out as a fresh contraction hit her. He pressed his cock to her belly, coating it with slimy sperm, pressing his cockhead down on her bellybutton and rubbing it from side to side in the mess. The tickling was agonising, her bellybutton wobbling beneath his cock, from side to side, the head slipping on the sperm-slick skin. Once more she screamed, and again, out of all control, and suddenly her whole middle seemed to lock in on itself as her uterus contracted furiously.

'No!' she yelled, and something inside her seemed to burst.

Fluid sprayed from her vagina across Toby's trouser leg and she screamed again, not knowing whether she was in agony or orgasm, but absolutely certain that her labour had started.

Autumn 1922, Chelsea, London

'A girl. Named Holly, if you please. I couldn't stop her,' Toby said, lowering himself into one of the more comfortable chairs in Cicely's drawing room.

'It's actually rather a pretty name,' Cicely answered. 'To go with the wet nurse's child, I suppose, if they're supposed to be twins. Hazel, isn't it?'

'If you mean the child, yes,' Toby replied. 'The wet nurse is called Catherine, and a damn fine piece she is, too. D'you know, I half suspect she's had Lottie's drawers apart. Certainly they spend a lot of time together in private, with the door locked to boot.'

'You do talk nonsense, Toby,' Cicely answered. 'As if Lottie would ever do such a thing with a maid.'

Toby responded with an amused grunt and helped himself to a cigar. Fighting down a pang of jealousy, Cicely tried to tell herself that he was simply trying to annoy her, something in which he always took pleasure.

'Was she all right?' she asked after a pause.

'Lottie? Oh, fine. She made a bit of a fuss, of course, but that's you girls all over, isn't it?'

'I should like to see a man do any better.'

'Oh, I'm sure we'd manage, but thank the Lord we don't have to. Speaking of men, how's Cyprian? For that matter, *where's* Cyprian?'

'Don't talk to me about Cyprian. No, do, at least I can tell you the truth. He's out chasing boys, as usual.'

'Well, that is only to be expected. After all, you knew what he was like when you married him, and vice versa.'

'Yes, well, it hasn't worked out very well. All his inverted friends think his being married is the most wonderful joke. They're always round, and in fact they're about the only people I get to speak to nowadays. My set take the opposite attitude, as if I were some kind of traitor. Frankly, they're all too damn serious.'

'Ah, I see. Tough luck, eh?'

'Tough is the word and, if that wasn't bad enough, Cyprian can't stand the sight of me like this, and he has no interest whatever in the child. We got on rather well before, you know.'

'I can imagine. So what's to be done?'

'I don't know. At present we can't seem to agree on anything. I tried to compromise. I even said the baby could have the nursery done in lilac if it made him happy. He said I was being flippant.'

'Difficult, no doubt. I know how pig-headed Cyprian can be. I, however, have to persuade Victor Cushat not to drag the Bomefield name through the mud, which is unlikely to be easy. Have you seen anything of him?'

'We hardly move in the same circles these days. In fact, I hardly move in any circles at all, save for the rather small ones around the floor of my room. What do you intend to do?'

'Well, I did intend to appeal to his better nature, but I'm not at all sure he has one, for all his much-vaunted moral principles. So I've decided that my best bet was to state my case in terms of political expediency, pointing out that to be linked to such a sordid scandal can only harm his career, that sort of thing.'

'What if he won't bite?'

'I don't know, but I feel sure he will. You see, I understand the Victor Cushats of this world. There's no good pleading with them, because it only gives them an excuse to get on their moral hobbyhorses. You can't bullyrag them, either: they're too damn conceited to back down; and, besides, nobody who's prepared to go from door to door pleading the Conservative cause in Stepney East can be considered a coward. Bribery's no good, I don't imagine, and certainly unsafe. No, reason is the answer. I shall be calm, diplomatic, steady; thus shall I triumph.'

Autumn 1922, Ashwood House, Somerset

Charlotte stood at the nursery window, looking out across the Somerset countryside. Behind her, both Hazel and Holly were fast asleep in their cribs, with Catherine fussing over them, adjusting blankets.

The scene in the foreground was pretty, with the leaves in a myriad shades of green, gold and red, pasture in rich green, with the blue of the sky reflected in patches of water. Not that her eyes were focused on the near scenery, but on the far, where the Blackdown Hills made a grey-green horizon, ragged with the outlines of trees. They had always seemed far away and somehow romantic, but now seemed more distant than ever, representing a boundary to her world that would be effectively closed if Toby failed to convince Victor Cushat of the need for silence.

It had been two weeks since he motored up to London, and there had been no call, nor a telegram, nor a letter, leaving her increasingly worried that he had lost his nerve, failed or, worst of all, abandoned her. All three seemed entirely possible, but as she gave a dejected sigh she caught sight of movement in the distance, bright yellow and moving fast. Her heart leaped as she realised that it was a car, and almost certainly Cicely's canary-yellow sunbeam.

Immediately, she ran downstairs and out on to the carriage sweep, waiting in mounting frustration until her hopes were confirmed by the sound of the car's engine and at last its appearance. There were two occupants, whom she first thought to be Toby until she realised that it really was Cicely, still in masculine clothes despite being in the last month of her pregnancy.

'Sissy!' Charlotte called out, waving frantically. 'Or rather George!' she corrected herself as the car drew to a halt beside her. 'Oh, I am so glad to see you! You have good news for me, I know you have!'

Cicely returned Charlotte's enthusiastic kiss, but didn't answer, instead pulling off her driving gloves one by one and removing her goggles.

'Well?' Charlotte demanded.

'News, yes, but not good news,' Cicely said. 'For a start I've left Cyprian.'

'You haven't! Oh my!' Charlotte exclaimed, trying her best to fight down a surge of delight.

'It was too much,' Cicely went on, 'simply too much. I mean to say, I was prepared to sit at home all bloody day and play the little wife. I was prepared to have him buggering boys right, left and centre. I was prepared to put up with his hideously bad taste, and even subject my child to the same. But I was not prepared to have that wretched man Quigley in the nursery dressed up as nanny Martha!'

'From *It*? Why?'

'Yes, well more or less, a nursemaid anyway. That's what Quigley wanted to be, the nursemaid. Can you believe it?'

'How extraordinary!'

'Too extraordinary for my tastes, darling. We had the most terrible row, which ended with him saying I was a worse example than Quigley. So I left him, and I've come to live with you. I hope you don't mind.'

'Mind!' Charlotte exclaimed. 'I don't mind at all, silly! Nothing could make me happier.'

'I'm glad,' Cicely went on, 'because that's not the only bad news.'

'Oh.'

'Toby has failed to win over Victor Cushat. In fact, he punched him in the nose.'

'He punched him?'

'Yes, rather hard.'

'Well, I shall know what to say to him, really!'

'I'm afraid you'll have to wait. It was all rather public, you see. Outside Berry Bros as it happens, which I think shows a measure of taste on Toby's part, if not discretion. He got pinched and the judge gave him ninety without the option.'

'Three whole months! My poor Toby!'

'Oh, he'll be fine. I dare say it won't be so terribly different from school.'

'And Cushat?'

'Ah. Now, there I fear that Toby miscalculated, assuming that any calculation went into the thing in the first place, which, it being Toby, I doubt. Barely had the bleeding stopped than Cushat made a speech in the house. "Moral Decline and the Prevalence of Illegitimate Birth" I think the title was.'

'Oh, my! He didn't!'

'I'm rather afraid he did. Your name wasn't actually mentioned, of course, but he's made damn sure everybody knows. It was quite a rousing speech, in fact, so I understand, much the best he has ever made. I suppose it must have been the memory of that punch in the nose.'

'You are a disgrace, Lottie Bomefield,' Cicely said. 'I mean to say, seducing a maid is bad enough, but milking one!'

'Catherine's very sweet,' Charlotte answered, 'and, anyway, I didn't seduce her. It just happened.'

Cicely laughed in dismissal and drew deeply on her cigarette before blowing a smoke ring towards the ceiling. They lay together on Charlotte's bed, where a cuddle intended purely for solace had very quickly turned into some of the most urgent, passionate sex of their lives. Locked together, top to toe, heads buried between thighs, they had fed on each other's quim, and in Charlotte's case on Cicely's bottom hole as well.

When they had finally come apart it had been for a longer, slower session, making up for all the time without each other. Charlotte had been given a firm spanking with the same shoe brush that had been put across her bottom so often at school. Cicely had sat spread-legged on Charlotte's back to do it, and taken her lover through tears and screams to an exquisite orgasm without thought for the Colonel or anybody else who might have been listening. The beating had been followed by a lengthy session licking Cicely's bottom and another climax for each of them, after which they had at last collapsed together on the bed, by then naked.

With more than a touch of guilt, Charlotte had told Cicely about Catherine and the milk.

'Well, she's pretty enough,' Cicely admitted, 'and I can see she'd make a good wet nurse. Maybe I'll have her myself.'

'She's quite tough,' Charlotte answered, 'and ever so motherly. She loves to nurse me, and to spank my bottom, too.'

'We shall see who gets her bottom spanked.' Cicely laughed. 'And you may be sure it won't be me. So the milk, it really works?'

'It does,' Charlotte replied earnestly. 'Don't you believe it?'

'Oh, I believe it all right. There are many things we ought to be able to learn from other cultures. Our own is so hidebound. You do look well too, and you've gained a little weight, in the nicest possible places. No, the thing is, I'm surprised it works when it's so simple. These things tend to be frightfully arcane.'

'Well, Francis did say the villagers used to . . . to do their stuff in it, but I'm sure he was just trying to make me behave for him.'

'Why should he lie? You suck willingly enough, God knows.'

'I'd been refusing. It didn't feel right, with me being engaged to Toby.'

'I see. Still, it might make sense. After all, sperm does give life.'

'That's what Francis said.'

'It's true.'

'Still, it would be hard to be sure. Scientifically, I mean.'

'Really, Lottie, I'm surprised at you! You still think like old Mebbin, with her "rational thought" and "process of deduction". There are some things you don't need to work out scientifically. Does love make sense in scientific terms, or beauty?'

'I don't know. Couldn't love be to make two people stay together so that they look after the children properly?'

'And how does that explain my love for you? Or think of Cyprian. I'd like to have seen old Darwin try to explain that one.'

'I'm sure you're right.'

'I am.'

Cicely went quiet, smoking and blowing the rings out above her head. Charlotte cuddled closer, letting her breath out in a long sigh. After making love with Cicely it was hard to take the awful news she had been given seriously, and now that the blow had fallen the agonies she had expected had failed to materialise. There was regret, and also anger, but with them a strong feeling that she would, in fact, be happier away from the censorious gaze of those who expected her to behave a certain way, of those who had always demanded that she conform.

'Such things will die, you know,' Cicely said suddenly.

'What things?' Charlotte demanded.

'The milk, the vital essence. I can see it now. Some missionary will come to the village. Someone like Lester Jerton, so certain in his own little world and so sure he knows what's best for everybody else. He'll build a church and preach at them from his silly wooden pulpit, and a school, too. Eventually they'll start to take notice, one or two, not because they believe it, but because it gives them influence. After that it'll soon be the end. They'll be taught about sin, and modesty, and weighed down with all the baggage of Christianity. The vital essence will be declared immoral, and banned. A few will hold out, I imagine, but not the young, and that will be that.'

'How horrid.'

'Horrid, but true. How I hate men like that. They kill everything romantic, everything different, and all the while they're so damn sure that what they're doing is right.'

'Like Cushat.'

'Yes, like Cushat, but there's a deal of jealousy and pique there, too, I'd imagine. Still, what do we care? None of them will speak to us now.'

'They speak *about* us though.'

'Oh, endlessly, with little scandalised remarks and whispers, pretending to be horrified and all the while delighted by the opportunity for gossip. Still, should you care? You have Ashwood, or you will, and you have your father's investments.'

'I have you,' Charlotte sighed, snuggling herself against her lover.

'For ever,' Cicely assured her.

Again they went silent, Charlotte thinking of what Cicely was saying and doing her best to reconcile herself to her future. It was true, with what she had and the prospect of marriage to Toby, she didn't need to fear

178

social ostracisation. Nor did it seem such a loss as she had imagined, especially in the case of the county set, who had always bored her. In fact, after she had spent the best part of a year doing her best to avoid people, in practical terms there would be little difference.

'We shouldn't let it die, you know,' Cicely remarked after a while.

'The milk drinking?'

'Of course the milk drinking. What have we been talking about?'

'I was thinking of something else.'

'Well, don't. It would be easy, you see, down here. Wouldn't that be wonderful, to know that we alone held the knowledge, the last flicker of the candle?'

'It would, yes, but –'

'Oh, there are sure to be difficulties, but we can overcome them, I'm certain of it. First I'll need to get the full story out of Francis, and we must try the vital essence.'

'With you know what? I'm not sure I care to.'

'You swallow it, why not in milk?'

'Catherine's milk is delicious. The other stuff tastes revolting – especially after asparagus.'

'Asparagus?'

'Yes.'

'Strange. Anyway, I fully intend to milk the pair of you.'

'The pair of us? Together?'

'Certainly together. You're in milk, aren't you?'

'Yes, look.'

Rolling on to her back, Charlotte cupped her left breast, squeezing gently until a prickle of white specks appeared on the skin of her nipple. For a moment Cicely watched, before leaning forward and taking the little bud of flesh into her mouth. Charlotte sighed, her eyes closing in the ecstasy of having her lover suckle at her breast.

'That is simply beautiful,' she said. 'Don't stop, ever.'

Cicely responded by sucking the nipple deep into her mouth, pulling up the flesh of Charlotte's breast. Cradling her friend's head, Charlotte pushed up her chest, enjoying the sensation of being suckled almost as much as she enjoyed doing the suckling.

'I can do this to you soon, darling,' she sighed. 'That will be more beautiful still.'

'Perfect,' Cicely said, disengaging herself. 'I don't remember cow's milk tasting like that at all.'

'It is different,' Charlotte assured her, 'or so Catherine says.'

'Catherine still eats meat?'

'Well, yes. I've tried to explain why she shouldn't, but she doesn't even seem to understand.'

'Typical country girl. We must change that, of course, and ever so many other things. We shall live a life according to our own plan, not that of society, with no cruelty, nor exploitation. We will recognise the rights of all living things, and their fundamental equality. Shall we dress and ring for tea?'

Colonel St John watched the deep red liquid rise in the glass as Spince filled it. Dinner had been excellent. With a pheasant stuffed with field mushrooms entirely to himself, he had for once been grateful for the girls' vegetarianism, while the steamed pudding had been above reproach and the cheese in perfect condition. Even the tinned asparagus soup had been served with plenty of pepper and a topping of sour cream, making an ordinarily straightforward dish into something special. There was no doubt in his mind that since her caning Mrs Mabberley's always competent cooking had taken on a certain flare. The same was true of service in general, both from the housekeeper and the butler, and as he raised the glass to his lips he drank a silent toast to himself.

As he put his glass down Cicely settled herself into the chair opposite him. She was in immaculate black tie, a masculine effect that would have been perfect had it not been for the prominent bulges of her belly and breasts, which a black silk cummerbund did little to hide. It had a disturbing image, but little more so than when she had been dressed as a man but not pregnant, while he still found it impossible to think of her as anything other than completely female.

With Charlotte there was no question that she was completely female. She was already beginning to regain her waist, although her gown, a red silk affair cut for her before her pregnancy, was definitely straining in places, the bust especially. During the dinner he had frequently allowed his eyes to stray towards the considerable amount of cleavage on display, and he had quickly begun to wonder what he might be able to persuade her to do afterwards.

Glancing from Cicely to Charlotte and back, he assessed his chances. Spince had placed the decanter on the table and was retreating slowly. Charlotte was giggling, her hand on Cicely's arm, both of them flushed with drink and apparently in high spirits. It seemed odd, considering the news Cicely had brought down from London, yet he was not about to lose an opportunity.

'So how about a nice story for your old uncle then, Sissy, eh?' he asked.

'Certainly, what would you like?' she answered.

'Well . . . I . . . I . . .' he stammered, taken back by her easy acquiescence. 'You know the form, something good and rude.'

'I shall choose,' Cicely said, rising. 'Lottie, why don't you help Francis undo his trousers, and I'm sure he'd like to see a little something.'

'Naturally,' Charlotte replied and immediately pulled the front of her gown down over her breasts.

The Colonel's cock twitched in response to the sudden exposure. Charlotte's breasts had at least doubled in size during her pregnancy, and were now notably plump if not large, two round handfuls of girl flesh topped by dark nipples. As he sat back in happy surprise she came to kneel between his open knees. There was none of the resentment that normally showed in her face at the beginning of their sessions, only a happy smile. Nor was there any hesitation. Her hands went straight to his fly, popping the buttons quickly open then reaching in to pull out his cock without hesitation or distaste. As she began to stroke it, Cicely turned from the bookcase.

' "The Romance of Lust"?' she asked.

'Splendid.'

'Very well, and as a special treat you may paw my bottom.'

'Well, I am honoured.'

Cicely perched herself on the arm of the Colonel's chair, her trim bottom in easy reach of his hand. The black material of her trousers was enticingly taut and round, yet it took a moment of conscious effort before he let his hand close on it. As she opened the book he began to grope, his cock stiffening quickly in Charlotte's hand.

'I shall choose a good bit, with the girls playing together,' Cicely announced, 'or would you prefer some flagellation?'

'Girls'll do nicely,' he answered, 'preferably with a little sodomy thrown in.'

As she searched for a place he continued to grope her and Charlotte continued to stroke his cock. She had taken one of the empty glasses from the tray, and he found his grin growing broader.

'Here we are,' Cicely announced. 'With Mary and Lizzie. Are you sitting comfortably?'

'Splendidly, thank you, my dear,' the Colonel answered, pushing his now fully erect cock up towards Charlotte's face.

Charlotte took the erect penis into her mouth, sucking softly as Cicely began to read.

' "We immediately began with a gamahuch, I taking Mary's cunt while Lizzie crossed her legs over her head, and was gamahuched by Mary, whose finger was at the same time acting postillon to her charming bottom hole, while I had the exquisite prospect before me of their operations. As soon as ever Mary spent I made Lizzie lie down on her back, with her head towards the bottom of the bed, Mary kneeled over her in the opposite direction, presenting her very full backside, which was daily developing larger proportions. I plunged into her cunt, plugging her little rosy bumhole at the same time with my middle finger . . ." Careful, Lottie, or he'll spend in your mouth.'

Charlotte nodded around her mouthful of cock and Cicely continued to read. For all the masculine clothes, Cicely's bottom felt unmistakably feminine, soft and cheeky, rounded and smooth. He had been cautious at first, uncertain how far her invitation extended, but as he continued to grope and she continued to read he grew slowly bolder. Having cautioned Charlotte, she moved a little, sticking her bottom further out, and he grew bolder still, pressing the material of her trousers down into the hot crease between her buttocks.

'Where was I?' Cicely said. 'Yes, here: ". . . while Lizzie did as much for me, at the same time rubbing Mary's clitoris with the fleshy end of the thumb, while Mary, at the same time she herself was fucked and frigged in two places, was employed in gamahuching Lizzie, and frigging her bottom hole with two fingers, Lizzie declaring that one finger felt as nothing . . ." You are becoming very eager, Uncle Francis. Should I pull them down for you?'

'Decidedly you should,' he answered.

'You might even follow the story a little, if you insist,' she said, rising. 'You are not to touch my cunt, though, just my bottom.'

His cock slipped from Charlotte's mouth as Cicely eased down her trousers, deliberately pushing out her bottom towards them to provide the best possible view. Beneath them she had on plain, masculine drawers, which came down with the trousers, exposing her ripe and undoubtedly feminine bottom, with a puff of hair showing between the cheeks. He had placed his open hand on the chair arm and she sat down on it, sighing as one of his fingers found her anus.

'You may put it in, if you wish,' she said, 'and wiggle it a little as I read.'

'What happened to the invert nonsense?' he demanded as his finger invaded the moist ring of her bumhole.

'Let us say that I have learned rather more about myself,' she said. 'Yes, like that, well in, thank you. Now, something suitable ... "Mary was gamhuched and bottom-fingered by Lizzie, while she employed herself with Lizzie's clitoris and my bumhole ..." No, this is better; pull at him, Lottie, hard ... "... removing my two fingers from her delicious bottom hole, and wetting it with my saliva, I withdrew my prick from the reeking sheaf of her cunt, and to her great delight slowly housed it in her longing and exquisitely delicious bottom hole ..." Oh, lovely, up her bottom hole, up mine. Oh deeper, deeper, wiggle it in me ...'

Cicely dropped the book, her hand going to her crotch as Charlotte watched open-mouthed, her hand still bobbing rapidly up and down on the Colonel's cock. As Cicely's bottom lifted he pushed a second finger into her, cupping her bottom with his hand as he masturbated her anus. She cried out in ecstasy even as he felt his cock jerk in Charlotte's hand.

The sperm fountained out, most of it falling into the glass or across his belly. Quickly, Charlotte collected what had spilled, wiping it up and smearing it into the glass. As Cicely's gasps and moans subsided, he pulled his fingers slowly from her bottom hole.

'I am sorry,' Cicely sighed after a while. 'I just . . . Oh, I don't know, but thank you, anyway.'

She kissed him and stood up, hoisting her trousers back into place. Already his cock was softening, while Charlotte had kneeled back with the glass in her hand.

'That should be plenty,' Cicely said. 'Now, a little milk.'

'Oh, so that's what you're up to,' the Colonel said. 'I thought so. Very sensible, too.'

'We were determined to try,' Cicely said as Charlotte placed the glass on the table and leaned across it. Holding her breast carefully to make sure the nipple stayed within the glass, she began to squeeze, milking herself. He watched in fascination as the tiny jets spurted out, pooling at the bottom on top of the much thicker come.

'You'll need to give it a good stir,' Cicely remarked.

Charlotte nodded, pursing her lips in concentration as she squeezed out the milk. The Colonel watched the glass fill, wishing that his cock was ready to allow him to get the most out of the sight. As the level reached halfway, Charlotte changed breasts, again squeezing out the drops and spurts of milk.

'Not too full,' Cicely cut in. 'It'll spill when you stir the jism in.'

'I'll stop, then,' Charlotte answered, standing again.

Her face was flushed, her nipples wet with milk. She made no effort to cover her breasts, but took up the glass, using a finger to stir his come into her milk.

'Uncle Francis?' Cicely asked as Charlotte withdrew her finger.

'Not for me, thank you,' he answered. 'You'll find the texture a bit like prairie oyster, which I could never stand.'

'Then you may drink first, Lottie,' Cicely went on.

The Colonel watched, trying not to grin too openly as Charlotte put the glass to her mouth, sipped, then swallowed. She made a face, her tongue darting out at the same time to catch a stray drop.

'What do think, my dear?' he asked.

'Perfectly horrid,' she answered.

'The best medicines often are, I'm afraid,' he remarked as Cicely took the glass.

She drank a little, made a face herself and then swallowed the remainder, including a last sticky streamer of come that for a moment clung to the glass.

Cicely sat back in her chair, trying not to retch at the taste of the mixture she had just swallowed. After quickly filling a fresh glass with port, she took most of it into her mouth, swilled it quickly around and swallowed.

'That's better,' she said, seating herself. 'Now, Uncle Francis, you must tell me everything.'

'Everything? How d'you mean?'

'About vital essence, of course. For instance, how much jism was put into how much milk? Did the women who were in milk eat anything special? Was there any sort of ritual involved in drinking it?'

'Great heavens! It was a while ago, you know, my dear – '87, if I remember rightly.'

'Do try, Uncle.'

'Well yes, certainly. Hmm, now, let me see.'

He paused, sipping at his port, his brow furrowed in thought. Cicely waited, hoping that his memory for long-past events was better than it was for things that had happened recently.

'D'you know,' he said after a while, 'I actually think I might have some notes from that period. Fancied myself as a bit of an anthropologist, I did, back in my early days. Soon gave up, mark you, but not before then, I think. No, I'm sure of it.'

'Notes?' Cicely queried. 'About the village?'

'Yes. Well, if I was making notes I'd have certainly remarked on such an unusual custom. Look, I'll have a poke about in the lumber room tomorrow, how's that?'

Again he took up his port glass, sipping thoughtfully before continuing.

'Now ritual, there's something I do remember. They did do something of that order. Not all the time, mark you, sort of high days and holidays thing, I suppose, but they definitely did. Yes.'

'What did they do?' Cicely demanded.

'Oh, it was frightfully complicated. Instead of just sharing the stuff about, the elder Johnny would do the milking, with all the girls lined up on a long bench as I remember – no, they'd kneel down, that was it. All the milk would go into one big pot, and then the young chaps, or some of them anyway, would come over and do their business.'

'Did they chant? Was anything added other than milk and the young men's sperm?'

'No, just milk and jism. It wasn't all the young men, though, just the most virile. I suppose it was a bit like the old customs that survive here and there about the country, you know, when all the young lads race to light a bonfire or gather a sheaf of corn or whatever.'

'For fertility?'

'Yes, quite. Fertility, that's the thing. After the young chaps, a few of the older fellows would have a go. For wisdom that was. Took a while, some of them. Needed a helping hand as often as not.'

'You witnessed all of this? There was no secrecy?' Charlotte asked.

'Ah, well . . . secrecy. No, not as such. There's no taboo about nudity, you see, or sex. A degree of reverence was expected, yes, but it was hardly a secret. To give you an idea, imagine a church service where some complete stranger walks in. They're perfectly welcome, so long as they stand quietly and don't do anything to interrupt. It was the same.'

'Did any of your own people try to interrupt?'

'Ours? Good heavens, no. Soames was far too much the old soldier, and Broderick and I did as he said. One of the first things you learn, out East, if you want to live, never meddle with local beliefs. Started the Great Mutiny, that did, meddling.'

'So they shared the contents of the pot?' Cicely asked.

'Yes, after a good stir. Everybody would take a sip, a bit like communion, really.'

Cicely stood on the lawn of Ashwood House, contemplating the grounds. Within her was a desperate need to keep busy, to drive the disaster of her marriage and the humiliations of London from her mind. Initially she had hoped to submerge her ill feeling in her love and lust for Charlotte, until the discovery of the facts of vital essence had provided a still better subject on which to expend her energies. Not only was it secretive and intimate, but magnificently defiant of the society she loathed.

Even the health-giving properties of the mixture linked in to her feelings. After all, if it aided her to live to ninety or even one hundred, she could confidently expect the pleasure of seeing all those who had snubbed her or ridiculed her die away. Society also seemed likely to change, and perhaps for the better. Certainly it had changed since her childhood, albeit largely as a result of the war.

'We might use one or other of the follies, when the weather is warm,' Charlotte said, breaking into Cicely's thoughts.

'The chapel would be better,' Cicely replied decisively. 'After all, we don't want any rumours spreading among the men who work on the estate.'

'We always know where they are,' Charlotte said, 'and I rather like the idea of doing it outdoors. It seems more natural.'

'Yes, that's true,' Cicely admitted, 'but to do it in the chapel would be wonderfully irreverent, don't you think?'

'We may use both, of course,' Charlotte said, 'according to what the weather permits, and we might also have some new hedges planted to screen the ground, which we can always explain away as windbreaks.'

'Ditches, too,' Cicely added, 'we shall quite cut ourselves off from casual intrusion. I don't suppose the hunt will be meeting here this year?'

'I would think not; certainly the secretary has not written.'

Cicely nodded and Charlotte turned at a sound from behind her to find Colonel St John striding briskly from the house, a sheaf of yellow papers clutched in his hand.

'Ah, girls! There you are. I've found my notes!' he called. 'It took simply ages, and of course they were in the last place I thought of looking, not in among my Indian things at all, but with the Nigerian stuff.'

'Is there much on the vital essence?' Cicely queried as he joined them.

'Plenty,' he answered, 'far more than I recall writing, certainly. It's remarkable how much slips from one's memory. For instance, I'd quite forgotten about the breast whipping . . .'

'Breast whipping?' Charlotte demanded.

'Yes, to stimulate the milk, don't you know?' he answered. 'Not hard, mark you, just enough to bring the blood up to the surface. It was done with a clump of bamboo shoots and the girl's arms tied up above her head to stop her putting her hands in the way and getting hurt.'

'It sounds ever so painful.'

'Quite stimulating, I imagine. You should try it.'

'I shall do no such thing!'

'We'll try it on Catherine, then,' Cicely put in. 'What else is there, Uncle Francis?'

'Plenty,' he replied. 'For instance, whipping the girls' breasts was only one of the ways to stimulate production. Another was to use a plant, a nettle of sorts. I imagine ordinary stinging nettles would do very well.'

'We must try that, too,' Cicely answered him.

'That was more for difficult cases than to get more production,' he said. 'You know, when it was hard to bring a girl into milk. Again, they'd string her up by her wrists to get an even shot at her titties, and her husband would tickle her with the nettles. I actually remember seeing it now. How the girl howled!'

'I imagine she would!' Charlotte exclaimed.

'It worked a treat, though,' he went on. 'It wasn't long at all until her milk was simply gushing out. In the end she was among the best milkers in the village.'

'Were her breasts large or small?' Cicely asked.

'Large,' the Colonel said immediately, 'not that it actually makes all that much difference in terms of milk production. Less than you might expect, anyway.'

'No?' Cicely queried, glancing down to her own breasts, which although swollen were still smaller than Charlotte's.

'Absolutely,' he assured her. 'Look at the thing for yourself. Catherine's must be a good eight to ten times the size of Lottie's, yet she produces what, twice as much milk?'

'More like three times,' Charlotte said.

'Still, not ten,' he went on. 'Don't worry, Sissy, my dear, you'll have plenty. Starting you off might be a different matter. It was usually the small-breasted girls who had difficulty there.'

'I must say, you seem to have remembered a great deal since last night,' Charlotte remarked.

'Well, yes, I've been reading the notes, after all. So, um . . . care for a spot of essence?'

'Why not?' Cicely answered him. 'We must do it properly this time, with plenty of milk and rather less jism. I want to try the breast whipping too, and see if it really works. Besides, it's about time I tried young Catherine for myself.'

'Catherine?' Charlotte asked.

'Yes, of course. Why not?'

'I . . . I don't know, really. Shouldn't we ask her?'

'Whatever for? She'll do as she's told, won't she?'

'I suppose so.'

'Then there is no difficulty. Now be a dear and run for some bamboo, just little bits, to make the switch. Where do you suppose Catherine is, Uncle Francis?'

'In her room, I would guess. That or the nursery. Look, er . . . d'you mind if I watch?'

'Mind?' Cicely answered. 'Naturally not. Why should I? She's only a servant.'

Catherine found herself grimacing as she folded the blankets, one by one, placing each on top of a growing pile. Both Hazel and Holly were deeply asleep, having fed to satiation, and her breasts were already becoming hard and sore. There was an hour to go before lunch and the relief of milking herself, while she was uncertain whether it was acceptable to offer to feed Charlotte from the teat when Cicely was in the house.

She knew that Charlotte and Cicely were lovers, which sparked a measure of jealousy. She also knew that Cicely's assumption of the masculine role went beyond dressing the part, and that full advantage of Charlotte's gentle and subservient nature was taken. It had surprised her to find that Charlotte needed to be spanked so badly, but she knew it came from Cicely's behaviour. The same was true of all Charlotte's joy in deliberately degrading herself, both by punishments and humiliations. All of it she blamed on Cicely.

She had watched the conversation on the lawn, wondering what they were talking about all the while, until the little group broke up. The Colonel had returned to the house, and as she finished a blanket she heard his footsteps in the corridor.

'Ah, Catherine, my dear, there you are,' he announced himself. 'We wish to borrow you for a while.'

'Yes, sir,' she responded.

'In the garden, if you would,' he went on. 'You're in good form? Plenty of milk this morning, I trust?'

'Plenty, sir,' she assured him, blushing faintly at his familiarity despite being used to it.

'Splendid, splendid,' he said. 'Now, do you happen to know the whereabouts of Spince and Mrs Mabberley?'

'Yes, sir. Both, sir. Mr Spince would be in his parlour, while Mrs Mabberley's gone shopping in the village.'

'Good, good. The yew garden is probably best, then. Come along.'

'The yew garden, sir?'

'Absolutely. We ... ah ... No, best to let Lottie explain. Come on, that girl, at the double.'

Catherine followed him down the stairs and out of the house, wondering what was expected of her. Both Charlotte and Cicely were already in the yew garden when she and the Colonel reached it, standing between two hedges and beneath one of the largest trees. As she saw the neatly tied bunch of bamboo in Charlotte's hand she realised that she was to be beaten.

'I ... I've not been bad, have I, miss?' she stammered. 'I've not earned a whipping, surely I've not?'

'This is not a punishment, Catherine,' Charlotte said soothingly. 'Just an experiment ...'

'For goodness' sake, Lottie, you don't need to explain it to the girl,' Cicely interrupted.

'I think I should,' Charlotte protested.

'Lottie's right,' the Colonel put in. 'Always best to have a willing subject, Sissy. Important lesson, that. Now, my girl, we're going to whip your breasts, but it's not a punishment, d'you see?'

'No, sir, I don't see at all, sir,' Catherine said, instinctively putting her hands up to her chest.

'It stimulates the milk production,' Charlotte explained. 'Don't be afraid: it won't be done hard.'

'I've plenty of milk,' Catherine assured them. 'They ache dreadfully, they do. I'll gladly give all I have, this moment.'

'No, that's not the point,' Cicely said. 'We want to see if whipping your breasts stimulates production, that is all.'

'Why?' Catherine asked. 'I've been giving my best, Mrs Yates. Is that not so, Miss Charlotte? You've never complained before.'

'That is Miss St John, thank you, Mullins,' Cicely snapped. 'It will be a punishment if you don't mind your tongue.'

'I'm sorry, Mrs . . . Miss St John,' Catherine stammered.

'I'm not complaining, Catherine dear,' Charlotte said softly. 'I'm very happy with you. Please, Catherine, for my sake? We shan't hurt you, I promise.'

Catherine looked doubtfully from one to the other. Charlotte seemed genuinely sympathetic. The Colonel was trying to look stern, and failing. Cicely looked impatient and rather excited. Remembering some of the things Charlotte had told her, and which she had been asked to do, she began to wonder if Cicely hadn't simply found an excuse to make her a plaything. Thinking of Mrs Mabberley, she reached a decision.

'Very well,' she said, 'if you must. I suppose Miss St John will be wanting to do it?'

'I might, as it happens,' Cicely answered her. 'Lottie?'

'As you please,' Charlotte answered, holding out the switch to her friend.

'A moment, darling, we are forgetting something,' Cicely said, pulling a hank of coarse twine and a handkerchief from the pocket of her tweeds. 'Hands crossed, please, Mullins.'

'I'm to be tied up?' Catherine queried.

'It's for the best,' the Colonel assured her. 'Stops you putting your hands in the way, don't you know?'

'I suppose . . .' Catherine managed, holding out her wrists to Cicely and placing one on top of the other.

Cicely quickly wrapped the handkerchief around Catherine's wrists, knotting first one pair of corners, then the other. The string was applied with the same certainty, making it quite clear that it was not the first time Cicely had tied a woman's wrists together. Catherine had begun to tremble slightly and, as the twine was knotted off to leave her bound, the reaction became stronger. A long end had been left, which Cicely tied to a stick and threw over a branch of the big yew above them. Taking the stick once more, she pulled on it, hauling Catherine's arms up until they were stretched high above her head, and then tied the twine off on to the tree.

'Perfect,' Cicely declared, 'and now to have these great, fat, peasant breasts out, or shall we strip her completely? What do you think, Lottie?'

'It's not a punishment, remember, darling,' Charlotte said.

'Strip her down,' the Colonel suggested. 'Best thing, you know, stops 'em soiling themselves.'

'Soiling?' Catherine queried.

'With sweat and such, don't you know? Not wanting to be indelicate,' the Colonel said.

'Well, perhaps it would be better,' Catherine admitted. 'Down to my drawers anyways.'

'Pretensions of modesty!' Cicely laughed. 'Whatever next?'

She stepped forward, put her hands into the crossed front of Catherine's maternity dress and tugged it wide, taking the chemise with it. Catherine's breasts fell free, to loll, huge and pale on her dress, the skin glossy with tension from the milk within, the nipples straining hard and already damp. Cicely took one, lifting with one hand, then two as her tongue flicked out to moisten her lips.

'Obscene!' she whispered. 'How can you bear to be so fat?'

'I can't help it, miss; I'm just built this way,' Catherine protested.

'It's all that disgusting meat you stuff yourself with,' Cicely went on. 'Look at yourself. They must weigh a stone each. I'm going to enjoy this, I really am.'

Catherine didn't answer. There were butterflies in her stomach and a lump of fear in her throat, while she was struggling not to react to the feel of Cicely's hands on her breast. Both of them were straining from her load of milk, sore and sensitive, badly in need of suckling.

Cicely finished the task of stripping Catherine. Her dress was tugged down, taking her drawers with it, to leave her standing in a puddle of cloth, nude but for her open chemise and knee stockings. Cicely stepped back, her eyes sparkling as they lingered on Catherine's naked body. Catherine said nothing, knowing that it was pointless protesting about the unnecessary and undignified removal of her drawers.

All three of them were watching her, and there was no mistaking the lust in their eyes. The Colonel had taken a hip flask from his pocket, his hands trembling as he removed the stopper. Charlotte was more transparent still, open-mouthed and moist-eyed, her hard nipples showing clearly through her dress.

'Obscene,' Cicely repeated with relish. 'So very, very fat. What do you weigh, Mullins?'

'Thirteen six by the kitchen scale, Miss,' Catherine answered. 'That's not so very large, not for a girl of my height . . .'

'Be quiet,' Cicely cut in. 'You're fat, obscenely fat, a great wobbling piece of suet. If it wasn't for your milk I'd have you put on a regime. Now, the switch, please, Lottie. Let's she how she reacts to having those fat breasts thrashed.'

Catherine shut her eyes, trying to stop herself shaking as Cicely took the switch from Charlotte. She had guessed that Cicely might be jealous of her, but not how deep it went. Now it was clear and, whatever Charlotte and the Colonel might want to whip her breasts for, it was equally clear that as far as Cicely was concerned it was a punishment.

'So, so fat,' Cicely said softly and the switch touched Catherine's breasts.

It tickled, making her muscles jump and setting her breasts quivering as the bunch of bamboo was trailed slowly across her skin. She shut her eyes tight, biting her lip. The switch came up, then down, patting her tight flesh, gently, more firmly and with a sudden, sharp smack full on to one nipple.

Catherine gasped, her eyes coming open with the sharp pain. Cicely was right in front of her, eyes bright, mouth in a tight smile. Again the switch came down and again Catherine jumped. Two irregular pink marks now marred her breasts, covering the nipples and much of the upper surfaces. Cicely was lifting the switch, watching Catherine's face as it came up, her smile growing wider then it changed to a vicious grin as the bamboo smacked down hard on bare breast flesh.

'Just look at yourself, Mullins,' Cicely said, flicking the switch over Catherine's orbs, 'so fat and soft. These are like two great jellies, the way they wobble, or like whale blubber, I imagine, two big, fat balls of whale blubber.'

Cicely brought the switch down again, laughing as the ripples spread through Catherine's breast flesh. Again she did it, and again, to the sound of Catherine's gasps and squeals and her own joyful laughter. It got harder, the red marks on Catherine's skin growing deeper, with goose-pimples springing up. Catherine began to jump on her toes, wriggling in her pain and shaking her chest to make her breasts bounce and quiver in a futile effort to avoid the switch. Cicely merely laughed the louder at the display, crowing in glee over Catherine's pain and misery.

The switching grew harder still, and Catherine's efforts to avoid it grew wilder, encouraging Cicely further. Soon she was dizzy with pain. Both her breasts were covered with a pattern of pink and scarlet marks, also hot and throbbing, while the tension from her milk had risen to a straining, unrelenting discomfort that grew worse with every bounce and jolt.

'She is wonderful, isn't she?' Cicely called out after Catherine had performed a particularly ludicrous gyration. 'Look at her blubber quiver, Lottie. Doesn't it just make you want to thrash the fat beast?'

As she finished she lashed the switch hard across Catherine's breasts. Catherine screamed as it hit, dancing back on her toes, losing her balance, and for one moment she hung from her hands before she recovered herself, panting and gasping in shock and pain, only for the switch to slap down once more and her control to go completely.

Cicely stood back, laughing as she waited for Catherine to recover herself.

'Must you be quite so cruel, Sissy, darling?' Charlotte asked, her words coming to Catherine through a haze of pain.

'Naturally I must,' Cicely answered pleasantly. 'We want to conduct the experiment properly, don't we?'

'Oh, nonsense, you're just being a beast!' Charlotte said.

'Would you love me if I wasn't?' Cicely answered.

Charlotte gave no answer.

Catherine had managed to stand properly and was hanging, panting, from her rope. Her head was hung down, her tawny hair trailing loose across her reddened breasts, dark with sweat. Her milk was coming, beading on her nipples, each drop growing larger in time to the heaving of her chest. There was sweat, too, prickling up from the whipped skin. She watched, her senses swimming, as two drops coalesced and ran down, reached a nipple and blended with milk until a thick, pearly white drop from the teat fell to her dress.

'It works!' Cicely declared. 'Look, she's milking like anything.'

'I say, so she is,' the Colonel added.

'Well done, Catherine,' Charlotte said. 'You are a good girl, and very brave.'

'I shall whip her a little more, then, as she is so very brave,' Cicely said.

The switching started again, slaps and smacks until once more Catherine's breasts were jumping, then her whole body as it became more severe. It hurt more than ever, and her gasps and screams rang out louder than before. The milk was coming, too, spurting from her nipples each time the switch struck home, spattering her tortured skin and dripping from her teats. Soon she was dancing in pain, an uncontrolled, urgent kicking of her legs and writhing of her body, making her breasts swing and the heavy flesh of her bottom wobble.

Yet her anguish only seemed to provoke Cicely, who drove the blows in hard and harder, until both Catherine's breasts were a mass of scarlet welts, the skin ridged and inflamed, the nipples swollen and throbbing. Milk was spraying everywhere, mixed with sweat, spattering out over her body and the ground beneath, even catching Cicely. Nor was the agony in her breasts the only pain, with her stomach muscles knotting and twitching, while her bladder had become a hot, angry ball in her lower belly. Her arms also hurt, her wrists yet more, with most of her body weight now hung from the tree.

Writhing, jumping and kicking, she danced under Cicely's blows, hardly aware of her tormentor's laughter and cruel remarks. They didn't matter, only the pain of the switch did, controlling her utterly, with her breasts two huge balls of agony on which her whole world was focused. Nothing else mattered, and as her self-control snapped completely her bladder burst in a great gush of pee, spraying out across the grass and over her dress and drawers. Cicely jumped back, but too slowly, gasping in disgust as the stream caught her shoe and the leg of her trousers.

'You filthy beast!' Cicely spat, slapping at her wet leg.

Catherine said nothing, too far gone to respond or to care, just hanging limp in her bonds as the contents of her bladder emptied out. She let it come, all of it, spurting from her quim, soaking her clothes and running down her legs. Most went on to the ground, but plenty found her boots, filling them with warm, wet urine until it began to spill from between the laces at either side.

'Disgusting!' Cicely snapped. 'She's done it all over my leg! For goodness' sake, Mullins, can't you even hold yourself?'

All Catherine could do was shake her head in miserable resignation to soiling herself. Nor did she try to stop, but let it all run out, down her legs and into her boots, bubbling out of the sides and over her sodden drawers. The others watched, silent, as at last it died from a gush to a trickle and finally stopped.

'Well, of all the disgusting, dirty little beasts!' Cicely said. 'Imagine piddling yourself!'

'I don't suppose she could help it,' Charlotte put in.

'Nonsense,' Cicely answered, 'she's just a dirty, fat beast.'

'Well, be that as it may, you've certainly stimulated her milk,' the Colonel remarked. 'Are you going to milk her now?'

'In a minute,' Cicely replied. 'I've yet to finish with those fat breasts of hers.'

'Oh, do stop: she's in a terrible way,' Charlotte pleaded.

'Her bottom, then,' Cicely said. 'I'm sorry, Lottie, but she's piddled on my leg and I'm sure it was on purpose. She simply cannot be allowed to get away with it.'

'Very well, thrash her backside for her,' the Colonel said, 'but no more than a dozen, d'you hear.'

'A dozen, then,' Cicely agreed, turning to Catherine. 'Stand up, girl, and stick that fat behind out.'

Catherine struggled to obey, dragging her feet together and sticking out her bottom. Cicely chuckled at the sight and patted the switch down across the crests of Catherine's cheeks.

'I suppose you need a fat bottom,' she remarked, 'if only to balance those ridiculous breasts. Now stick it out further; come on, girl, make a target of yourself. Legs apart, too, well apart, in case I want to whip your cunt. That's better. You see, you can be obedient when you want to.'

Catherine was now in a pose as revealing as it was vulnerable, bottom stuck out behind, burning breasts hanging from her chest, legs wide to let the air to her quim. She heard Cicely give a wicked chuckle and the switch came up between her legs, against her quim, gentle, tickling as it was drawn slowly back.

'Shall I whip it?' Cicely asked. 'Shall I whip your fat cunt, Catherine?'

'No, please, miss, no,' Catherine whimpered.

She gasped as the switch was tapped against her sex, just hard enough to sting before being pulled away, leaving her with her eyes shut tight and her muscles jumping in an agony of anticipation.

'No, please, miss, not that, not there!' she faltered, once more starting to tread up and down on her toes.

A last burst of piddle escaped her, pattering down on her ruined dress. Again Cicely chuckled.

'Very well, my fat little coward, I shall let you off, for now. But remember what you might get if you're not very, very good.'

'Yes, miss, I will,' Catherine managed.

Relief flooded through her and she sighed, only for the noise to turn to a squeal of anguish as the switch came down across her bottom with all the force of her tormentor's arm. Her balance went and she fell forward, scrabbling frantically at the ground with her toes. Cicely struck again, and again, thrashing away at Catherine's bottom, in peels of laughter at the uncontrolled antics of her victim.

Catherine screamed and thrashed, writhed and struggled, hanging almost entirely from her wrists as she kicked and swung in a desperate effort to get her balance back, all the while with the horrible switch smacking down over and over on her tortured body, her bottom, her legs, even her belly as the rope twisted above her. As Catherine was beaten, so Cicely laughed, the sound taking on a wild tone in her delighted cruelty. A dozen strokes passed, and two dozen, until Catherine had lost all sense of how many there had been or anything else beyond her pain and Cicely's demented laughter. Finally it stopped, leaving Catherine struggling for balance and Cicely panting with the effort.

'I think that's enough, my dear,' the Colonel said, his words coming faintly through the haze of Catherine's pain. 'You shouldn't exert yourself so, not in your condition.'

Cicely hurled the tattered remnants of the switch to the ground, nodding as she bent to rest, her hands on her knees. Hanging limp in her bonds, Catherine again felt a great wave of relief. Her skin was wet with sweat, also milk on her breasts and belly, pee and quim juice down her legs. She was panting, her whole body aching, her bottom on fire, but more than anything her breasts, with the hot sting of the bamboo weals and the strain of the milk within making them feel as if they were about to burst. Slowly the world around her became clear, Cicely resting, the Colonel smiling quietly to himself, Charlotte closer, face flushed pink with excitement.

'You are hurt?' Charlotte asked softly.

Catherine nodded.

'Yet ever so wet,' Charlotte went on. 'Do you feel as I would, do you? When you have spanked me?'

Catherine shook her head, then nodded, knowing her denial for a lie. Cicely gave a cruel laugh.

'Of course she is excited, Lottie. She is a slut, and she knows it. Wonderful, I do love it when they're really well beaten and they realise what it is they actually want.'

'Shall I make her spend?' Charlotte suggested.

'Oh, yes, do.' Cicely laughed. 'That will be funny.'

'I will, then,' Charlotte answered and stepped close to Catherine.

A finger found Catherine's sex, pressing in between the swollen lips. She moaned in response.

'You are so, so wet.' Charlotte giggled. 'Now don't wriggle so: I'll soon have you off.'

Catherine let it happen, her body responding to Charlotte's tickling, probing finger, the pain of her tormented body changing as her clitoris was attended to, growing warm, turning to a hot, urgent pleasure until her feelings turned to gratitude for the beating and for Charlotte's touch, bliss and at last ecstasy as her body tensed in burning, exquisite climax. She screamed, her vision red and blurred, her head thrown back and her teeth clenched, unable to bear what was being done to her but unable to stop it. Even then Charlotte kept on frigging, until at last the contractions stopped and Catherine collapsed completely.

As she came down from her orgasm she was close to fainting. Nothing seemed real, even the aches of her body dull and distant. Her whole weight was on the twine, until it went slack, suddenly, and she collapsed, sitting down heavily among her pee-soaked clothes, indifferent to the wet, squashy feeling as her bottom settled on to the sodden fabric of her dress. Even sitting was too much, and she slumped down on to her side, lying half on fresh grass and half on pee-soaked cloth.

Charlotte kneeled down beside her to untie the knot at her wrists, the others approaching, too. The knot undone, Catherine began to massage life back into her aching arms. They waited, watching her, until at last she blew out her breath and rolled on to her side in exhaustion.

'Get up,' Cicely ordered.

'I can't,' Catherine muttered. 'I'm spent.'

'Get up, will you? We wish to milk you,' Cicely demanded.

'I can't,' Catherine repeated. 'I'm sorry, miss, I really can't.'

'Don't be too harsh, Sissy,' Charlotte put in.

'I don't wish to be harsh, Lottie, but what are we to do?'

'Suckle her,' Charlotte replied. 'Then she need not get up.'

'And the jism?'

'Francis must do it in my hand. I'll wipe some on each nipple.'

'Why not straight on her breasts?' the Colonel grunted. 'What d'you say, Catherine?'

Catherine said nothing, but rolled fully on to her back, leaving her smarting breasts poking up into the air. The Colonel gave a pleased snort, his hands going straight to his fly. His cock came out, close to erection as he brandished it over Catherine's naked body.

'Very well, Uncle Francis, spend on her,' Cicely said. 'A bit on each.'

'My pleasure,' the Colonel grunted.

He sank down, swinging one leg across her body, straddling her. She watched as he began to masturbate, his cock protruding from his fly into his hand, the head an angry red colour. He was jerking at the thick shaft, directly over her breasts, his eyes fixed to them, his knuckles brushing her tortured skin, his face growing slowly redder with effort.

Suddenly sperm erupted from his cock, splashing out over one nipple and across her breast in a long line. He jerked it away with a grunt, moving to the other breast and leaving a streamer hanging between them, which broke as his next spurt caught her. With both her nipples soiled with sperm in addition to the milk and sweat, he sat back, squeezing the last of his come out into his hand before plastering it over a clean area of her breasts.

'Good enough for you?' he panted, getting slowly to his feet.

'Very neat,' Cicely said, gazing down at Catherine's come-topped breasts.

Charlotte was already sinking to her knees. Her mouth went wide as she took Catherine's left breast in her hands. Her lips closed on the nipple and she began to feed, sucking the teat deep into her mouth. Cicely came down more slowly, tasting the Colonel's sperm on one finger and making a face before joining her friend. Catherine lay still, allowing the soothing feel of being suckled to build up against the aches and pains of her body. Her nipples hurt, stinging where the bamboo had left ridges and even tiny cuts, yet being suckled was still a relief, with the strain in her breasts fading slowly away as the girls guzzled down her milk.

On the first day of November Cicely gave birth to a baby girl. Despite the Colonel's vigorous resistance to the idea, the child was named Sappho. She was then given over to the care of Catherine.

A week later found Cicely seated on her bed beside Charlotte, her shirt open, squeezing irritably at one small breast. She had not come into milk, despite her best efforts, even to the point of allowing Charlotte to apply a gentle whipping. Nothing had happened, and despite squeezing and rubbing, suckling and stroking, her nipples had remained obstinately dry. Now, with her frustration rapidly submerging what little pleasure she had gained from the evidence of her masculine character, she found herself close to tears.

'I can't do it!' she complained. 'I just can't!'

'Have patience, darling, these things come with time,' Charlotte said soothingly.

'I don't have any patience!' Cicely snapped. 'Imagine if we didn't have Catherine. Poor Sapphie would have no milk to drink.'

'I'd feed her for you,' Charlotte replied, 'and besides, we do have Catherine. Really, you needn't worry at all.'

'I want my own milk!' Cicely retorted.

'I could try whipping you again,' Charlotte suggested.

'It stings so,' Cicely protested, 'and it's undignified. Catherine guessed, I'm sure she did.'

'Does that matter? You did whip her.'

'That is hardly the same! Oh, I don't know, maybe you should, but they do feel awfully tender. I'm not sure I could bear it.'

'Certainly you could. Didn't Catherine?'

'She's a servant; it's different. They're not as sensitive as we are. After all, look how beastly cold it gets in their passage in the winter. I know I could never stand that. Still, maybe gently.'

'I think it has to be quite hard to work. Hard enough to make the skin rough, anyway.'

'Ow!'

'Or we could try the other way, with nettles.'

'Ow again!'

'It might not be so bad. Anyway, do you want your milk to come or not?'

'You know I do, more than anything. I just can't bear pain.'

'Maybe if you had a glass of brandy first?'

'Well maybe, or something stronger. Does Uncle Francis still keep laudanum in the medicine cupboard?'

'Yes, but it's been there for simply years, from before the war. Brandy would be better.'

'I'm not sure . . . It's . . . Oh, very well, bring me a bottle, if you would.'

Charlotte patted Cicely's hand and got up, then left the room. Alone, Cicely turned her attention back to her breasts, massaging one and then the other until the skin had started to turn pink. Not so much as a trace of fluid showed on either nipple, while her fear of the nettles made the frustration worse.

Before long Charlotte had returned with the brandy decanter, full of old cognac, of which she poured a liberal glass. Cicely drank it with trembling fingers, already imagining the hot pain of the nettle stings on her tender flesh. Charlotte kissed her and left once more.

A second glass of brandy followed the first, and a third, before Charlotte returned, now with a bunch of long, straggling nettles in one gloved hand. By then Cicely was beginning to feel the effects of the brandy, with a warm, groggy sensation stealing up on her. The sight of the nettles was still a shock.

'They're enormous!' Cicely protested. 'You'll get me everywhere!'

'I'm sorry, darling,' Charlotte answered her. 'They were the best I could find. It's really too late in the season. Look, I'll pull some of these little side branches off, shall I?'

'Yes, do. How do you want me? Do you think I need to be tied?'

'That all depends if you're going to struggle. Do you think you can keep your hands away from your chest?'

'I don't know.'

'We'll see, and if you can't manage it I shall tie your hands behind your back.'

'Well, lock the door, then. I don't want to be seen like that.'

Charlotte placed the nettles on the window ledge and locked the door as Cicely removed her shirt completely and sat back against the wall. With their privacy assured, Charlotte began to remove the side branches from the nettles, quickly gathering a neat bunch.

'I don't suppose they'll hurt so very much,' she said, studying the bouquet she had made critically. 'They're always so much worse in the spring.'

'Are you sure?'

'Yes. Don't you remember making me stuff my drawers with them at school?'

'Yes I do. Sorry.'

'Don't be. It hurt at first, but it was nice in the end. It'll be the same for you, you'll see.'

'I doubt it,' Cicely said miserably, but pushed out her breasts as Charlotte came to kneel on the bed.

She shut her eyes, her body tensing as she waited for the pain. Nothing happened, only a gentle tickling sensation across her chest, back and forth as Charlotte stroked the bunch of nettles from breast to breast.

'It just tickles!' she complained. 'It's not working at all.'

'Wait,' Charlotte said. 'It will.'

'I . . . Oh!' Cicely gasped as the sensation on her breasts changed, to warmth, then heat, and a sharp, insistent throbbing as her hands came up to protect herself.

'Ow!' she exclaimed. 'Oh, my goodness! Lottie! Ow! I'm on fire! They're burning!'

'Don't touch,' Charlotte said. 'I nearly got your hands then.'

'I had to!' Cicely protested. 'It hurts so much, Lottie! Oh, my goodness, look at them!'

Her breasts were covered in stings, tiny bumps that rose as she watched, growing and merging to form whole areas of raised flesh an angry pink in colour. It hurt crazily, a hot, throbbing pain that made her want to tear at her skin, and in particular at her nipples, which had popped out into hard, smarting buds, their surfaces rough with nettle stings.

'Shall I go on?' Charlotte asked.

'No,' Cicely answered, and then abruptly changed her mind. 'Yes, but pour me another brandy first, and tie my hands.'

Charlotte nodded, quickly filling Cicely's glass. Cicely drank, her hand shaking so hard that Charlotte had to help her with it. With the cognac inside her she leaned forward, crossing her wrists behind her back. Charlotte obliged, using the sleeves of Cicely's shirt and knotting them tightly. With her arms secured, Cicely once more stuck out her chest, closed her eyes and nodded.

Again the nettles were applied, tracing lines across her flesh, lines that tickled, then stung, and finally burned, until at last she could no longer stand the pain, screaming in reaction and pulling away. Her whole chest was throbbing, her breasts swollen and bright pink, her nipples angry points of furious pain.

'It hurts so much!' she gasped. 'Oh, Lottie, it hurts!'

'There, there,' Charlotte said, reaching out to stroke Cicely's hair. 'Take a deep breath, just relax.'

'I can't,' Cicely sobbed. 'It hurts too much. Ow! Hold me, Lottie; hug me.'

Charlotte came in close, throwing down the nettles as she put her arms around Cicely, briefly kissing one inflamed breast before cuddling in close. Cicely tried to fight down her feelings, with the pain in her chest blending with the swimming sensation in her head. Her breasts felt huge, heavy and hot, really burning, while the nipples seemed to be on fire. The tears were starting in her eyes, and not just from her pain, but also her frustration.

As Cicely burst into tears, Charlotte cuddled closer still, stroking and whispering soothing words in tune to the gasps and broken sobs. Her emotions filling her head, Cicely let it all out, crying freely, only to find the pain changing, with an urge to push out her breasts and open her thighs rising up beneath it. At the sensation her thoughts went back, to the playing field at Wilton-heath, the agony of six cane cuts, the awful shame of having a bare bottom in front of her friends and a group of leering field hands and, worse, the dreadful need to give herself up to their lust.

'Not me!' she gasped. 'It doesn't happen to me!'

'What is it, darling?' Charlotte asked.

'This is beastly! I'm starting to wet. I can feel it!'

'Of course you are, darling. That's what happens.'

'No. To you, maybe. Not to me. Not to me!'

'To everyone, Sissy, darling, everyone. Shall I kiss you, there?'

'No.'

'Let me. It'll be nice.'

'No.'

'Oh, don't be so silly.'

Cicely gave a weak groan as Charlotte moved down the bed. Fingers tugged at her trouser buttons, opening them, and the fly. Hands took hold of her trousers, tugging at them, pulling them down, off her hips, off her bottom, to her knees.

'Do play, Sissy, for me,' Charlotte said. 'Now roll up your legs like a good girl.'

With a last, abject moan, Cicely gave in to what she so desperately needed. Pulling up her knees, she made herself available. Charlotte lost no time, tugging open the split of Cicely's drawers and burying her face in her quim. Cicely sighed deeply, cocking her legs wide as Charlotte started to lick, lapping eagerly at Cicely's anus and vagina before going higher.

As the sharp little tongue began to flick at her clitoris, Cicely knew she was completely lost. Her breasts were in agony, throbbing and hot, the nipples engorged and smarting. Yet it was no longer bad, no longer something to be hated. Instead it had become the focus of her pleasure as Charlotte's expert mouth worked her slowly up towards orgasm. Her head was full of shame, but there was nothing she could do, thinking of the way she had been nettled, of her exposure, of her burning breasts. Being tied became part of it, having her wrists bound with her own clothes not an annoyance but a delight, something to make her torture more painful, more effective. She was still crying, even as she felt her orgasm coming and her back arched in ecstasy, her quim pushing hard into Charlotte's face. It hit her and she screamed, blending rapture, misery and pain together in an explosion of emotion that left her sobbing weakly on the bed.

With her orgasm past, the pain once more became unpleasant, less strong than before, but a constant, nagging throb. Nor was there any sign of milk, despite both her nipples being swollen, with the teats distended to nearly twice their normal size. Despite their tenderness, she tried massaging, and letting Charlotte suckle, but to no avail.

'It's no good!' she sobbed. 'It just won't come! I'm useless, Lottie, I'm no good at all!'

'There, there,' Charlotte soothed. 'I'm sure you can do it. I remember old Mrs Mullins saying it sometimes takes several days.'

'Oh, what would she know? She's just some stupid old commoner. Anyway, it's been a week! It's me, Lottie: there's too much of the man in me.'

'Nonsense. You've had a baby, haven't you? What could be more womanly than that?'

Two days later, with Cicely's breasts once more returned to their normal dimensions and colour, there was still no milk. In contrast Catherine was not only feeding all three babies but had enough over to provide a glass each at bedtime. That left Charlotte's milk for the production of vital essence.

Milking herself and masturbating the Colonel had become an evening ritual, always in the library, with each of them in their allotted role. Only in the last days of her pregnancy had Cicely stopped reading, and since the birth she had not begun again. Charlotte had managed the awkward task of reading holding the book with one hand and working on the Colonel's cock with the other, but it had not been to his satisfaction.

'Do you feel up to reading me a spot of "The Pearl" this evening, my dear?' he asked Cicely as they settled into their chairs. 'You are rather good at it, you know.'

'I really couldn't,' Cicely sighed.

'Whatever is the matter?' he demanded. 'You ought to be happy, I'd have thought, not moping about the house all day.'

'It's delicate, Francis,' Charlotte put in.

'Aha,' he said. 'Cunt still sore, eh? Don't want to get excited?'

'It is not that at all!' Cicely snapped.

'No? You didn't split, then?'

'Francis, really!' Charlotte protested.

'Happens, you know,' he went on blithely. 'So what is it, then?'

'As I said, it is delicate,' Charlotte insisted.

'Look if you must know, I can't make milk,' Cicely said curtly.

'No?' he replied. 'Well, don't be upset, my dear. As I think I explained, there are ways to help.'

'I've been nettled, thank you.'

'And no luck?'

Cicely shook her head.

'No,' Charlotte answered. 'I'm afraid not. Sissy's dreadfully upset.'

The Colonel gave a thoughtful nod and busied himself with the port. For a long while none of them spoke, Charlotte feeling torn between loyalty to Cicely and the need to milk herself, which was becoming acute. Eventually it was the Colonel who spoke.

'I'm surprised the nettles didn't work as it goes. Now look, I didn't mention it before, but there was another way, or rather there was supposed to be. Not that I actually saw it, but one of the elders described it to me. It had been done to a girl whose case was a bit like Sissy's. The stingers wouldn't work, try as they might, so they used bees.'

'Bees?' Charlotte demanded.

'Yes, honey bees. After all, they sting like billy-o.'

'But wouldn't that be terribly dangerous?'

'Well, they didn't just upend a hive over her tits, you know. Nothing so crude. It was done carefully. The girl's breasts are coated with honey, which the bees come to collect. A little smoke annoys them enough to make them sting.'

'So like the nettles, yet stronger?'

'Much stronger. I imagine you have to be damn careful.'

'Well yes, naturally. Sissy, what do you think?'

'I don't know,' Cicely answered. 'The nettles hurt so very much. Can you be sure it will work, Uncle Francis?'

'Well, no,' he admitted. 'Not certain. All I can say is that the Indian fellows used to consider it pretty well foolproof, a last resort, but foolproof. As I say, I never actually saw it done.'

'I don't know,' Cicely sighed. 'I'm tempted, but I'm scared, too. Maybe with enough brandy.'

'You're welcome to as much as you please, I'm sure.'

'So how do we go about it?' Charlotte asked.

'Well, we've no shortage of bees, but we don't want to wait. If the weather clamps down they go in.'

'We really need someone who knows what they're doing,' Cicely said, 'and I'm not having old Thomas Dunn anywhere near me.'

'He's a good beekeeper,' the Colonel remarked. 'But no, see your point, quite. We need someone who knows what we're about. Catherine Mullins, she's the girl for you. Used to look after the hives at home. Told me so herself.'

* * *

Cicely stood in the orchard, looking doubtfully at the row of beehives to one side. It was moderately warm, and the insects were busy, flying this way and that with the faint buzzing sound of their wings. She had dressed in the house and was ready. A fine net hid her face and neck, her long school dress the rest of her body, leaving just her breasts bare. They felt impossibly vulnerable, the skin tingling with the memory of the nettles and the anticipation of what was to come.

Charlotte and Catherine stood nearby, busy with the preparations for Cicely's ordeal. Charlotte held a small pot, into which she was pouring thick, dark honey. Cicely could smell it, her nose twitching and her nipples stiffening in reaction to what was going to be done with it. Catherine, also protected, but fully clothed, was inspecting the beehives. Further off was the Colonel, seated in a wrought-iron chair, apparently paying no attention to her at all as he filled the cap of his hip flask with brandy. She had drunk plenty herself, and not only brandy. Lunch had involved champagne and sherry, to both of which she had done full justice. The brandy had followed, and more as they had walked out to the orchard, at the back of which stood the beehives. Now her head was spinning gently, but the drink had done nothing to ease her fear, only to make it harder not to show it.

'There we are, that should be plenty,' Charlotte announced, twisting the honey pot to catch the last strand. 'Now, Sissy, I think it's time you were tied to the tree. The big apple would be best: it has the straight trunk.'

Cicely nodded dumbly in response.

Wondering if those luckless enough to be burned at the stake had felt at all similar, she let herself be led to the tree. Standing against it, straight-backed, she waited patiently as Charlotte prepared her, first attaching her to the tree at her waist, then her ankles. That done, her hands were strapped behind the trunk, leaving her not just helpless but unable to do more than waggle her breasts.

'There we are,' Charlotte declared, 'nice and snug. Now, the honey.'

There was more than a little satisfaction in Charlotte's voice, which Cicely promised herself would earn a suitable revenge in due course. Meanwhile, she was at her friend's mercy, and it was hard not to think of all the tortures and degradations she had subjected Charlotte to across the years. There were countless spankings and other punishments, as well as plenty of bottom kissing, licking and wiping. There was also shoe polishing, tidying, endless chores, minor humiliations.

Taking a brush, Charlotte began to slap honey on to Cicely's breasts, plenty of it, cool and sticky. Soon it had began to run down over her stomach and hang in long drips from her nipples.

'Isn't that enough?' Cicely asked.

'Oh, the more the merrier, I dare say,' Charlotte said happily. 'Catherine says the more honey there is the more likely they are to sting when they get angry. Now, are you sure about this?'

Cicely managed to nod, unable to speak for the sudden lump in her throat.

'We're ready, Catherine,' Charlotte called.

'Yes, miss,' Catherine replied and Cicely turned to watch.

Catherine took a length of bamboo and brushed honey on to it, coating it liberally. Twisting it between her fingers as she went, she stepped quickly to one of the hives, pulled up a section and pushed it within. There was an immediate angry buzzing and the lump in Cicely's throat grew. It was all too quick, too sudden, and the choking sensation in her throat was growing unbearable. She swallowed hard as the stick came out, black with bees, at the sight of which Charlotte made a hasty retreat, to stand behind the Colonel's chair.

Smiling happily, Catherine stepped across, holding the stick up in front of Cicely, whose flesh had started to crawl and jump, making her breasts quiver, with the erect nipples twitching. Without waiting a moment, Catherine put the stick to its target, against Cicely's breasts, from nipple to nipple.

Cicely's jaw was trembling as the bees began to crawl on to her honey-laden breasts, buzzing their wings, their legs tickling through the honey. It was impossible to stop shaking, and her breasts were wobbling, despite her desperate efforts to keep still. More bees moved on to her skin, and more, until both of her honey-smeared globes were crawling with rounded black-and-gold bodies. She could feel their legs, the tickling growing to a maddening peak as they began to collect the honey.

'There we are, miss, and not one off your titties,' Catherine said cheerfully. 'Now for the smoke and it'll soon be over.'

Catherine walked away, unhurriedly, to the small bonfire of leaves and twigs they had lit in the corner of the orchard. Cicely was left to her torment, her jaw shaking and her flesh crawling as the bees fed on her honey-covered breasts. Her nipples had come right out, rock-hard, making two stiff little promontories on which the bees were having trouble, scrabbling with their feet and buzzing their wings to keep in place. It was impossible not to watch, certain that at any moment one would lose patience and sting her in an effort to keep her still. Yet that was going to happen, it was what was supposed to happen, and as she watched the bees crawl over her skin a sick fear was rising inside her, until the tears had started in her eyes and she had begun to whimper. At the fire, Catherine took her time, throwing on damp leaves and waiting until the smoke had become thick and yellow before sucking it into the bellows. Twice she blew it out and sucked more in before she was satisfied.

Cicely was crying freely, big oily tears running down her cheeks, close to panic as the bees writhed and clutched, growing more and more agitated with the quivering of her breasts. Without warning, her bladder went, spraying out piddle into her drawers, to trickle down her legs and soak into her dress, making a very obvious stain. Too far gone even to think of trying to stop it, she let it come, her head hung in shame as she wet herself.

'Oh, dearie me. Well, accidents do happen,' Catherine said as she approached.

Cicely looked up through a haze of tears. Catherine was holding the bellows up, towards her breasts, then slowly she closed her hands and smoke puffed out over Cicely's breasts. She caught the scent of burning leaves even as the noise of the bees took on a new, angry tone. Her mouth came open in a cry of despair as the bees became a furious, writhing mass. She felt real panic, her stomach knotting hard, fresh piddle spurting out into her drawers, her anus opening to emit a loud fart even as she felt a sudden stab of pain in the tender flesh of one breast.

She screamed, as much in shock as pain, then again as another stung her, another and she was thrashing her head from side to side, writhing against the tree trunk, screaming and sobbing and shaking her breasts in a frantic, futile effort to dislodge the bees. Again her anus opened, and her drawers filled with hot, squashy dung as she emptied the contents of her bowels into them, blind with fear and panic, in unbearable pain as her whole chest began to burn and a great cloud of thick yellow-grey smoke blew out into her face.

Her panic ebbed slowly away as the bees dispersed, one or two more getting in their stings until a single individual was left, clinging to the tip of one erect nipple. She saw it as her eyes came open, the six legs held wide around the little bump of flesh, its abdomen

216

coming up, the tiny point of the sting turning down, pressing to her flesh and driving home into the very tip of her nipple. Once more she screamed, the sound ringing out around the orchard as she threw her head back in pure agony for one awful moment before it all became too much and her senses slipped into merciful blackness.

As she came round the first thing she saw was Charlotte staring at her chest, face set in an expression of absolute delight. Catherine was beyond, also looking thoroughly pleased, and the Colonel was approaching, brandy flask in hand.

'You've done it!' Charlotte called. 'Look, Catherine, look. Milk!'

Cicely could say nothing. Her muscles were still slack, her quim running pee and her bumhole open, adding to the heavy load of dung in her drawers. She hung her head, watching the white beads of milk grow on her bee-stung nipples, mixing with the honey and the yellow pollen from the bees' legs until beads of pearly yellow fluid hung from the tip of each. Both Charlotte and Catherine had gone behind the tree and were working to untie her, drawing the rope at her waist tight to squeeze out a last piece of dirt into her drawers. Released, she slid slowly down the tree to sit squashily down at the base of the trunk.

'You had better clean her up. I think she's soiled herself,' Charlotte said to Catherine.

'Really, Miss Cicely, couldn't you even hold yourself?' Catherine asked as she sank down by Cicely's side.

Still Cicely could find nothing to say. Her breasts were burning, the skin red and lumpy, still glossy with honey. They were throbbing, too, with her hard nipples dripping the mixture of milk and honey on to her stomach. Yet, as with the nettles, the pain was warm and arousing, an undeniable pleasure, which brought her more shame than her sodden dress or even the feel of the disgusting, squashy mess in which she sat.

'We'd better get you in the bath,' Catherine said, wrinkling her nose. 'Come now, put your arm about my shoulder. That's right.'

Cicely let herself be lifted. Clutching on to Catherine, she was carried to the yard and dumped unceremoniously into the trough beneath the pump. There was an immediate shock as the cold water rose up her body and she gasped, only for the sound to turn into a sigh as her breasts went under. She lay back, letting the cool water soothe her chest. Above her, Catherine was rolling her sleeves, face set in a stern, matter-of-fact expression with just a hint of satisfaction.

The cleaning up was done briskly and thoroughly. Cicely's clothes were loosened and pulled off, Catherine tutting all the while, and most of all when she reached down to pull the filthy drawers off Cicely's bottom. What it wasn't was fast, with Cicely left to lie nude in the tub as Catherine scrubbed at the dirty clothing before dumping it into a tub to soak. Only then did she turn her attention to Cicely's body, using her fingers, carbolic soap and a coarse scrubbing brush as Cicely's arousal and humiliation rose slowly, the one warring with the other.

Her breasts were done first, soaped gently in Catherine's hands until the honey had come off. They hurt, the flesh unbearably tender as they were moulded and massaged, but her nipples remained obstinately hard, with her desire growing and growing until she knew that if Catherine decided to have her there would be nothing she could do about it.

With her breasts clean, Catherine started on Cicely's bottom. The awful feeling of humiliation grew sharply worse as the mess was scooped out from between her buttocks, a good handful, which Catherine held up for Cicely's inspection.

'Disgusting!' Catherine said. 'And in your pretty drawers. Really, Miss Cicely.'

'I couldn't help it,' Cicely said weakly.

'Well I've a mind to rub it in your face, just to teach you a lesson,' Catherine went on. 'But I shan't, seeing as I'm so kind-hearted. Now turn yourself over and stick that dirty bottom up. I need to get at the tricky places.'

Cicely obeyed, rolling on to her front and sticking her bottom above the surface of the water as Catherine washed her hands at the pump. Her breasts were still underwater, making the pain bearable, and her arousal was threatening to get the better of her.

'Now if I was you,' Catherine went on, eyeing Cicely's lifted bottom, 'and you had me like that, I dare say I'd soon be feeling a dozen smart ones across my arse. It's not nice having to clean up your dirt, not nice at all, and if I wasn't so soft I'd give you what you deserve, lady or no lady. Now say you're sorry and we'll have done with it.'

'I'm sorry,' Cicely said miserably, choking out the words despite herself.

In answer Catherine depressed the handle of the pump, spraying freezing water across Cicely's bottom. She gasped in shock, and once more as the process was repeated, before Catherine's hands went to her bottom. The soap was applied vigorously, rubbing into Cicely's cheeks and up her crease, over her quim and into her pubic hair. The brush followed, buttocks and belly scrubbed firmly until the skin was pink and tingling. Then came more soap, on to the tender skin of Cicely's vulva and anus, stinging as it was rubbed in. Fingers followed, prodded roughly into bumhole and vagina, taking soap with them until Cicely was open-mouthed with the stinging pain, now of breasts, sex and anal area.

'That hurts!' she protested. 'It stings so much!'

'Oh, does it now?' Catherine answered. 'Well, you should have thought about that before you did your business in your drawers, shouldn't you? And now, Miss

High-and-Mighty, I'm going to frig your little cunt, and we'll see who's a slut, shall we?'

'No,' Cicely managed, but she made no move to turn over.

The answer was a stinging slap to her bottom, then the rough insertion of a thumb to her vagina.

'Oh God, no,' she moaned as Catherine's hand closed on her sex, two fingers catching the bud of her clitoris between them.

Catherine began to rub, and as she rubbed she spanked, slapping happily at Cicely's bottom to make the wet cheeks bounce and quiver. As the frigging grew harder, so did the slaps, until Cicely was gasping at each.

'You said you wouldn't punish me!' she wailed.

'Who's to say this is a punishment?' Catherine answered. 'This is what you do to sluts, as you and I well know, Miss Charlotte also.'

Cicely sank down with a moan. Somewhere in the back of her mind a voice was screaming at her to get up, to slap Catherine's face, to make the maid strip and grovel at her feet, babbling a string of apologies under a dog whip or riding crop. She didn't do it, but merely stuck her bottom higher to the sharp slaps, wiggling it against Catherine's fingers in a display she knew was as wanton and subservient as anything she had made Charlotte do. It didn't matter: she couldn't stop it and, as she took her burning breasts in her hands and began to rub at the bee stings, she knew she was lost.

The orgasm came in a great rush, rising in her sex and travelling up her spine to make her scream. Catherine kept frigging, rubbing mercilessly at Cicely's clitoris and smacking away at the wet pink bottom, until at last Cicely's legs went and she fell forward into the trough, spent, exhausted and utterly humiliated. Above her Catherine laughed.

Cicely was put to bed, where she stayed for two days, with Catherine or Mrs Mabberley bringing up her food on a tray and Charlotte visiting to apply a soothing ointment to her bee-stung breasts, also to provide her twice-daily does of vital essence. Ironically, the milk she had been so desperate for was now coming well, wetting her bedclothes in the night and leaving her breasts swollen and taut with pressure.

On the morning of the third day she found herself growing bored and irritable, with the tension of her milk load worse than the fading ache of the bee stings. Her skin was still pink in places, with low bulges of redder flesh where the stings had gone home, yet the temptation to scratch had given way to one to stroke and squeeze, anything to relieve the pressure.

Her emotions had been as battered as her body, but, if her body had recovered, then they had not. It was impossible not to think of Catherine as her torturer, in the same way she had always seen herself with respect to Charlotte, a torturer and a lover at the same time, providing what was needed. In the trough, in the extreme of her anguish, she had been unable to resist, and she had a nasty suspicion that should Catherine ever again catch her unprepared it was more than likely to happen again.

The self-knowledge provoked resentment and shame, much as had her discovery that she enjoyed the feel of a man's penis up her bottom. Since being put to bed she had thought of little else, despite her best efforts, and at night it had taken all her willpower not to masturbate over what Catherine had done to her. Now, with her swollen breasts aching and her mind numb with boredom, the temptation to simply spread her thighs as wide as they would go and let her imagination take control was once more becoming hard to resist.

She bit her lip, thinking of the way Catherine had masturbated her in the trough, so roughly, and without a thought for the possible intrusion of Spince or Mrs Mabberley. That had been dreadful, but maybe no worse than the feel of sitting down in her own dung while the maid looked on in a mixture of amusement and disapproval. Turning to the window, she wondered whether it would count if she just masturbated over the memory of being tied up and tortured, yet she knew that it was only the presence of Catherine that made the experience a sexual torture rather than a painful therapy.

Just as she had decided that it was impossible to hold herself back, she heard the sound of footsteps in the corridor. A moment later the door swung open, admitting Charlotte with the lunch tray.

'How are you, darling?' Charlotte enquired happily.

'Better, really,' Cicely answered. 'I think I'll get up after lunch.'

'Catherine says another day would be good for you,' Charlotte replied.

'What does it matter what Catherine says?' Cicely demanded.

'She's very good with that sort of thing,' Charlotte replied. 'It's remarkable how much she does know, in fact.'

'Old wives' tales, most of it,' Cicely said sulkily.

'Well, she made the ointment for your titties, didn't she?' Charlotte asked.

'Yes, I suppose so.'

'And it is ever so efficacious. How are they?'

'A lot better, thank you. Look.'

Cicely let the piece of ointment-soaked flannel she had been given to cover her breasts fall, exposing them. Charlotte made a little sympathetic noise.

'Nearly better, then. You'll soon be as right as rain, you'll see. It was worth it, though, wasn't it? I knew the bee treatment would work.'

'Yes, it was; I suppose it was,' Cicely answered, smiling ruefully as she cupped one small breast and gave it a gentle squeeze to release tiny sprays of milk from the teat. 'Ow! They're so tender!'

'You poor thing. Well, I feel the same if it's any consolation, and it's hours to dinner. Speaking of dinner, poor old Francis is feeling a bit drained, and his cock's dreadfully sore. I didn't dare ask this lunchtime, and I'm sure he wouldn't have had much to give if I had. There was barely more than a dribble yesterday, the third time. Catherine had to run down to the pantry and give old Spince a helping hand. Apparently he was ever so grateful.'

'Spince? The butler?'

'Yes, of course, what other Spince do you think it might be?'

'Lottie! Drinking a gentleman's jism is one thing, but a butler's!'

'I'm sorry; Francis hadn't made anything like enough.'

'Had to be Spince, then, I suppose, but you'll regret that, when I'm better. So you told Catherine, too?'

'Everything. She's wants to have some, too, but I said there wasn't enough to go round for now.'

'No, there isn't. Francis is getting on, of course, and besides, from what he said we're not really making it properly. We need a young man, for virility.'

'Toby would oblige, I feel sure.'

'I dare say he would, unfortunately not while he's enjoying His Majesty's hospitality.'

'No, but he'll soon be out.'

'I'd rather not wait. I've been thinking about it as it happens. We might get some from one of the village lads. If it would be a bit infra dig, but no worse than a butler.'

'I'm certainly not helping any of them!'

'Not you, silly. Catherine could do it. She can suck him, and keep it warm in her mouth while she runs back. We shall have a bowl ready, into which she can spit the jism and then milk herself.'

'She might, I suppose. I wonder if she'd be willing.'

'For goodness' sake, Lottie, she's a servant! You're letting her get above herself.'

'Well, you're a fine one to talk, Cicely St John, moaning away in the water trough with your bum stuck up in the air and her hand you know where!'

'I couldn't help it,' Cicely said, more sulky than ever.

'I'm sure you couldn't,' Charlotte answered tartly, 'but don't preach at me when you can't keep your own feelings in.'

'She took advantage of me; it wasn't fair! Besides, how do you know so much? Has she told you?'

'No, silly, I was watching. You were so carried away with it all that you never even noticed us.'

'Us? Not Uncle Francis, too?'

'Of course, well, he had asked.'

'Only about the bees, not that! Oh, no!'

'Oh, don't pout so, Sissy. You had fun, and you should be grateful for it.'

'You don't understand.'

Cicely sank back against the pillows, thinking of the wanton display she had made of herself. Charlotte having seen was bad, but the idea of the Colonel watching, and undoubtedly coming over what he had seen, was truly unbearable. She blew out her breath in a long sigh, wishing fervently that she could be as cool and poised as she liked to pretend.

'Look, jolly well cheer up,' Charlotte said after a while, 'or I shall ring for Catherine and ask her to do the same again.'

'No, please,' Cicely answered in sudden panic.

Charlotte laughed. 'You're not scared, are you? Not you, surely?'

'Naturally I am scared. I've always been scared of that. Do you remember my fight with Miss Mebbin?'

'Yes, of course.'

'I was dreadfully scared. Scared she'd do it to me, you know, spank me. All that week, all that term really, I'd been growing more sure of myself, more certain that I'd never have to feel it again.'

'What?'

'That. What you feel when you're punished.'

'But it's wonderful. With a lover anyway – with you.'

'It is, I know; that's the worst thing. When Miss Mebbin punished me that time on the sports field I hated her so much for it, but I wanted more at the same time. I couldn't help myself, and that made me hate her even more. That was why I was so cruel to Catherine.'

'I thought you were jealous of her and me.'

'I was, a little. I still am, as it happens, Lottie.'

'And do you hate her?'

'No, I can't hate Catherine, but I do intend to exert my authority over her.'

'You do?'

'Certainly I do. What can be done to me can be done to her.'

Catherine gave the butler's cock a last few vigorous tugs and opened her mouth to catch the ejaculation. Most of it went in, leaving her face clean but for a small blob that clung to her upper lip. She caught it with her tongue, then leaned forward, sucking at the meaty cockhead and holding what came out in her mouth.

'Thank you, Catherine,' Spince puffed. 'You are a very obliging girl.'

She gave a muffled response and got quickly to her feet, running from the parlour. Snatching up the mixing bowl she had set ready in the kitchen, she emptied her mouthful into it, the gagging sound drawing a chuckle from Spince.

Climbing quickly to her room, bowl in hand, she shut the door and freed her breasts, milking one and then the other on top of the little puddle of sperm. A brisk stir completed the process, leaving a creamy liquid with a fair bit of froth on the top. She looked down at it doubtfully, thinking of how she had always hated the taste.

Grimacing, she put the bowl to her lips, tilting it to pour the essence down her throat. It tasted richer, and seemed thicker than the milk alone, with a salty, meaty aftertaste, making her think of bacon, then cheese. Nodding thoughtfully, she licked her lips and put the bowl down.

'Cheese?' Cicely queried. 'Girl's-milk cheese?'

'Yes, miss,' Catherine answered. 'It tastes better that way.'

'Well, maybe, but do you suppose it has the same effect?'

'I don't see why it shouldn't,' Charlotte put in. 'It's the same stuff, after all.'

'Just what I said to myself, Miss Cicely,' Catherine agreed, 'and a sight nicer and all. Here, try some.'

Cicely sat up in bed, watching as Catherine cut the little white pat of cheese deftly into three pieces. Taking one, she popped it into her mouth, squashing it against her tongue. It was like no other cheese she tasted, sharp and rich at the same time, quite salty, and with a distinctive flavour all its own. Without doubt it was nicer than the plain vital essence.

'Very nice,' she said, swallowing. 'Lottie?'

Charlotte nodded and swallowed her own mouthful before speaking.

'Yes, not bad, different. Do you know, I've tasted this before, I know I have.'

'Come on, Lottie, that's hardly likely.'

'No, I'm sure of it, I even remember when. Yes, that's right. You remember Alice, from school, Alice Challacombe?'

'Yes, very well.'

'Well, whenever she had tuck from her people there was cheese in it. It tasted the same, I swear to it.'

'You're imagining things, Lottie.'

'I am, probably, but it is a little peculiar. When Francis was trying to persuade me to take milk as part of my diet, he mentioned a man called Archie Maray. I knew I'd heard the name before, but I couldn't put my finger on it. Now I can. Alice's mother used to work for the Marays.'

'Oh, you do talk nonsense, Lottie.'

'It is a little like goat's cheese,' Catherine remarked.

'There we are, then,' Cicely said. 'Alice's cheese came from goats.'

Charlotte shrugged. 'Well, anyway,' she said. 'I think it's very clever of you, Catherine. Now, Sissy and I were saying earlier that we really need the help of a virile young man, one of the boys from the village, perhaps, preferably more than one. I do wish you'd help.'

'Yes,' Cicely added, 'you're to go down this morning, and do make sure to choose the strongest and best formed of them. There's a lad call Sam who will do very nicely.'

'Sam Mullins is my brother,' Catherine answered.

'He is? Does it matter?'

'Certain sure it matters!'

'I thought you village girls and boys more or less behaved as you pleased.'

'Not at all, Miss Cicely, and besides, he's married now, to Eliza Burridge, who was always a good friend to me, even when I got in trouble.'

'Very well, what of the boy who got you into trouble?'

'John Dunn, miss, and I wouldn't touch him with a ten-foot pole, miss. He should have married me, he should, and he wouldn't, just on account of us not being sure who Hazel's father was.'

'There's another, then, Luke I think his name is. The biggest of the boys who are working on the new ditch.'

'My brother, miss.'

'Well, we are running a little short, aren't we, Catherine? The one with the very black hair, then, who is at least handsome if less than sturdy.'

'Peter Fitch, you mean. He's married to my sister, Rebecca.'

'Now you are being unreasonable, Catherine. You must choose one or another of the four I have suggested.'

'None of them four, miss. It can't be done.'

'Catherine, I don't think you understand me. I wish you to do as I have asked, and it is not a request but an order.'

'Be that as it may, Miss Cicely, it can't be done, not with any of them.'

'Are you being wilfully disobedient, Catherine?'

'If that's how you choose to put it, miss, then yes, I am.'

'Well, I shall know what to do about that!'

'Indeed?'

'Don't you dare take that tone with me, girl! You need not suppose, Mullins, that simply because I allowed you to take advantage of me in a weak moment you are any less subject to my discipline. Now, on the bed with you, and let's have no more nonsense. I intend to beat you.'

'Begging your pardon, Miss Cicely, but you've no right to do any such thing. This is Colonel St John's house, and Miss Charlotte's, not yours. You've no right.'

'I have every right! However, if you insist on being so exact . . . Lottie, pray order this impudent girl to make herself ready for punishment.'

'Well, I . . .' Charlotte began.

'Lottie!' Cicely hissed.

'Oh, very well, Sissy, if you must. Catherine, please don't be awkward. Get on the bed as Cicely asks. It won't hurt so very much.'

'I'll not go,' Catherine answered defiantly. 'I'll not.'

'You will do as you are told!' Cicely snapped.

'And if I won't?'

'I shall . . .' Cicely hesitated, knowing perfectly well that dismissing Catherine was out of the question. Not only was she privy to a great many secrets, but she had become essential to the running of the house, in a way that Mrs Mabberley never had been. Nor was it desirable. She had imagined that Catherine would accept her punishment and, once punished, could easily be put in the same subservient position as Charlotte. Catherine had refused, which left her with the choice of backing down or enforcing her will physically.

Charlotte put her hands out, trying to think of something she could say to defuse the growing anger between Cicely and Catherine. The two women were glaring at each other, Cicely in outrage, Catherine in defiance.

'Very well,' Cicely said, getting to her feet, 'it seems that I shall be obliged to teach you a lesson.'

'Sissy, stop. Really, is there any need?' Charlotte stammered.

'Certainly there is need,' Cicely replied. 'She needs to learn her place, here and now.'

As Cicely spoke she reached out for Catherine's sleeve, catching hold of it and pulling. Catherine resisted, tugging her arm away, which came close to making Cicely lose her balance. With an angry click of her tongue, Cicely grabbed out again, catching Catherine's dress and jerking her forward. Catherine went down, on to the bed, but rolled to stop herself being put into a convenient spanking position, taking Cicely with her.

Charlotte jumped back as the two girls rolled together on the bed. Catherine was on her back, Cicely grappling with her, trying to pull her over. It didn't work, and Catherine took hold of Cicely's wrist, jerking it free. Cicely sprawled down across Catherine with a gasp of anger, and a second of shock as Catherine grabbed her around the waist, struggling to get a proper grip. Catherine was trying to sit up, and, if she succeeded, it was obvious what would happen: Cicely would get spanked, a prospect that had Charlotte's hand at her mouth.

'No, you little bitch!' Cicely spat and lashed out backhanded, catching Catherine across the face.

Catherine gasped and went back, clutching her cheek and letting go of Cicely. Immediately Cicely was over, rolling and grappling for Catherine, pinning her on to the bed and planting another hard slap full across her face. Catherine yelped in pain and smacked back, missing, and for a moment the two of them were flailing at each other's arms, smacking and clawing. Catherine's hair was pulled loose, then the front of Cicely's pyjama top, buttons torn away to expose one small breast. At that she went wild, clawing and swearing and slapping, until Catherine's hands came up in front of her face in a vain effort to protect herself. Instantly Cicely had grabbed Catherine by the hair, pulling hard even as she cocked up her leg. Catherine squealed as she was forced to roll over, turning beneath Cicely until she was face down on the bed. Mounted astride her victim, Cicely was grinning, panting, red-faced, but triumphant, her hand still twisted firmly into Catherine's hair.

'Get off me, you brat!' Catherine howled. 'Let go of my hair!'

'No!' Cicely answered. 'Not until you say you'll take a spanking, a hard one, and admit you deserve it, you fat slut!'

'I shan't!' Catherine gasped. 'Never!'

'I shall make you!' Cicely spat, twisting her hand harder into Catherine's hair. 'I shall!'

'No!' Catherine answered, and twisted her body hard underneath Cicely.

Cicely squealed and fell to one side, sprawling across the bed, still with her fist locked in Catherine's hair. Catherine squealed, clawing for Cicely's wrist, but Cicely was already scrambling around, holding on with desperate determination as she once more threw a leg over Catherine.

'You see, quality will always show in the end!' Cicely panted. 'Now, let us have your dress up and that fat bottom out of your drawers!'

Charlotte watched in absolute delight as Cicely settled her trim bottom on to Catherine's head, pinned the maid helpless to the bed. One firm tug had Catherine's dress up, drawing out a muffled squeal of consternation. Another tug and Cicely had burst open the button that held Catherine's drawers together, the curtains falling wide to reveal the maid's big, white bottom to the sound of a yet more furious squeal. With a crow of triumph, Cicely brought her hand up, and down, to land with a resounding smack on the pale surface of Catherine's bottom. The maid squealed, clawing at Cicely's leg, only to get another, harder smack and the spanking had begun.

Catherine was cursing and squealing, tossing herself up and down, her legs kicking, her fists hammering on the bed. Cicely was laughing, struggling to keep her balance, smacking down over and over at the maid's fat white bottom, the cheeks bouncing and jumping, the skin reddening. Catherine, her face squashed down into the bedclothes, was having trouble even breathing, but she continued to kick and struggle helplessly as Cicely rode her and spanked away. Her drawers fell down, then off, kicked away in her helpless struggling.

Charlotte could only watch, thrilled, and at the same time shocked by her own reaction. Her quim was wet, her heart pounding, her eyes flicking between where Cicely's bottom was spread over Catherine's head and the victim's bouncing, wobbling bum cheeks. Slowly, the fight was going out of the maid, her struggles subsiding in apparent acquiescence to the humiliating punishment, the noises she was making turning from anger to suffering, her legs still kicking in pain, but not resistance.

'Not so uppity now, are we?' Cicely puffed happily, and paused.

Her skin was flushed pink, sweat running down her face and chest. With two deft flourishes she opened the waistband of Catherine's dress, separating skirt from top and opening the lower part to leave her plump target completely vulnerable to further punishment.

'And now the bitch will beg,' she said, and reached out to grab at the long-handled hairbrush that lay on Charlotte's dressing table. 'This is for your impudence and your airs. For daring to ape your betters, and most of all for what you did to me with the bees!'

Suddenly Catherine lunged to the side, catching Cicely completely off balance. Cicely went down, on to the floor, with a yelp of shock and annoyance. Cicely was off, and Catherine had rolled before she could recover herself, and bounced up. Cicely sprawled over the edge of the bed, legs wide, pyjama-clad bottom stuck up high. Instantly Catherine took hold of the seat of Cicely's pyjamas, and wrenched them down to expose a trim, bare bottom. Cicely screamed in outrage, grabbing for her trousers, but too late. They came down, and off, leaving her to fall to the floor, bare from the waist down, for one moment making a full show of hairy sex lips and wrinkled pink bottom hole.

'Now you're really going to get it!' Cicely spat as she struggled to her feet.

Taking the hairbrush, Cicely launched herself at Catherine, face red with fury. Catherine caught her and they went down on the bed, clawing and scratching, each struggling to get on top. The last of Cicely's pyjama buttons was wrenched away, leaving her top flapping open, both breasts bare as well as everything below her waist. Catherine's top was loose already, and quickly came open, spilling out her huge breasts as she tumbled on to Cicely, smothering her in flesh.

Cicely slapped out, catching one fat breast hard, to leave a red print and draw a furious scream from Catherine. Again Cicely slapped, this time full in

Catherine's face. The girls went into a frenzy of smacks and slaps, clawing and tearing at each other, cursing and spitting as they rolled on the bed, first one on top, then the other.

Charlotte had retreated into the corner, open-mouthed as she watched the girls struggle in a flurry of legs and arms, hair and cloth, bottom and breasts. For a moment it seemed as if Cicely was going to pin Catherine down once more, only for a particularly vicious slap to catch her in the face. Cicely's hand went to her cheek, her eyes going wide in fury even as Catherine lunged, caught Cicely by the wrist, twisting even as she threw her body to the side. Cicely went down, yelling in fury as her arm was twisted tight into the small of her back and she was forced down on to the bed. Catherine lost no time, climbing on to Cicely's back then settling her bottom across her victim's shoulder blades.

Cicely was pinned helpless, one arm pulled up into the small of her back, the other pinned beneath Catherine's leg. She was still kicking and struggling, red-faced with fury, but try as she might she could not shift the maid's weight. Catherine clung on, her chest heaving, her breath coming in long, ragged pants. Both girls were red-faced, their skin glossy with sweat and milk, red with the marks of slaps and scratches. Beads of crimson blood showed in places, on Catherine's breasts and belly and across Cicely's face.

'Get off me, Mullins, now!' Cicely spat.

'No,' Catherine answered. 'I shan't get off you! I shan't! I'm going to punish you, you spoiled, uppity little brat! I'm going to spank you and spank you and spank you . . .'

'Don't you dare!' Cicely hissed. 'Get off me, I say! Get off me this moment!'

'No,' Catherine repeated.

Again Cicely's body jerked as she tried to throw Catherine off and, again, Catherine held on, twisting at

Cicely's arm to draw out a squeal of pain and rage. Cicely went limp.

'Tell her to get off, Lottie,' Cicely said, still angry, but with a note of pleading in her voice.

Charlotte shook her head, unable to admit her fear, or admit that, of all the things she most wanted at that moment, it was to see Cicely get spanked.

'Please?' Cicely said. 'Tell her, Lottie! Tell her to get off!'

'Don't you dare, Miss Charlotte,' Catherine said. 'I'll not stand for it!'

'Lottie, please!' Cicely begged. 'She's going to spank me! Stop her!'

'I can't!' Charlotte managed. 'I really can't!'

'That's right, Miss Charlotte,' Catherine said. 'You be a sensible girl and stay out of it. Now, where did that hairbrush go?'

'No! Not the hairbrush!' Cicely squealed.

Catherine just chuckled and reached for the hairbrush where it lay on the bed. Panic began to show in Cicely's face, a muscle in her cheek twitching, her eyes wide in horror as she tried to look back.

'Don't do it, Catherine, please!' Cicely begged. 'I'm sorry I was a beast to you. I'm sorry I punished you . . . I'm sorry, I'm sorry, I'm sorry, just please, no, not that . . . Ow!'

Her pleading broke off as the hairbrush landed on her bare bottom with a loud smack. Charlotte stifled a nervous giggle and the hairbrush came down again, hard on Cicely's naked flesh, making the cheeks jump and leaving a broad red impression.

'Ow!' Cicely wailed. 'That hurts, Catherine, that really hurts! Spare me, I beg you! Do something, Lottie! Ow! Ow! Ow!'

Catherine had begun to lay in with the hairbrush, ignoring Cicely's frantic protests. Smack after smack landed on the trim bottom, making the cheeks bounce and part. Cicely began to kick again, and to struggle, her dignity evaporating with her self-control until she was squealing and thrashing, her face contorting, her mouth opening and closing like a fish. Catherine smacked away, harder and harder, until Cicely's cries and yelps had turned to screams and hot, angry tears of pain and dismay.

Still Catherine carried on, ignoring her victim's outbursts, spanking and spanking, until Cicely was truly howling, face red and screwed up, tears spraying from tightly closed eyes, legs wide apart and kicking, quim and bumhole wide and wet. Yet still Catherine continued, smack after smack, until the whole of Cicely's bottom was flushed crimson, the flesh blotchy and rough with marks, prickly with goose pimples and glossy with sweat. Several times Cicely's bumhole opened wide in response to her pain, emitting loud, rasping farts to make Catherine laugh with glee for her victim's sorry state and miserable humiliation.

Charlotte watched it all, one hand clutched to the front of her skirts, unable to look away from the awful expressions on Cicely's face as her friend blubbered her way through the spanking. She was getting more and more aroused as well, until she could no longer hold back and moved to where she could get a better view between Cicely's legs, at the open, wet quim and pulsing bumhole.

At last Catherine stopped, throwing the hairbrush to the side. Cicely's thrashing subsided, her legs going still, her bottom no longer wriggling. Slowly, her howls and screams turned to gasps and a miserable, broken snivelling noise, until at last she lay still and silent, legs still well apart to show the wet mush of her sex and the sweaty dimple of her anus. She was utterly defeated, as limp as a broken doll, tears trickling from her eyes, nose wet with mucus, saliva running from her open mouth.

'And now, Miss Cicely,' Catherine declared. 'You are going to lick my bottom hole, nice and clean, and you're to do it well.'

Cicely answered with a broken sob that might have been a refusal, but as Catherine lifted her weight she made no move to free herself. Instead she let herself be rolled over, face up, to lie across the bed with her tear-streaked face upwards. All the while Catherine held on, but only when the maid had climbed back on top and swung one chubby thigh across did any emotion register on Cicely's features. Then, with the maid's huge pink flushed bottom directly above her face, her eyes went wide in horror, fixing to the great cheeks and the deep cleft between them as Catherine began to lower it. Charlotte caught a last look of utter dismay as Cicely's face disappeared beneath the broad cheeks of Catherine's bottom.

'Now lick,' Catherine ordered, 'and don't be prissy about it. I want to feel your tongue well inside. Come on, lick. Lick, Cicely, you little brat!'

Catherine wriggled her fat bottom into her victim's face, and at that Cicely once more came alive. Her legs beat a frantic tattoo on the floor, her fists clutching at the bedclothes. Catherine laughed and grabbed at one of Cicely's legs, catching it under the knee and pulling it high. Cicely continued to kick, her free leg waving wildly in the air, and once more Catherine began to spank.

Smack after smack rained down on the trim buttocks, many of them also catching the lips of Cicely's quim where they poked out between her thighs. Charlotte watched in delight, admiring Cicely's red bum cheeks, swollen pink sex and sweaty bottom hole. The position was incredibly undignified, delightfully so, with Cicely's leg rolled up to show everything and her face smothered beneath Catherine's broad rear end. An amusing touch was added by the ridiculous way Cicely's free leg kept kicking and waving in the air, and Charlotte found herself sharing a smile with Catherine.

'Come on, Sissy, lick her, then she'll let you go,' Charlotte urged.

'Come on, there's a good girl,' Catherine added, 'lick it, Cicely.'

As Catherine spoke, she lunged for Cicely's free leg, catching it and pulling it up alongside the other, forcing her victim to roll up tighter still, with the full spread of her bottom exposed to Charlotte's gaze.

'I'll hold her, you slap her bottom and cunt,' Catherine suggested, nodding to where Cicely's furry quim poked out between her thighs.

Cicely responded with an angry wriggle, but Charlotte was too excited to resist and began to slap gently at her friend's rolled-up bottom and the lips of her sex.

'You know how to stop this,' Catherine said, 'just get your tongue up my hole and give me a good licking. Now come on, Cicely, or I shall tell Miss Charlotte to use the hairbrush.'

Again Cicely gave an angry wriggle, but Charlotte carried on spanking, aiming the slaps at the crests of Cicely's buttocks and on to her quim, which had begun to redden.

'I do enjoy seeing a good cunt slapping,' Catherine said happily. 'Now come along, Cicely, best to get it over with, don't you suppose? Fuck her with the hairbrush, Charlotte, or put it up her bottom.'

Cicely kicked, but succeeded only in wiggling her bottom. Charlotte giggled, her tongue flicking out to wet her lips as she took hold of the hairbrush. Cicely's vagina made a fine target but, after all the times the same hairbrush had been pushed up Charlotte's bottom hole, the struggling girl's anus was an even better one. Smiling, Charlotte pressed the rounded handle to her friend's bumhole, which twitched in response, closing tight, dislodging a bead of quim juice, which ran into the little pit.

'Open up, now, Sissy,' Charlotte said, 'or you know what happens.'

At her words the little hole relaxed, opening to a mushy pink cavity, wet with fluid. Catherine giggled and

237

Charlotte put the hairbrush to the hole. The handle went in, and up, sliding smoothly into Cicely's rectum as the sweaty, juice-slick ring of her anus gave way. With it up as far as it would go, Charlotte let go, stepping back.

'My, but you do look a sight, Miss Cicely.' Catherine laughed. 'What with your bottom and cunt all red and Miss Charlotte's hairbrush sticking out of your hole.'

Cicely gave an angry jerk, making the brush in her bottom waggle from side to side. Charlotte took it in her hand again and began to bugger her friend, feeling a little guilty, but telling herself that Cicely had done the same to her many, many times. It felt good, anyway, to see the little hole going in and out and think of all the times she had been in similar rude, humiliating situations, under punishment while Cicely enjoyed her helplessness and degradation.

'Lick her bottom, Sissy!' she ordered. 'Come on, lick it!'

This time there was no answering protest, and a moment later Catherine gave a deep, pleased sigh.

'Oh, she's doing it!' Catherine gasped. 'Oh, she is! Oh, I can feel her tongue! Oh my . . .'

Catherine's face set in a mask of pure pleasure, her eyes closing and her mouth going slowly slack. Charlotte watched, her arousal and delight growing stronger still, her arm moving mechanically to work the hairbrush in Cicely's anus.

'Spend in her face,' Charlotte urged.

Catherine nodded, and moved, easing herself back to rub herself in Cicely's face, using it to masturbate on. Charlotte smiled to herself, full of a delicious sense of cruelty as she began to work the brush faster in Cicely's anus. Still Catherine had hold of Cicely's legs, pulling on them as she rode on the defeated girl's head, back and forth, plump wet quim pressed hard to nose and mouth.

'Oh, she's willing now,' Catherine moaned. 'That's good, yes, suck on it . . . yes, lovely. Now back in the dirt.'

Catherine moved again, once more smothering Cicely's face with her bottom to allow her anus to be licked. Seeing her friend's final surrender, Charlotte abandoned the hairbrush and began to strip, pulling at the fastenings of her clothes in her eagerness to be nude.

'Good girl,' Catherine said. 'Charlotte's stripping, Cicely, and soon I'll make her put her face to your cunt, if you're very good and tongue me properly. That's right, right up, lick it all up . . .'

Catherine trailed off with a deep sigh and let go of Cicely's legs. Taking her breasts in her hands, she began to play with the nipples, stroking her fingers across them then squeezing to send little jets of milk out across Cicely's prone body. Cicely had made no move to break free, but set her feet well apart, to keep her sex wide to Charlotte. She was moving her hips, too, the hairbrush still protruding obscenely from her anus and waving up and down to the motion.

Charlotte was down to her stockings and drawers, but could wait no longer. Grabbing the hairbrush, she once more began to bugger Cicely, then to lick, burying her face in her friend's open quim. Cicely responded by pushing her hips up, pressing herself to Charlotte's face.

Catherine was getting urgent, grinding her bottom into Cicely's face and squeezing at her breasts. Milk was running down both, and over her rounded belly and sex, wetting her skin and Cicely's beneath. Her face was set in ecstasy, her mouth wide, her eyes closed as her rubbing motion became a frantic bucking, squashing her sex over and over into Cicely's face with a meaty slapping noise until at last she cried out in rapture. Charlotte heard, but licked harder as Catherine settled her bottom slowly down over Cicely's face, reaching back to spread her big cheeks as wide as they would go. Cicely's legs came together, locked over the back of Charlotte's head, and she too was coming, squirming and bucking her hips, her tongue pushed to its full extent up Catherine's open bottom hole.

Only when Cicely's writhing had died down did Charlotte pull back, going on to her knees. As her friend came she had been touching her own sex, which was wet with juice and ripe for entry. Orgasm would have been easy, but she had held off, wanting some of the attention for herself.

As Charlotte stood up, Catherine dismounted, revealing Cicely's face, the skin pink and wet, smeared with fluid around her mouth and over her nose. Charlotte giggled, and received a sulky look in return, but Cicely said nothing, merely propping herself on to one elbow.

'Now don't pout,' Charlotte said. 'You know as well as I do that you deserved that, and besides, say what you will, but the state of you between your legs doesn't lie. So stop sulking and play sweetly, because it's my turn now.'

'In good time, young lady,' Catherine said. 'For the now, you're going to suckle me, the pair of you, properly. Now come along.'

She moved back on the bed as she spoke, and propped herself against the pile of pillows Cicely had made earlier.

'Come along,' she repeated, patting her lap, 'and you can take those silly drawers off, Miss Charlotte, I want you bare.'

Charlotte obeyed, hastily peeling off her drawers and stockings as Cicely extracted the hairbrush from her bottom. The sulky look on Cicely's face held, but she went obediently into Catherine's arms, allowing her head to be cradled. The big nipple was fed into her mouth and her eyes closed as she started to suck. Charlotte followed, cuddling up to Catherine and taking a mouthful of breast, the big nipple between her pouted lips.

Catherine sighed as the girls began to suckle, cradling both their heads and stroking their hair as they fed. Charlotte let the feelings of security and comfort steal up on her, knowing all the while that Cicely would be feeling the same emotions, and that, once they had fed together as they were, their relationship with Catherine would never be the same again. She would still be a maid, but their nursemaid, suckling them when they needed it, comforting them when they needed it, spanking them when they needed it. The thought was bliss, and as the warm milk filled her mouth her leg came up, over Catherine's, pressing her sex to the big, firm thigh.

As Charlotte began to masturbate on her leg, Catherine gave a little tolerant chuckle, clearly amused by the reaction. In response Charlotte cuddled closer, rubbing more urgently and sucking harder. Catherine continued to stroke Charlotte's hair, soothing her as she masturbated, showing her that it was all right to be naked and wanton, to rub her sex on the leg of the woman she was suckling. Never had Charlotte felt so cared for, so wanted or so understood, as she wriggled herself towards orgasm, naked in Catherine's arms, mouth full of firm, milky nipple, bare bottom stuck out behind and, best of all, with Cicely quietly watching and suckling on their nursemaid's other breast.

When the climax came it was exquisite, rising slowly as her rubbing got faster and faster and her mouth filled with milk, a bubble of pure pleasure that grew and grew, then burst, even as her mouth came open and milk splashed out over Catherine's breast and belly. Again she shut her mouth, pressing her face to Catherine's soft flesh and sucking hard, drawing more and more milk into her mouth as the orgasm tore through her, lifting her to peak after peak until at last it began to die and she slumped down, still suckling, with milk trickling from the corner of her mouth. Catherine sighed, hugging the two contented girls to herself as Charlotte's orgasm died away.

For a long while they lay together, saying nothing, Charlotte and Cicely with their heads cradled on Catherine's chest, occasionally suckling or stroking each other's skin. Beneath them the bedclothes were wet with milk, and the scent was strong in the air, mixed with the rich musk of their quims. For Charlotte the contentment was perfect, representing an idyll that she had no desire to leave, ever. If Cicely felt any different she did not show it, and when Catherine began to test her authority, ordering them to kneel up and milk each other, neither resisted.

It was done into a chamberpot, the girls taking turns to kneel on the bed, bottoms high as they squeezed and pulled at their breasts, expressing the milk. Catherine watched them indulgently, occasionally patting one or other bottom or stroking a pouted quim. Before long they were giggling as they did it, with little regard for accuracy, the milk spraying up from their breasts as they competed to get the little squirts of fluid into the pot. It was getting everywhere, their skin wet with it, the bedclothes sodden, when Catherine called a halt, ordering Charlotte to pass her the pot.

'Now,' she said, 'I'll show you a special version of this vital essence, the sort you'll drink when you're not well behaved!'

She took the pot, placing it at the centre of the bed and rising to squat over it, her intention as obvious as it was dirty. Charlotte watched, open mouthed as a stream of golden pee erupted from Catherine's quim, splashing into the milk, and Cicely gave a little moan. Catherine laughed, reaching down to spread her sex lips and show them her sex as the pee gushed out, splashing and gurgling in the pot until at last it stopped.

'There we are,' Catherine said, wiggling her bottom to shake the last few drops loose. 'Now drink up, girls, every last drop.'

Charlotte took the pot as Catherine lifted it, sharing a look with Cicely, who made a face.

'Now come along,' Catherine urged. 'Or do I have to spank you again?'

'No,' Cicely answered quickly.

'No,' Charlotte agreed, and quickly put the pot to her lips.

She tilted it, her eyes fixed on the milky yellow fluid, her nose full of the strong, female scent. It touched her lips and she tasted it, sweet and sharp, rich and acrid, of milk and urine mixed. With a last thought for the utter subservience that drinking another girl's pee represented, she tipped further, opening her mouth, filling it, and swallowing, in an ecstasy of submission as it flowed down her throat.

Only wanting to watch Cicely do the same had prevented her from drinking it all. She stopped, and held out the chamber pot to her friend. Cicely swallowed, but took it, her hands shaking as they closed on the smooth white china. Holding it, she put it to her lips, and tilted, and she was drinking. Catherine gave a peal of delighted laughter as the mixture of her pee and girl's milk flowed down Cicely's throat, slapping her thigh in merriment.

'Good girl!' she crowed. 'That's right, all of it, taste my piddle! Oh, that is fine! Now together, on the bed, head to toe and in go your faces!'

They obeyed without hesitation, curling together and burying their faces in one another's quim as Catherine came to kneel over them.

'Good girls!' She laughed. 'Now plenty of tongue, and don't forget each other's bottom. I want to see you good and dirty.'

Charlotte obeyed, pushing out her tongue to lap at Cicely's anus. The little hole was already juicy and wet, and her tongue went in easily, well up, to taste her lover's bottom as she had so many times before, only now Cicely's own tongue was in the same place. It felt wonderful, with the little muscular tip delving into her anal cavity, physical ecstasy, and mental, from the knowledge of what was being done to her and who was doing it. Cicely, who had brought her to the depths of erotic torment so often, now with her own tongue firmly where she had so often made Charlotte put hers.

'Good girls!' Catherine repeated, in sheer glee. 'Now make each other spend!'

Neither girl needed encouragement. Both were licking urgently, clutched to each other with their tongues working on quims and bumholes. Charlotte had rolled on top, her hands curled around Cicely's thighs to pull open the little bum cheeks, while Cicely's hands were on Charlotte's bottom, also spreading it wide. Above them Catherine shook with laughter, and as she took hold of her breasts she began to squeeze.

Charlotte felt the patter of milk on her back, then in her hair as Catherine moved. A moment later two huge balls of pink flesh were being pushed against her face. Pausing in her licking, Charlotte sucked a teat into her mouth. Milk flowed out, dribbling from Charlotte's mouth on to Cicely's quim and into the open hole. Catherine giggled and squeezed the other breast, spattering Cicely's sex with milk. More came, spurting into Cicely's open hole as Charlotte began to take turns between nipples and quim, her face wet with juice and milk, and all the while with Cicely's tongue well up her bottom.

Catherine kept on squeezing, until Cicely's vagina was full, milk bubbling and spurting from the gaping hole as it began to contract. Charlotte was lapping urgently, slurping up the milk, sucking at Cicely's clitoris and Catherine's nipples. Her own clitoris was sucked suddenly between Cicely's lips and she screamed, starting to come immediately, even as Catherine pressed one big nipple to the open quim in front of her and began to rub. Charlotte screamed again, her whole body locking in unbearable climax, even as Cicely's hole contracted hard and a fountain of milk erupted into Catherine's face. A finger found Charlotte's bottom, driving deep up the little hole as a thumb found her vagina and she screamed again, both holes full, her clitoris held between Cicely's teeth. Burying her face in the wet, soft flesh between breasts and quim, she sucked and lapped at anything she could reach, clitoris, nipples, vagina, anus, desperate for all she could get as she rode her orgasm, on and on in a welter of perfect ecstasy, broken only by a resounding crash from the next room.

Winter 1923, Ashwood House, Somerset

Toby, Lord Cary, brought his car to a stop on the carriageway of Ashwood House. Colonel St John was ill, dangerously ill according to the doctor, whose telegram had led to Toby's early release on compassionate grounds.

As he climbed from the car the front door of the house swung open, and a young woman in a yellow dress and a fur muffler stepped out. She was too tall for Charlotte, and he took a moment to realise that it was his sister.

'Toby,' she called, stepping across to him.

'Sissy?' he queried. 'Good heavens, I hardly recognised you. You're in a dress. What happened to the male bit?'

'Oh, I grew bored with it. Besides, I realised that I was being silly. I am who I am – mere clothes do not make me a man. Oh, and you needn't worry about dinner tonight, either. Mrs Mabberley has been instructed to roast a sirloin.'

'That's decent of you, especially if you're on nut pie and boiled greens.'

'I'm not, not any more. I have been shown the error of my ways and will be eating beef.'

'Sensible girl. So what's up with Uncle Francis? Nothing too serious, I trust.'

'I'm rather afraid it is. Old Borrowdale thinks he had a seizure of the heart. In any case, he took a bad fall, in his bedroom. Caught his head on the grate.'

'Good heavens.'

'We heard him, fortunately. Look, I'd better tell you. The thing is, he was standing on a chair, watching Lottie, Catherine and me, through a spy hole in the wall.'

'Watching you? Watching you do what, exactly?'

'You may guess.'

'With the two of you I can guess very well. The maid as well?'

'Catherine, yes. You know how it is.'

'After the last few weeks I don't think I dare imagine. So, this spy hole, from his room into Lottie's?'

'In the panelling. It just looks like one panel has parted from the frame a little way. We'd never have noticed, except that the one on his side was bigger, hidden behind that old picture of the Charge, and obviously it was still open when he fell. It wasn't the only one, either. He had a whole system of them, in just about every room, the bathrooms, most of the bed-rooms. I always did wonder how he seemed to know exactly when Lottie or I was about to come out of the bathroom.'

'Good heavens! So you mean he'd been watching everything?'

'For years, it seems. Including, well, you know . . .'

'Oh, dear. Maybe not, though. I mean to say, how would he have known?'

'He would have guessed,' Cicely said with certainty. 'Anyway, you had better come up and see him, and best not to mention the spy holes.'

'Absolutely,' Toby agreed, 'let bygones be bygones.'

They made their way into the house and up to the Colonel's room. He lay in bed, pale and spent, yet still with a hint of the fire that had always marked his personality. Charlotte was beside him, his hand in hers, and at Toby's appearance she gave a weak smile.

'Hullo, old thing,' Toby managed. 'Uncle Francis.'

'Ah, Toby, my boy, there you are,' he said. 'Glad they let you out.'

'I've you to thank for that, Uncle,' Toby joked. 'Compassionate grounds, you know.'

'Compassionate grounds? You shouldn't have been there in the first place. Prigs and puritans, the lot of them. By God, but what's the world coming to when they lock a gentleman up for punching a cad. I tell you, I'm not so very sorry to be leaving it. Not the same, you know. Not my world.'

'Don't talk such nonsense, Francis,' Charlotte said soothingly. 'You have years ahead of you. Now do try to relax. You mustn't excite him, Toby.'

'Nonsense yourself,' the Colonel snapped. 'I heard what the quack said. If it happens again I'm a goner, dead, damn it. Now look, I've something of a confession to make.'

'Don't worry, Uncle Francis. We know about the spy holes. This is no time for recrimination.'

'No, not the spy holes, although God knows they might be reason enough to set you against me. No, I'm afraid I've been damn cruel to you, Sissy. You too, Lottie, in a way.'

'Nonsense, Uncle Francis,' Cicely said. 'Not at all.'

'I have, believe me,' he went on. 'Never could resist it, you see. It was the terrible tempers you always got into, you know . . . so lovely.'

'Don't mind that, Francis. Do try not to excite yourself,' Charlotte said.

'No, no. Let me tell you. D'you recall that I mentioned a fellow called Archie Maray? Used to virtually live on milk.'

'Now, Francis . . .'

'Shut up for a moment, damn you. Well he did, and the thing is you see – according to rumour, anyhow – the milk came from a couple of girls living out on one of the moor farms, and it wasn't cow's milk. It was their own. I knew, you see, heard it from his son. Seemed a fine idea. When I saw young Catherine Mullins and just how damn big her bosom was . . . Well, I had to give it a try, and this vegetarian business made the perfect excuse for suggesting it.'

'I don't mind, Francis, dear. What matter if the Marays also drink girls' milk?'

'You're not listening. The thing is, old Archie Maray wasn't after the milk for the sake of his health, more for the sake of his cock, if you follow my meaning. So was I.'

'Yes, you took pleasure from it, as we all did. We didn't mind, no more than we have minded reading for you. It seems a small enough price to pay for such a secret as vital essence.'

'No, no. Listen, will you, girl? It was a pack of lies. The whole thing.'

'The whole thing?'

'How do you mean?'

'The business with the milk girls in India, the vital essence, everything. Made it up, the lot of it.'

'No, surely not, Francis!'

'I wanted to see young Catherine in milk, d'you see, and you, Lottie. Then, when you started to get prissy about helping me with my needs, I added the bit about the jism.'

'There's no such thing as vital essence?'

'Load of nonsense. Made it up. All of it. The whole damn lot.'

'No, surely not! But your notes.'

'Forgeries, I'm afraid, my dear. Old paper from your papa's writing cabinet and black ink mixed in with red to make it look brown.'

'The breast whipping? The nettles? The bees?'

'Pack of lies, the lot it.'

'Everything?'

'Everything.'

NEXUS BACKLIST

This information is correct at time of printing. For up-to-date information, please visit our website at www.nexus-books.co.uk

All books are priced at £5.99 unless another price is given.

Nexus books with a contemporary setting

ACCIDENTS WILL HAPPEN	Lucy Golden ISBN 0 352 33596 3	☐
ANGEL	Lindsay Gordon ISBN 0 352 33590 4	☐
BEAST	Wendy Swanscombe ISBN 0 352 33649 8	☐
THE BLACK MASQUE	Lisette Ashton ISBN 0 352 33372 3	☐
THE BLACK WIDOW	Lisette Ashton ISBN 0 352 33338 3	☐
THE BOND	Lindsay Gordon ISBN 0 352 33480 0	☐
BROUGHT TO HEEL	Arabella Knight ISBN 0 352 33508 4	☐
CAGED!	Yolanda Celbridge ISBN 0 352 33650 1	☐
CANDY IN CAPTIVITY	Arabella Knight ISBN 0 352 33495 9	☐
CAPTIVES OF THE PRIVATE HOUSE	Esme Ombreux ISBN 0 352 33619 6	☐
DANCE OF SUBMISSION	Lisette Ashton ISBN 0 352 33450 9	☐
DARK DELIGHTS	Maria del Rey ISBN 0 352 33276 X	☐
DISCIPLES OF SHAME	Stephanie Calvin ISBN 0 352 33343 X	☐

------ ✂ --------------------------

Please send me the books I have ticked above.

Name ....

Address ....

....

....

.... Post code..................

Send to: **Cash Sales, Nexus Books, Thames Wharf Studios, Rainville Road, London W6 9HA**

US customers: for prices and details of how to order books for delivery by mail, call 1-800-805-1083.

Please enclose a cheque or postal order, made payable to **Nexus Books Ltd**, to the value of the books you have ordered plus postage and packing costs as follows:

UK and BFPO – £1.00 for the first book, 50p for each subsequent book.

Overseas (including Republic of Ireland) – £2.00 for the first book, £1.00 for each subsequent book.

If you would prefer to pay by VISA, ACCESS/MASTERCARD, AMEX, DINERS CLUB or SWITCH, please write your card number and expiry date here:

....

Please allow up to 28 days for delivery.

Signature ....

Our privacy policy.

We will not disclose information you supply us to any other parties. We will not disclose any information which identifies you personally to any person without your express consent.

From time to time we may send out information about Nexus books and special offers. Please tick here if you do *not* wish to receive Nexus information. ☐

------ ✂ --------------------------